The Girls of St. Cyprian's

BY

ANGELA BRAZIL

Author of "The School by the Sea"
"The Leader of the Lower School"
"The Youngest Girl in the Fifth"
&c. &c.

With frontispiece

BLACKIE & SON LIMITED
LONDON AND GLASGOW

Printed in Great Britain by Blackie & Son, Ltd., Glasgow

THE GIRLS OF ST. CYPRIAN'S

CHAPTER I

The United Schools Alliance

"If there's one slack, slow business in this wide world," said Bess Harrison, stretching her arms in the exigencies of a combined sigh and prodigious yawn, "it's coming back to school after the Easter holidays. Tame isn't the word for it! It's absolute milk and water. September start is some sport, because one's generally in a fresh form, and there are always changes; and even January is fairly lively; but now! Why, there's scarcely even a new girl to make a small excitement, and altogether it's about as stale as beginning again after half-term week-end."

"Worse," agreed Maggie Orton. "At half-term one hasn't had time to get out of things. One feels a little sorry for oneself, but that's all. But when one's had nearly three weeks off it's far harder to fall into harness again."

"And the burden's heavier!" urged Mona

Bradley. "I've just told Miss Pollock so. We don't start in September with such a grind. No! They keep laying straw after straw on our unfortunate backs, here an exercise and there a problem, or some bit of extra prep., till in the aggregate it's more than mortal girl can bear! We're victims of over-pressure—that's what it is!"

"You don't look a victim—with cheeks like two streaky red American apples!" laughed Maudie Stearne.

"Appearances are deceptive, my good child! You'll often find the thin, wiry sort of folk can stand more than the nice, plump, rosy ones. As for me, I contend that this special botany class is the last straw. The camel's back is bending visibly, and I mean to throw over either Latin or music."

"Not music, surely!" said Kitty Fletcher. "Why, you'd miss half the fun of the school! You'd be out of all concerts and choral meetings, and you needn't flatter yourself the Dramatic would take you up instead. No, you'd just have to squat with the kids, and act audience, and I don't think that's much in your line, Mona Bradley! You're not the one to covet a back seat, as a rule."

"Why, of course I didn't intend to be out of the concerts," protested Mona plaintively. "I only thought I might drop my lessons and give up practising for a while — just during the tennis season, you know."

"Oh! I dare say! And you think Miss Jackson will let you play at recitals when you've never practised a note? Happy are the ignorant, indeed! Don't you know she wouldn't allow Margaret Hales a part in that trio, when poor old Mag had only been away ten days with 'flu'? As for putting on a girl who actually wasn't having lessons, why, the idea's preposterous! No, take your granny's advice, and knock off maths. or chemistry, or anything you can induce Miss Cartwright to let you throw overboard, but stick tight to your piano."

"True, O Queen! Yours are the words of wisdom, I admit. It's the half-hour's practising before breakfast that I so particularly loathe and abhor."

"Well, now the mornings are light, you needn't growl!"

"What a Mentor you are! You'll be quoting Dr. Watts to me next:

> "'Tis the voice of the sluggard, I heard him complain,
> 'You have waked me too soon, I must slumber again!'

I don't mind confessing that I hate getting up in the mornings; however sunny they are, it makes no difference. And to have to do it every day for a whole term, and peg away at scales and arpeggios! Ugh! I sometimes wish I'd been born a savage in Central Africa!"

"Then they'd have made you learn the tom-tom, and no doubt that's an instrument that needs perseverance. You can't get out of it, Mona mine! I see nothing for you but a dreary prospect of early rising, and the pursuit of five-finger exercises. It's your hard, cruel, inexorable fate, the chain from which you can't escape."

Mona laughed rather unwillingly: her mirth was never very spontaneous.

"I know it's slavery! Well, I suppose I must

live for the summer holidays! They let me lie in bed as long as I like, and it's my ideal of bliss."

"Then keep it, you old slacker!" said Bess Harrison. "We'll leave you to your dreams of a Mahomet's paradise. I like something livelier, and to go back to my original proposition, I think every school ought to provide a new sensation after the Easter holidays, just to wake us up, and keep us from stagnating."

"Of course there are tennis and cricket this term," suggested Maggie Orton, half apologetically.

"That I admit—but so far at St. Cyprian's we've only carried them on rather languidly. I wouldn't for the world confess it outside, but between ourselves I don't mind saying that we're far and away behind other schools at games. In music I grant you we can give anyone the lead, in languages we're fair, but at athletics we're a set of duffers."

"We oughtn't to be, then!" exploded Nell Hayward. "We're surely as physically fit as most girls, and if we laid ourselves out to train we'd astonish people. It's merely a matter of management. No one's bothered much about it before, or tried to keep us up to the mark, so of course we slacked. It's not our fault!"

"But the fact unfortunately remains the same!"

"We want some new life, certainly, put into the tennis and cricket," said Maudie Stearne. "Something to make it go. It's never been the same since Miss Pritchard left."

"She was A 1."

"We shan't get another Miss Pritchard!"

"None of the Sixth seem over-keen."

"We may make up our minds that St. Cyprian's is no good at games!"

"Cease these jeremiads!" interposed Kitty Fletcher. "I'll tell you something to cheer you up. Yes, it's news — real, creditable, veritable news! Why didn't I tell it before? Because I've been keeping it up my sleeve for the pleasure of giving you a complete surprise."

"Are we to have a professional to coach us?"

"Or a special games mistress?"

"Are several female athletes going to join the school?"

"Go on, Kit, and tell, can't you?"

"I haven't heard of either athletes or games mistress, but Miss Cartwright has a grand scheme on hand. We and five other schools are to join together in an alliance, and to meet each other for all kinds of things—hockey, cricket, tennis, concerts, debates, photography, gymnasium, arts and crafts, everything that's going, in fact."

"A kind of Olympic contest? Oh, what sport!"

"Exactly. You see, one school's generally keen on one thing, and another on something else. This is supposed to spur us on, and make us more 'all roundish'."

"Hem—a little wholesome competition!" quoted Maudie, with a fair imitation of Miss Cartwright's rather scholastic voice.

"You put it in a nutshell. We won't call it rivalry, but it would certainly touch us up to be beaten in anything by Newington Green or Marston Grove!"

"Ra—ther!"

"And no doubt they'd feel the same, so it will put us all on our mettle."

"I think it's a gorgeous idea; but how's it going to be run?"

"That's just the point. Each school is to have its own separate committee, and then send delegates to a general committee. There are to be five departments: Musical, Dramatic, Arts and Handicrafts, Literary, and Games, and we're to choose two delegates for each."

"Who's to do the choosing? Miss Cartwright?"

"No, it's to be put to the vote of the upper school. One must be from the Sixth and one from the Fifth, each form to vote for its own delegate."

"That sounds fair enough."

"Can we choose the same delegate for two subjects?"

"I shouldn't think so."

"Let me see — Musical, Dramatic, Arts and Handicrafts, Literary, and Games," said Maudie Stearne, ticking them off on her fingers. "Yes, I have somebody in my mind's eye for each. Mildred Lancaster, of course, for music."

"Mildred Lancaster? No, Lottie Lowman."

"She's not in it with Mildred."

"But she's a better organizer. There's no comparison, in my opinion."

"Nor in mine."

"Talk of people and they're sure to turn up! Here they both come."

"And as different as chalk from cheese!" murmured Maudie under her breath.

The two class-mates who entered the room at that moment were certainly entirely unlike as regards personal appearance, and the dissimilarity went deeper. Lottie Lowman, the elder by six months, was a brisk, alert-looking girl with a fresh complexion, a rather long, pointed nose, a thin mouth, and a square, determined chin. Her forehead was broad and intelligent, her light hazel eyes were very bright and sparkling, and her brown hair held just a suggestion of chestnut in the warmth of its colouring. Lottie's general effect was one of extreme vivacity. She loved to talk, and could say sharp things on occasion—there was hardly a girl in the Form who had not quailed before her tongue—and above all she adored popularity. To be a general favourite at once with mistresses, companions, and the Lower School was her chief aim, and she spared no trouble in the pursuit. Her flippant gaiety appealed to a large section of the Form, her humorous remarks were amusing, even though a sting lurked in them, and if her accomplishments were superficial, they made a far better show than the more-solid acquirements of others. She could do a little of everything, and had such perfect assurance that no touch of shyness ever marred her achievements. She knew absolutely how to make the best of herself, and she had a *savoir faire* and precocious knowledge of the world decidedly in advance of her sixteen years.

Mildred Lancaster, though only six months Lottie's junior, seemed a baby in comparison, where mundane matters were concerned. She was slightly built and rather delicate-looking, with a pale, eager face, a pair of beautiful, expressive brown eyes, a small mouth, and silky, soft, dull-gold hair, with a natural ripple in it. The far-away look in the dark eyes, and the set of the sensitive little mouth, suggested that highly-strung artistic temperament which may prove either the greatest joy or the utmost hindrance to its possessor. Mildred was dreamy and unpractical to a fault, the kind of girl who in popular parlance needs to be "well shaken up" at school, and whose imagination is apt to outrun her performance. Gifted to an unusual degree in music, at which she worked by fits and starts, her lack of general confidence was a great impediment, and often a serious handicap where any public demonstration was concerned. The feeling of having an audience, which was like the elixir of life to Lottie, filled Mildred with dismay, and was apt to spoil her best efforts.

The two girls, who had already heard of Miss Cartwright's scheme, came into the room full of the exciting news, and anxious to discuss it with their class-mates.

"The very thing for St. Cyprian's!" declared Lottie. "I'll undertake we'll give the other schools points! 'Nulli secundus,' second to none, shall be our motto. We'll practise and rehearse till we're tiptop, and can take the shine out of anybody. The five departments give such splendid opportunities. When's the election, by the by?"

"To-day at four," said Mildred. "And Miss Cartwright has just made up her mind that VB is to vote. She says it will be fairer, and give a better representation of the school."

"Oh, goody! We shall have to hurry up about canvassing."

"Is there to be canvassing?" objected Mona

Bradley. "I thought Miss Cartwright didn't like it?"

"We can't get on without it," said Lottie promptly. "Why, how else are you going to put the candidates' points to the electors? There are so many things to be considered if you take an all-round view. Besides, the fun of it! We'll have speeches!"

"Tub oratory's a cheap way of catching the crowd!" growled Kitty Fletcher.

"You shall give us a deep discourse, then!" flared Lottie. "No doubt you'll convince VB with some learned remarks. Well, if anything's to be done, we'd better be doing. Nell, old girl, you'll be on my side? Let's come and organize a plan of campaign. O jubilate! Here are the others!"

About seven more girls entered the room at the moment, all hotly engrossed in the new scheme, and anxious to discuss it. The company broke into groups, representing fairly well the various sets of the Form, and began eagerly to weigh the advantages and disadvantages of the various members proposed for the delegateships.

"It's a responsibility," said Kitty Fletcher, "because a good leader is half the battle. Don't let's allow any personal feeling to creep in. Vote for your enemy, if she's 'the man for the job'."

"May we vote for ourselves?" chirruped Eve Mitchell. "Oh, there! I was only in fun!" as the general scorn of the Form descended upon her. "Don't utterly spiflicate me! I'm not going to write 'Eve Mitchell' on all my five papers! Honest, I'm not!"

"You've a good chance for the Music, Mildred,"

whispered Kitty to her friend. "There isn't a girl in the school can play like you, and they know it. I'll back you up for that, if you'll put in a word for me at Games—that's all I'm good for!"

"And enough too," replied Mildred, "considering we can only be a delegate for one subject. I'll do my very best, Kit. I'll go at eleven and harangue some of those slackers in VB. Joan Richards and you would make an ideal couple; you'd work well together, and pull up the standard to what it was before Miss Pritchard left. Trust me to do all I can!"

There was little time for canvassing if the election were to take place at four o'clock on that very day. Perhaps Miss Cartwright had intentionally arranged it so, wishing to avoid too great seeking for favour among the girls. Competition she considered wholesome, but she did not want it to degenerate into rivalry. At eleven o'clock "break", and during the dinner interval, the supporters of the various prospective delegates worked hard, impressing the merits of their particular candidates upon the electors, and trying to secure promises of votes. The poll was only to be among the members of the Upper School, who, in the Principal's opinion, were likely to be better judges of each other's capabilities than would the younger girls. Juniors, she argued, might be swayed too easily by influence, but she trusted to her seniors to take an open-minded and unbiased view of the situation.

Soon after four o'clock, therefore, Forms VI, VA, and VB assembled in the lecture hall. A monitress dealt out papers, and in a moment or two Miss Cartwright, the Principal, stepped on to the platform.

"I should like to remind you, girls, of the few essential rules of our election," she began. "They are very simple. No one, of course, must vote for herself. Each girl is put on her honour not to be influenced by personal bias, but to choose for the good of the school. On your papers you will find five divisions—Musical, Literary, Dramatic, Arts and Handicrafts, and Games. Opposite each you are to write the names of one member of the Sixth Form and one of the Fifth. You must sign your own name to the paper, but this will be treated as confidential. I shall myself count the results."

"You vote for me, Mildred, for the Musical, and I'll vote for you," whispered Lottie Lowman, who happened to be sitting next to Mildred Lancaster. "We can't vote for ourselves, so exchange is no robbery, is it?"

Mildred coloured with embarrassment. She had already scribbled "Maudie Stearne" on her paper, not "Lottie Lowman", and it was tiresome to be thus cornered.

"These are the secrets of the confessional!" she murmured, trying to pass it off as a joke.

"Nonsense! We can't be so strict as all that. See, I've put 'Mildred Lancaster'. Let me look at yours."

As Lottie advanced her paper, Mildred hastily snatched hers away, but not before her companion had obtained a glance which told her of its contents. The slight rustle attracted the notice of Miss Cartwright, who fixed such a glare upon the two girls that each at once sat at stiff "attention", and as if unaware of the other's existence. In dead silence the voting was finished, the papers carefully folded, collected, and handed in.

"It will take me about ten minutes to count," said the Principal. "You can all go to the dressing-room. I will pin the result on the notice board as soon as I possibly can."

The girls filed from the lecture hall with a sense of relief. To sit waiting for the news would have been a sore trial of patience; it was far more satisfactory to spend the interval in donning hats and coats. Besides, in the dressing-room they could talk, and they certainly did not neglect the privilege. No sooner were they clear of the silence bounds than they broke into a perfect babel of chatter, discussing the pros and cons of the election. Some openly avowed how they had voted, some stuck to their privilege of secrecy, but all were ready to debate the chances of others. Mildred sat lacing her shoes and listening to the various scraps of conversation that reached her. She hardly dared to hope for her own success, yet among the whole Form no one more ardently desired a delegateship than herself. To be a representative of the musical side of St. Cyprian's particularly appealed to her. She felt it was almost in the nature of a sacred trust.

Close by Lottie Lowman and a few satellites were washing their hands.

"Some people's meanness is hardly to be believed!" Lottie was saying. "I'd voted for her, and told her so, so she hadn't the excuse of not knowing, and I think the least she could do was to vote for me—it only seemed fair!"

Mildred abandoned the neat "tennis knot" in which she was tying her shoelace, and sprang up in defence of her character.

"You'd no right to look!" she protested. "Surely I could put any candidate I liked? There was no coercion!"

"Not for those who weren't candidates themselves," said Sheila Moore; "but when you were standing for the Musical, you were in rather a different position."

"It was ever so generous of Lottie to vote for you!" urged Nora Whitehead.

"I certainly call it stingy not to vote for her!" added Eve Mitchell. "I should have thought it an obligation!"

"Oh, it's too bad of you! I can't see where the obligation comes in. Our votes were to be quite private. I think you're horrid!"

"Horrid yourself!" retorted Eve, and would have added more, but at that moment a scout announced that Miss Cartwright was in the very act of pinning the results upon the notice-board, so there was a general stampede for the corridor. As it was impossible for everyone to see the precious paper at once, the news was proclaimed aloud for the benefit of those on the outskirts of the crowd.

MUSICAL.—Ella Martin, Lottie Lowman.
LITERARY.—Phillis Garnett, Laura Kirby.
DRAMATIC.—Dorrie Barlow, May Thornett.
ARTS AND HANDICRAFTS.—Alice Lightwood, Freda Kingston.
GAMES.—Joan Richards, Kitty Fletcher.

"So I've won, even without your vote!" said Lottie to Mildred, with a spice of triumph in her tone.

"I'm very glad, I'm sure. I congratulate you heartily!" replied Mildred, turning back to the dressing-room for her books, and hurrying away, professedly in urgent quest of a tram-car.

Most of the others lingered, and started more slowly for home.

"I'm at the tiptop of bliss to have won the Games," said Kitty Fletcher to Bess Harrison. "I thought Mildred would have got the Musical, though. I can't understand it. She's miles ahead of Lottie, really."

"Yes, but I'm not sure if Lottie won't make the better delegate. Oh! I grant you Mildred has ten times the music in her, but I doubt if she'd get up a concert so well. She hasn't enough push and go —she's always dreaming. She'd play her own piece divinely, but she'd probably forget all about other people's."

"Yes, she is unbusinesslike," groaned Kitty, "but it seems such a shame that the most musical girl in the Form shouldn't represent the music section."

"Lottie knows exactly the public taste!"

"And plays trash!"

"She plays it well, though."

"In a way."

"You'll see her appointment will be very popular; she'll make things hum!"

"Likely enough, but I'm sorry for Mildred. I'm afraid she'll be fearfully disappointed."

CHAPTER II

St. Cyprian's College

AMONG the six day-schools which were to form the "Alliance" none was more important in the city of Kirkton than St. Cyprian's College. Though in numbers it was much smaller than the High School, it possessed a unique and thoroughly-well-deserved reputation of its own. St. Cyprian's specialized in music, and just as at many large educational establishments there is a classical and a modern side, its course of study was arranged for "collegiate" and "musical". No girl was received under twelve years of age, by which time, it was considered, her natural bent ought to have declared itself, and her parents could determine which branch would suit her best. Those who looked forward to a University degree, or any career in which public examinations must play an important part, were placed on the "Collegiate" side, and trained accordingly in the necessary classics, mathematics and physics, which would fit them for matriculation, or as candidates for certain scholarships. In this department St. Cyprian's had done well, and scored several brilliant successes. On the musical side Miss Cartwright considered she met a crying need. She was apt to wax enthusiastic when she discussed her favourite point.

"The time and attention devoted to music in most schools are totally inadequate," she would say. "Take any girl with a moderate amount of talent: the years from thirteen to eighteen are of extreme importance in her musical education. Now if she attends an ordinary High School, she may with great difficulty put in an hour's daily practice, but no allowance at all is made for this in her table of home work, and it must come out of her recreation time. She will probably have about forty minutes' choral singing weekly, and possibly—though this is by no means the rule—half an hour at theory, but of real music she does not understand even the rudiments. Pick out any ordinary girl of sixteen, take her to a concert, and ask her to name for you the various instruments in the orchestra: the chances are a hundred to one that the violin and the 'cello are about the limit of her knowledge. She could not tell you the difference between a sonata and a symphony, or give you the vaguest idea of the bass for such a simple tune as the National Anthem. Though, of course, girls differ greatly in musical capacity, I contend that the utter lack of any adequate training is largely responsible for the pitiable ignorance and bad taste in music which is a reproach only too justly flung at the British by other European nations. If all schools would give this subject the prominence it deserves, at the end of a generation the present popular songs would not be tolerated at all, and we could once more produce something of the quality of the old English, Scotch, and Irish melodies which have lived among our national tunes. I hope that we shall one day restore music to its proper place."

In accordance with her system, therefore, Miss Cartwright arranged that any pupil who was entered on the musical side of the school had a specially-prepared curriculum. Certain lessons, which were compulsory on the collegiate side, were in her case omitted, and the time given to classes in harmony and counterpoint. Each girl practised for at least half an hour daily at school, under the supervision of a mistress, who was present while she received the weekly or bi-weekly lesson from her master, and who would see that his instructions were carried out to the letter. The home practising was considered of such vital importance that every pupil received a weekly time-sheet, which she was required to fill up with the amount done daily, and to bring signed by a parent or guardian. By this method real and thorough work was ensured, and a record of progress carefully kept.

With regard to its special cult of music, St. Cyprian's was particularly fortunate in being situated at Kirkton, one of the biggest provincial cities in England. Kirkton offered peculiar facilities for a musical education. Owing to its important commerce and wide area, it could boast of an unusually large population, who were sufficiently wealthy and influential to support a magnificent series of classical concerts. The "Crawford" orchestra, so called in memory of its founder, was world-famous, and comprised some of the best instrumentalists from various parts of Europe, while its conductorship was considered an honour sufficient to tempt leading musicians from Vienna or Paris. There was also in the city the Crawford Academy of Music, on the lines of a foreign conservatoire, where members of the celebrated orchestra gave lessons, and students who were judged of sufficient talent could be adequately trained for the musical profession.

To this "Academy of Music" Miss Cartwright passed on the most brilliant of her pupils. Several of its professors taught at St. Cyprian's, and she endeavoured as far as possible that all the instruction given at her College should be on "Crawford" lines, and therefore preparatory to the more advanced work which was to follow.

Among the girls who comprised the musical section of the school there were, of course, vast differences. Some were not possessed of any very great capacity, and would never attain more than ordinary proficiency, but one or two were really talented. The standard was so high, and the pains taken with the pupils were so great, that almost any average girl could be taught to play well, up to a certain point. There is a difference, however, between music that has been learnt and music that is inborn, and no amount of cultivation can supply what nature has not implanted. At present there were only about five girls at St. Cyprian's whose performance was of outstanding merit.

Ella Martin, a member of the Sixth, played the violin with considerable skill; but though her technique was good, she had no power of expression, and the result was brilliant, but cold. Elizabeth Chalmers, of VB, was the counterpart of Ella Martin, but on the piano. Her rendering of most compositions was excellent as regards execution, but purely mechanical, and therefore soulless. May Fawcett, a child of barely thirteen, who had only joined the school at Christmas, showed talent, but was yet in the initial stages of Professor Delacluse's particular system, and, until she had forgotten the faults developed under her former teacher, was being kept almost entirely at exercises and studies.

In VA two girls came easily to the fore. Lottie Lowman had acquired rather an all-round reputation in the College. She played the piano well, with a crisp, firm touch and a certain amount of feeling. She was an excellent reader, and could dash off almost anything at sight, and as she had, besides, the power of memorizing, she always seemed at home on her instrument. She sang also, with a clear soprano voice, pretty, popular drawing-room ballads, into which she threw much sentiment, and which never failed to delight an ordinary audience. Her extreme confidence stood her in good stead, and her bright, taking manner added a further charm to her undoubtedly clever performances.

If Lottie was certainly the favourite of the school, it was Mildred Lancaster who, in the opinion of those really competent to judge, was likely in the future to do credit to St. Cyprian's. Mildred had shown talent amounting sometimes to inspiration, and every now and then she rose to the point of genius. She learnt both piano and violin, but it was at the latter instrument she excelled. Hitherto she had only worked when she chose, and was alternately the pride and the despair of her master, Herr Hoffmann. There was, unfortunately, no relying upon Mildred's industry. One week her practice sheet would record three hours daily, and the next would show a deplorable series of blanks. When she felt in the mood to play she could astonish her professor with her extraordinary flashes of brilliancy, but at other times she would seem absolutely apathetic and uninterested.

She had been three years at St. Cyprian's, and her general school record was fairly good. She never rose beyond the average of the Form, but was not regarded as amongst the drones. Perhaps one reason for this was her friendship with Kitty Fletcher. Kitty had a thoroughly sensible, practical character. She was a hard worker, and being one of a large family, was not given to whims or fancies. Her influence over dreamy, romantic Mildred was excellent; she would spur her on to fresh efforts, both in lessons and athletics, and by a combination of sympathy, chaffing, and sheer will power often prevented her from falling into the slough of inertia to which her disposition was prone. Bright, jolly Kitty was well liked in her Form, and her appointment as Games delegate proved popular. Her enthusiasm was catching, and already the girls promised under her leadership to try to retrieve the lost glory of the College, and raise it again to its former standard.

All at St. Cyprian's knew that the United Schools Alliance was not a thing to be taken lightly. If they wished to shine in comparison with other schools, they would have to work, and devote far more energy to their various undertakings than they had yet troubled to give. Their five rivals were not at all to be despised. The Kirkton High School, averaging six hundred to their two hundred, by its very numbers offered a good pick of champions for hockey teams or tennis tournaments. The Marston Grove High School, a suburban branch of the former, had improved on its parent establishment, and cultivated an almost Olympic keenness for athletic contests. The Newington Green School was famous for its Arts and Handicrafts. The Templeton School had given several excellent dramatic entertainments in aid of charities; while the Manor House School, noted for its French, could certainly win the palm in respect of languages.

"The fact is, except in music, we're rather a rotten set. We shall have to buck up!" said Kitty at the first committee meeting. "If we don't, we shall get a slap in the face."

Though they might not endorse her slang, the other nine delegates were inclined to agree with her sentiments.

"There hasn't been enough competition just amongst ourselves," argued Ella Martin.

"And it's been so hard to make anyone enthusiastic!" sighed Alice Lightwood.

"Or get them to do anything," echoed Joan Richards.

"Well, they've just got to enthuse now. Slackers must turn sloggers, for the credit of St. Cyprian's," declared Kitty. "Each department needs thoroughly organizing, and the best workers picking out. If possible we must try and not overlap. It stands to reason the same girl can't be champion at everything, and it's better to make her decide on her bent, and stick to it. If she's A1 at drawing, she mustn't unsteady her hand by over-practice at tennis; but if she's a record bowler, for goodness' sake don't let her waste her time pottering over photography. I vote we take a census of the school, put down everybody's speciality, and place her on one of our five lists."

"An excellent suggestion," said Dorrie Barlow. "We divide the school into Literary, Musical, Dramatic, Arts, and Athletics, and as heads of the various departments look after our own protégées."

"But surely all will play games?" objected Joan Richards.

"Oh, yes! they'll play, of course—one must have a rank and file—but the ones we select for special training must not be those who are working in another division. Can't you see that if a girl's in the 'Dramatic', or practising for a concert, she may play cricket or tennis for health and recreation, but she can't give her whole mind to it, as she ought to if she wants to be a champion?"

"A boarding-school with compulsory games has the best chance."

"Well, thank goodness, we're not competing against boarding-schools. The others are as much day girls as ourselves, and no doubt as hard to make keen. If we can keep up the general interest we shan't do badly, and I dare say we may hold our own with fair credit."

Kitty's plan was at once adopted by the committee. A census was taken of the school, and each girl was asked to decide upon which subject she meant to devote her surplus energies. The delegates were enthusiastic, and allowed nobody to escape from their net. They formed five special societies with sub-committees, drew up rules, enrolled their members, and insisted upon keeping them up to the mark. Any girl who was not clever in the more-cultured branches of the Alliance was relegated to athletics, and under Kitty's tutorship made to develop her muscles. At first the habitual idlers grumbled, and tried to evade the hard work, but public opinion was against them. St. Cyprian's was on its mettle, and the busy bees would not tolerate drones in their hive. Any girl who did not try her best in one of the five new societies speedily found herself unpopular, and to be unpopular in a large school is an unpleasant experience. Each society was working for a definite object. The "Dramatic" was getting up a play, the "Literary" meant to publish a magazine, the "Arts and Handicrafts" were working for an exhibition, the "Musical" meant to give a concert, and the "Athletic" was training its cricket and tennis champions.

Lottie Lowman certainly was capable of rendering good service in the Musical department. She discovered several juniors with promising voices, and taught them each to sing a solo with great effect. If her style was not quite of the best, she was enthusiastic, and could communicate her own enthusiasm to others. The younger ones practised away at light opera songs with keenest enjoyment, learnt, in their spare time, to play the accompaniments, and were always to be heard trilling snatches of melody about the school. Ella Martin was concentrating her efforts upon the instrumental parts, and left the vocal to her co-delegate. "Lottie's choir", as her flock was called, was entirely a separate institution from the College Choral Classes, and had nothing to do with Mr. Hiller, the singing master. Lottie organized the whole business, chose the songs, conducted practices, and coached her pupils entirely independent of any supervision at head-quarters. She threw herself heartily into her task. The work entirely suited her. She loved to lead, and was extremely happy in her new rôle of training mistress. The girls had gathered very readily round her musical standard, with one exception. Mildred Lancaster held herself aloof, and, under plea of needing all her time for instrumental work, refused to attend the choral practices.

It had been a great blow for Mildred that she was not chosen as a delegate. She was conscious that her talent greatly surpassed Lottie's, and she did not altogether approve of the latter's methods. Her marked lack of enthusiasm for the new scheme drew down comment from her friend Kitty Fletcher.

"You might help, Mildred! You could do so much if you liked, and it's all for the good of the Coll. Why can't you train some kids, or give a shove to the thing somehow?"

Mildred shook her head gloomily.

"I know you think me mean, but the fact is I can't work with Lottie. Her style sets my teeth on edge. She's giving those juniors the most trashy, rubbishy set of songs, and teaching them to sing with that horrible perpetual vibrato—and you know Mr. Hiller's opinion of that! She lets them thump accompaniments anyhow, with the bass all wrong. Ugh! The whole thing is too music-hall-y for me."

"Of course we all know your taste is classical," sighed Kitty; "but on that very account I thought you might be so useful in keeping up the standard.

Miss Cartwright never meant them to howl pantomime songs. You'd be a check on Lottie."

"A check she won't acknowledge. If I say a word, she'll ask me who's delegate, and tell me to mind my own business. I don't court snubs, thank you! No; if they chose Lottie, they must stick to Lottie, and abide the consequences. I'm not going to do the spadework and let her reap the harvest. I've plenty of practising to do on my own account, quite enough to fill my spare time."

"Yes, if you'd do it," retorted Kitty, who was public-spirited, and therefore rather angry with her friend.

But Mildred only shrugged her shoulders, and turned away. Kitty said no more at the time, but she made an opportunity to see Ella Martin, and poured forth her complaints.

"Mildred's slacking all round," she said. "I don't know what's wrong with her. She's letting her own work go. Her practice-sheet is a disgrace. She's the most musical girl we have at the Coll., and she's simply doing nothing for herself or anyone else."

"Yes, I've noticed she's gone off lately," replied Ella. "She's a curious girl. I can't make her out. I sometimes think she's incorrigibly lazy. She plays when she feels inclined, and she's so clever that it's no effort to her, but real solid work she doesn't understand. If I'd half her talent I'd undertake to do more with it than she does. Sometimes she makes Professor Hoffmann absolutely rage with wrath; she has her lesson just before mine, you know, so I don't bless her when she leaves him in a bad temper. Professor Daneport gets pretty savage too when she won't practise, though I think he realizes that her piano is only understudy to her violin, and doesn't expect too much."

"I wish something would happen to wake her up!" declared Kitty.

CHAPTER III

The Story of a Violin

MILDRED LANCASTER, with whose history this book is largely concerned, was an orphan, and had been brought up from her babyhood by an uncle and aunt who had no children of their own. Her uncle, Dr. Graham, was a busy man with a large practice, who managed nevertheless to spare a little leisure to keep up the scientific side of his profession. He was a prominent member of Health Congresses, Sanitary Commissions, and Medical Societies, and was full of schemes for the better housing of the poorer people, the opening of gardens and pleasure-grounds in crowded slum districts, the care of cripples and pauper children, or any question which affected the well-being of the poor people among whom his work chiefly lay. In all these things Mrs. Graham was his most earnest right hand.

She had a very strong sense of her responsibility towards those who were less-well equipped for the world's battles than herself, and she tried to take some of the light and beauty and culture of her own well-ordered life into those sad, sordid homes, where no dawn of higher things had ever shone. It was quiet, unostentatious work, that sometimes seemed to show small reward for the trouble spent over it, but she went on patiently all the same, knowing that the result might often be there, even if she were not able to see it herself.

To both Dr. and Mrs. Graham, Mildred stood in the place of a daughter. She could remember no other home, and knew no other friends, for her mother's relations had hitherto ignored the very fact of her existence. It was a happy little household, with a great deal of love in it, but the life was plain and simple, with few luxuries or extra indulgences. The Grahams were not rich people, and everything that they did not need for absolute necessities was devoted to helping forward the many causes they had at heart. On Mildred's education, however, they spared no expense. They sent her to St. Cyprian's College because it was the only school where she could spend an adequate time on the music which they hoped might some day prove to be her career, and they were prepared later on to give her the best possible advantages.

On the very afternoon when Ella Martin and Kitty Fletcher were talking about her, Mildred, quite unconscious of their concern on her behalf, was at home, trying to make up some arrears on her practising sheet. The cosy upstairs sitting-room of the corner house in Meredith Terrace was a cheerful place, though the carpet was worn and the curtains were faded. The long rows of shelves on either side of the fire-place were overflowing with books; on the walls hung prints, etchings, and water-colour sketches, most of them unframed, and pinned here and there, without any definite order as to arrangement, so as to secure the best light available. An unfinished red-chalk drawing stood on an easel by the open piano, a pot full of tulips made a rich spot of colour against the old green table-cloth, and a large grey Persian cat slept peacefully and luxuriously in the arm-chair.

It was a congenial atmosphere for study, and Mildred, who stood with her violin in the bow-window, had the dreamy, far-away expression in her eyes which, to those who knew her, meant that her artistic side was uppermost. Her long, thin, supple fingers were bringing real music from her instrument. Though her gaze might be fixed upon the piece placed upon the stand before her, she was paying no heed to it, for the snatches of melody, now bright and joyful, now soft and sad, which floated through the room were of her own improvising, a kind of reflection of the spring sunshine and the twittering of the birds outside that found its expression in the notes which flowed so richly and easily that it almost seemed as if her violin were speaking with a human voice. One cannot live long, however, in a world composed only of sweet sounds, and Mildred found her day-dream quickly and suddenly dispelled by the opening of the door and the brisk entrance of her aunt.

"Mildred, dear! Do you call this practising? I thought you had promised me to keep strictly to your concerto. When I last heard it there were still a great many mistakes, and I'm afraid Herr Hoffmann will be anything but satisfied when you go for your next lesson."

Thus brought back to the practical side of life, Mildred put down her violin with a sigh.

"Such a lovely idea came into my head, Tantie!

I just had to try it over at once, for fear it should go out again. I thought I might enjoy myself for ten minutes!"

Mrs. Graham did not look approving.

"How many scales and arpeggios have you played?" she enquired gravely.

"Well, not any yet. I can do them after tea."

"And your exercise?"

"Oh! there'll be plenty of time to learn that before next Wednesday. It's quite an easy one."

"It may be easy, but it will need practice all the same. Have you tried your new piece?"

"The 'Frühlingslied'? It's much too difficult. I shall take it back and tell Herr Hoffmann I can't possibly manage it. It's one of those terrible things that go with an orchestra. I simply hate them. The Professor plays to represent the other instruments, and he's always more than usually fussy and particular. He scolds most abominably if I play a false note, or happen to come in at the wrong place."

"I'm very glad to hear it. I think you need more scolding than you get at home."

Mildred screwed up her mouth with a rather humorous expression, then flung her arms round her aunt's neck and gave her an impulsive hug.

"Sweetest darling little Tantie, you can't scold! So please don't begin to try. I know I'm horribly bad. I ought to have been grinding away at that wretched concerto all the time, but it isn't very pretty, and it has such nasty catchy bits in it. I like making up pieces for myself so much better than proper practising. The tunes just come into my head, and then I feel as if I must play them over before I forget them. If I wait, they're gone, and I never can catch them again."

"I don't blame you, dear child, for liking to compose. What I find fault with is that you always want to shirk the hard part of the work. Scales and exercises are not pleasant, I own, but they train your fingers in a way which nothing else can do. How often has the Professor told you that, I wonder?"

"About fifteen dozen times, I dare say!" laughed Mildred, cajoling her aunt into one of the cosy basket-chairs which stood near the hearth, and installing herself in the other, with Godiva, the Persian cat, on her knee. "That doesn't make the scales and exercises any more interesting, though. It's no use, Tantie! I love music, but I detest the drudgery of it. Why need I spend so much time over the part I don't like? Why can't I just play my own tunes, and be happy?"

"Because we all hope you are worthy of better things. Simply to amuse yourself is not the highest ideal, either in music or life. Your violin was the only possession which your father could leave to you, and you must think of it as an inheritance, not as a toy."

"I know so little about my father," said Mildred, leaving her seat, and throwing herself down on the hearth-rug, with her head against her aunt's knee. "You scarcely ever talk about him."

"Because it's a sad remembrance, dear," said Mrs. Graham, stroking the golden hair with a gentle hand. "I've shrunk from speaking of it before, and yet I have often felt lately that you ought to know the story. I would rather you heard it from me than learnt it from anyone who might tell it to you with less sympathy than I should."

She paused, with a far-away look in her eyes, as if memories of the past were living before her. For a moment or two there was silence in the room, only broken by Godiva's purrs and the twittering of the birds outside.

"Please go on!" said Mildred impatiently.

"Your violin has a history," began Mrs. Graham. "You know already that it is a very old and valuable one, made by Stradivarius himself, whose skill was so marvellous that nobody since has ever been able to equal the instruments which he turned out from his workshop at Cremona. I can't tell you who was the earliest owner, or how many hands, long since dead, have brought sweet music out of it; but when I first made its acquaintance it was the most cherished possession of a strange old gentleman who lived in the cathedral city where I was born. No one knew anything about Monsieur Strelezki, for though he had been an inhabitant of Dilchester for several years, he remained to the last as great a mystery as on the day he arrived. His housekeeper, an elderly Frenchwoman, always alluded to him as 'Monsieur le Comte', and he was generally believed to be a Polish nobleman, who for some political reason had been exiled from his native land. He spoke excellent English, and was apparently well off and accustomed to good society; yet he lived the life of an absolute recluse, refusing to exchange visits with any of his neighbours, who, after their first curiosity had worn off, shunned him with an almost superstitious horror, whispering many tales about him under their breath.

"My brother and I would look with a kind of fascination at the gloomy old dwelling just outside the precincts which the Comte had bought, and at once surrounded with such a very high wall that it went in future by the name of 'The Hidden House'. We used to pass it every day on our way to school, and I remember how, by a mutual understanding, we always crossed the road exactly at the corner near the lamp-post, so as to avoid walking too close to what, in our childish imagination, might be the abode of a wizard or a witch. Your father was my only brother, five years younger than myself, my greatest companion, and my special charge after our mother's death. He had the most charming, lovable, careless, happy-go-lucky, and irresponsible disposition that I have ever known. I fear both my father and I spoilt him, for he was very winning, and when he would ask in his coaxing way it was difficult to refuse him anything. From a little child he had shown the most wonderful love for music. He seemed to learn the piano almost by instinct, and his greatest amusement was to play by ear all the chants and anthems which were sung by the cathedral choir. An air once heard never escaped his memory, and he would put such beautiful harmonies to it, and make such elaborate variations upon it, that I have often listened to him with amazement. Our father was proud of his boy's talent, and, wishing him to play the organ, made arrangements that he should take lessons from the cathedral organist.

"At first Bertram was pleased to have the great

instrument respond to his little fingers, but he found the stops and pedals were troublesome and confusing to manage, and he did not make the progress we had hoped for. His one longing was to learn the violin. He used to implore our dancing-teacher to allow him to try the small instrument by which we were taught to regulate the steps of our quadrilles and polkas, and he would even bribe the blind old street musician who played before our house on Saturday mornings to lend him his fiddle and bow. There was no one in the town, however, whom my father considered worthy to teach him, so he was obliged to content himself with trying to pick out tunes on a guitar which had belonged to my mother, and which he had found stowed away in the lumber-room. One day my brother and I were walking down the narrow paved street on our way home from the cathedral, when, passing by the mysterious 'Hidden House', we heard the wailing strains of a violin. Bertram at once stopped to listen, and seeing that the door in the high wall, which was generally fast locked, to-day stood open, he crept inside the garden, so that he might hear the better. I followed, to try and persuade him to return, but I, too, was so attracted by the enchanting music which flowed through the open window that together we stood concealed behind a syringa bush, almost holding our breath for pleasure.

"I know now that it was a composition of Rubenstein's that Monsieur le Comte was playing, but we had never heard it before. It was a style of foreign music quite new to us, and the wild romance, the weird beauty and pathos, the bewitching, haunting ring of the melody, rendered by a master hand, together with the strangeness of the unusual rhythm, roused my brother to a degree of excitement I had never seen him show before. As the last soft notes sank quivering away, he rushed from his hiding-place, and running up the steps to the French window, dashed impulsively into the room where Monsieur Strelezki stood with his violin.

"'Oh, thank you! Thank you!' he cried. 'I've never heard anything so wonderful in all my life. Will you please tell me what it's called? And oh! if you would play it over again!'

"To say that the Comte was astonished will very poorly describe the scene that followed, but finding that the boy was in earnest, he bade us be seated, and gave us such a bewildering and utterly charming selection of quaint Polish and Hungarian airs that Bertram was wild with delight. He sealed a friendship then and there with Monsieur Strelezki, and whenever he had a half-hour to spare he would hurry away to the 'Hidden House' to listen to more of the fascinating music.

"It was perhaps only natural that the Comte, seeing my brother's enthusiasm, should offer to teach him the violin; and though my father was somewhat doubtful about allowing him to accept so great a favour from our eccentric neighbour, he could not, in the end, resist Bertram's pleadings, so the lessons began. I think teacher and pupil enjoyed them equally, and the boy's progress was simply marvellous. He not only learned with a rapidity which astonished even his master, but about this time he began to compose pieces himself, and could hardly contain his joy in this newly-discovered talent. I would often beg him to write them down, as he was apt to forget them; but he did not like the trouble of transcribing music, and would declare with a laugh that it did not matter, as he always had a new one in his head. His school work suffered very much. He would spend over his violin hours which ought to have been given to preparing Greek and Latin, and my father was often angry over his bad reports. It seemed little use, however, to scold him; he was full of promises of amendment, but he never kept any of them.

"This had gone on for perhaps three years, when one day my brother went round early to the 'Hidden House'. He found everything in a state of confusion and upset. Monsieur Strelezki had died suddenly of heart failure during the night. The old housekeeper had discovered him, when she entered the dining-room in the morning, sitting, as she supposed, writing, with his violin on the table by his side; but the eyes bent over the paper were sightless, and the fingers that still held the pen were stiff and cold. On a half-sheet of note-paper he had written in a shaky hand:

"'To Bertram Lancaster.

"'Farewell, dear pupil and friend! The King of the Musicians has called me. We shall meet no more in this world. I bequeath you my Stradivarius. May it prove for you the key to fame. Remember always that there is only one secret of true success, and that is . . .'

"But here the messenger had come for Monsieur

le Comte, and he had obeyed the summons, leaving the secret he had tried to tell for ever untold.

"As my brother grew older his passion for music seemed only to increase. My father wished him to study law, so that he might in time give him a partnership in the steadygoing old-fashioned solicitor's practice which had been in our family for several generations, but Bertram utterly refused. He had set his heart on a musical career, and after a bitter quarrel with his father, he left home altogether, taking with him the small fortune he had inherited from our mother, and went away with the avowed intention of devoting himself to his violin.

"'I feel I have a future before me, Alice,' he said, as he bade me good-bye. 'I shall solve the Comte's secret yet. If it was talent he referred to' (and he flushed a little) 'I think I've my fair share of that, so perhaps the Stradivarius may really prove the key to fame, in spite of everything!'

"It is a very sad part of the story that comes now, but I must tell it to you all the same. Bertram left us in high hopes, and for a time, while his enthusiasm was fresh, and the change still new, I believe he studied hard at his music. But he had a curious lack of any real effort or steady concentrated purpose. He was always going to do great things, which somehow were never accomplished. I cannot tell you how many operas and oratorios he began to compose, which were to take the public by storm; but none of them was ever finished, though the fragments which I heard were of so rare a quality that they were fit to rank among the works of men of genius. Sometimes he would be at the very height of exaltation, and sometimes in the lowest depths of despair; there were periods of wild ambition, when he was determined to have the world at his feet, but they never lasted long enough to carry him through the whole of an opera.

"A few of his shorter compositions were published, and were very highly thought of by musicians, and he had splendid opportunities of playing at concerts and recitals. His appearances in public were always successful; yet he so often refused to fulfil his engagements, for no apparent reason except the whim of the moment, that the managers grew tired of him. He fell under the influence of bad companions, who led him to neglect his work, and to think of nothing but pleasure, and he had not the moral courage to say 'No' to them. His little fortune was soon spent, and as my father refused to help him, he was obliged at last to earn his bread as a teacher of music. It was in this capacity that he made the acquaintance of your mother, whose father, Sir John Lorraine, could not forgive her runaway match with one whom he considered utterly unworthy of her, and forbade her name to be mentioned again in his presence. You cannot remember her, Mildred, for she only lived long enough to put her little golden-haired baby into my arms, and beg me to be a friend to it—a trust that I have never forgotten, both for your sake and hers.

"After this matters went from bad to worse. Your father, in his grief, took no trouble over his teaching, pupils slipped away, and he also lost the post in an orchestra which for some time had been his chief resource. I helped him to my uttermost, but it was little enough, after all, that I could do for him. His health, never robust, seemed suddenly to fail, and before the year was out he had died, broken-hearted, in the prime of his youth, the success he had dreamt of still unwon. I was with him at the last, and as he put his poor worn hand in mine, he said:

"'Alice, I discovered the Comte's secret too late! Give the Stradivarius to my child. It's the only inheritance I have to leave her. Perhaps my wasted life may teach her to use hers to better advantage, and some day she may meet with the fame and success that I always hoped for but never gained.'"

Mildred sat very silent for a moment or two when Mrs. Graham had finished her story.

"What was the Comte's secret?" she asked at length, with a break in her voice.

"Perseverance and hard work. Talent is of very little use without these. Nothing can be gained in this world without taking pains, and any success worth having must be at the cost of the best effort that's in us. Do you see why I've told you this to-day?"

"Yes," replied Mildred thoughtfully. "I didn't know my violin had such a history. I loved it before, but I shall love it ten thousand times better now. Tantie, I think I'll tussle with the 'Frühlingslied' after all. I believe if I really slave at it I can manage it. It'll be hateful, but I declare I'll try, if I break every string, and wear my bow out in the attempt."

"That's my brave girl! Shall we have a resolution, not only for the 'Frühlingslied', but for all-round work at school? Miss Cartwright says you can do so well when you choose. Won't you promise?"

"Honour bright, Tantie! I'll do my best!"

CHAPTER IV

Concerns VA

MILDRED'S resolution to work was a huge effort to her easy-going, unpractical temperament, but she could not have made it at a more favourable time. The new Alliance had aroused a general wave of enthusiasm at St. Cyprian's, and many girls who before had been inclined to shirk were now determined to put their shoulders to the wheel. There is a great deal in public opinion, and while a do-as-you-please attitude had hitherto been in vogue, keenness and strenuousness now became the fashion. The school was divided into "Sloggers" and "Slackers", and the latter were looked down upon, and made to feel their inferiority. Among the seventeen girls who composed VA there was of course every variety of disposition, from Laura Kirby, who was nicknamed "the walking dictionary", to Sheila Moore, who was a byword for silliness. Naturally they had their different little sets and cliques, but these were only affairs of secondary importance; as a Form they were remarkably united, and anxious to maintain the credit of VA against the rest of the school.

It was especially with regard to their seniors that they felt an element of competition. To beat juniors was always a poor triumph, and nothing much to boast of, but the Form perpetually cherished the ambition to (as they expressed it) "go one better than the Sixth". The Sixth were not disposed to lay aside their laurels, so the struggle went on, in quite an amicable fashion, but with a spirit of rivalry all the same. It was the custom every few weeks for each of the three top forms to give a short dialogue in French or German. These had nothing to do with the Dramatic Society, being merely part of the school course, to accustom the girls to converse in foreign languages, and they were performed with very little ceremony before an audience of teachers and juniors. This month a German scene had been apportioned to VA, and Kitty Fletcher, Bess Harrison, Mona Bradley, and Mildred Lancaster were chosen by Fräulein Schulte to represent the principal characters. It was not difficult to learn their short parts, and last term, when once they had committed them to memory, they would have thought no more of the matter until the afternoon of the performance. Now, however, in view of the generally-raised standard, they were disposed to take more trouble.

"I'd just like to show the Sixth what we can do," said Kitty. "Suppose our dialogue turned out better than theirs? It would be such a triumph!"

"It strikes me the Sixth intend to turn the tables, and spring a surprise on us," said Mildred. "I'm quite sure they're concocting something."

"Oh, how did you get to know? What is it?"

"That I can't say, but I heard them murmuring something about a rehearsal, and they all scooted off to the small studio."

"Are they there now? I vote we go and see," suggested Bess Harrison.

The four girls hurried upstairs at once, only to find the door of the studio locked, and the Sixth firm in their refusal to open it.

"I want to get my drawing-board!" wailed Mona through the keyhole.

"Then you ought to have got it before. You'll have to wait now," was the stern reply.

"But I must have it. And my chalk pencils. Let me in just for an instant!"

"I tell you I can't!"

"What are you all doing in there?"

"That's our concern."

"Oh, you are mean!"

"Go away this minute, and leave us in peace. What business have you intruding here?"

Finding knocks and thumps on the door as useless as their entreaties, and that the keyhole had been carefully stopped up with a piece of soft paper, the four beat a retreat. They were consumed with curiosity, however.

"I just mean to get to know, somehow!" exploded Bess.

"Look here," said Mona, "I've an idea. Let us creep out through that skylight window on the landing, crawl over the roof, and then we can peep right down through the studio skylight. We'd see for ourselves then. It would be better than keyholes."

Mona's brilliant suggestion was hailed with joy. The only obstacle which offered itself was the difficulty of climbing up to the skylight. But Mona was resourceful. She remembered the housemaids' cupboard at the top of the stairs, and promptly purloined the step-ladder which stood there. Fortunately it was a tall one, so without any superhuman display of agility they were able to reach the roof. A narrow parapet ran round the edge of the house, which afforded some slight security, but perhaps all four girls felt qualms when they found themselves at such a giddy height. Not one would confess her fear, though, so they commenced to creep cautiously forward in the direction of the studio.

"It's like Alpine climbing!" gasped Kitty as they ascended the steep angle. "We've got to go over that ridge! Oh! I say, aren't the slates hot?"

Giggling a little to hide their tremors, the adventurous four reached the chimney-stack, and paused for a moment to survey the prospect. They could obtain a truly bird's-eye view of the playground and the street beyond.

"I know what it must feel like to see things from an aeroplane," said Mildred. "You just get the tops instead of the sides. Look at those hats down there!"

"Oh, don't let us waste time in looking!" said Mona. "Suppose the Sixth should have gone when we get to the studio? It would be such a stupendous sell!"

Urged by the mere idea of such a fiasco, the girls plucked up their courage again, and pursued their caterpillar-like progress. They soon reached the studio skylight, and, peering down, were able easily to see into the room. The Sixth were still there, and very busily employed. Apparently they were holding a rehearsal, and they were dressed up in costumes suitable to the occasion. Dorrie Barlow wore a large French peasant cap, Kathleen Hodson sported a cloak and top-boots, and Edith Armitage, in a blue silk dress with a train, was evidently a lady of high degree. Sublimely unconscious of the four spies above them, the seniors went on complacently with their work. Most of their conversation only ascended as a general buzz, but every now and then a remark in a louder tone than usual was audible on the roof.

"That's capital, Gertie!"

"No one's an idea what we're doing."

"We routed those Fifth-Formers!"

"Cheek of them to come prying here!"

"They went away no wiser, though!"

"We must hide these costumes."

The spectators above absolutely gurgled with joy, but they were careful not to betray their presence. Making a sign to the others, Mona motioned them to withdraw their heads.

"We've seen enough!" she whispered. "They might look up at any moment. Better beat a retreat now."

Four very satisfied girls climbed back over the ridge of the roof. They had gained exactly the information they wanted, and they meant to act upon it. They considered their action was a benefit to their Form.

"We've done it so quickly," said Mona, who was leading the way, "we shall have time to scoot downstairs, and be just innocently loitering about the playground before the Sixth have finished. They'll never guess!—Oh, I say, here's a go!"

"What's the matter?"

"Why, if the wretched skylight isn't shut!"

This was bad news indeed. With consternation in their faces they crept closer, and tried to lift the skylight up. They pulled till their fingers were sore, but with no success.

"Somebody must have come along the passage and shut it," said Kitty. "It's a nuisance to have to give ourselves away, but I can't see anything for it but to knock and get the window opened."

"Someone's sure to be going along the passage," said Bess hopefully.

So they knocked quietly at first, and then thumped with energy sufficient to break the glass. There was no response, however; not even a solitary junior passed down the passage.

"What are we to do?"

Kitty's face was blank in the extreme.

"The step-ladder's gone too!" squealed Bess.

At that moment the big school bell clanged loudly for afternoon call-over. Waxing absolutely desperate, the girls not only thumped on the glass, but shouted. To their intense relief their signals were heard, and the figure of Rogers, the upper housemaid, hove into view. Calling to them to keep clear of the window, she opened the skylight.

"Whatever are you doing up there?" she enquired tartly.

"Oh, Rogers, do be an angel, and fetch the steps quick!"

The expression on Rogers's face was not at all angelic.

"You've no business out on the roof, and you know it."

"Yes, that's why we want to come down," returned Kitty, "if you'll only let us. Do fetch those steps, please!"

Grumbling to herself, Rogers brought the step-ladder, and held it steady while the girls descended.

"I shall tell Miss Cartwright," she announced. "Larks like these are beyond a joke."

"Oh, Rogers, don't—don't, please!" implored the sinners. "We'll vow on our honour never to do it again. Honest—honest, we won't!"

"I can't have the steps taken out of my cupboard."

"We won't so much as peep through the chink of the door again, far less touch anything."

"Do, please, promise not to report us. Oh, we're going to be late for call-over! There's the second bell."

"Late you'll certainly be, and serve you right!" snapped Rogers. Then, relenting a little: "Well, I won't report you this time; but mind, if I ever catch you meddling with this window again, or touching anything in my cupboard, you needn't expect to get off."

Thankful to escape with nothing worse than a scolding, the four tore downstairs in the hope that they might just be in time to answer to their names, but Miss Pollock was closing the register as they entered the room, and had already marked them down "late". Rather crest-fallen, they went to their various classes—Mildred to practise, Mona to her drawing lesson, and Bess and Kitty to Latin preparation. At four o'clock they met to compare notes.

"After all, I think we scored," said Mona. "We found out what the Sixth were doing."

"Yes, and what we've got to do now is to get up our own dialogue in costume, and not let the Sixth have a hint of it beforehand."

"It will take the wind out of their sails when they see us all dressed up."

"Especially if we do the thing better."

"That goes without saying. I've a far nicer dress at home than Edith's blue silk."

"We shall have to tell Eve and Maudie."

"Of course, but no one else in the Form need know. It can be a surprise for everybody."

As a rule, though the school was obliged to be present to act audience at the monthly dialogues, everybody considered them rather a bore. Even the girls who were taking part had not hitherto been very enthusiastic. They had been regarded strictly as lessons, and not in any sense recreation. This time, however, both the Sixth and the Fifth had a secret—a possession which adds a charm to any undertaking. The Fifth held the decided advantage of knowing their seniors' intentions while preserving silence about their own. They held delightfully mysterious committee meetings in the dressing-room, and private confabulations in the playground. Long-suffering relations at home were induced to set to work with needles and thread, or to lend a variety of articles that would come in for the occasion. On the day of the dialogues several bulky packages were smuggled into school. The girls had been obliged at the last moment to take Miss Pollock into their confidence, and beg her to lock up the costumes in her cupboard until the afternoon, and to secure them the use of a small practising room for a dressing-room. Five out of the six performers stayed to dinner at the College, so they had a little extra time for last arrangements. By dint of hard pleading they had managed to change places with VB, so that their dialogue came third on the list instead of second.

"That's good biz," said Kitty. "Now we shall be able to sit all through the Sixth's performance, and do our robing while VB are on the platform. Then we'll just walk on and astonish everybody."

Punctually at three o'clock the whole school assembled in the big lecture-hall, and took their places, small girls in front, and older ones to the back, with a row of chairs reserved for teachers. In spite of the discretion of the performers, some little hint had leaked out that the afternoon's proceedings were to be of an extra special character, and there was considerable whispering and expectation among the audience. The six players in VA had seats at the end of a bench, so that they could make an easy exit when necessary. They watched with keenest anticipation as the door behind the platform opened and the actors in the French dialogue entered. The rank and file of the school had not expected costumes, and clapped heartily at sight of the quaint figures who were standing bowing and curtsying with eighteenth-century dignity. Kathleen Hodson as Monsieur le Duc de Fontaineville was stately in her top-boots, an evening cloak of her mother's flung across her shoulder, and a sword at her side.

"Silk stockings and buckled shoes would have been more in keeping with the period than those boots," whispered Bess to Mildred. "They haven't taken any trouble over details."

"Dorrie Barlow's cap is only made of tissue-paper," triumphed Mildred. "Wait till they see Eve's."

The wearing of the dresses seemed decidedly inspiring to the performers, who gave their short piece with far more spirit than was their usual custom. To be sure, Monsieur le Duc forgot his sword, and, tripping over it, nearly measured his length on the platform, but he recovered himself with admirable calm, and went on with his speech as if nothing had happened. Susanne, the peasant woman, clattered about in a real pair of sabots, but had the misfortune to step on the train of Madame, her mistress, with rather disastrous results, to judge from the rending sound which ensued. Gertie Raeburn was seized with stage-fright, forgot her lines, and had to be prompted; and Hilda Smith, who enacted the Abbé, was distinctly heard to giggle under her ecclesiastical vestments. In spite of these slight flaws the piece was immensely appreciated, and brought down a storm of applause, under cover of which our six heroines of VA slipped quietly from the room.

There was no time to be lost, for they knew VB's dialogue was only short. Miss Pollock had placed their parcels in readiness, so they opened them with utmost speed and began their toilets. They all helped one another, and made such a record of haste that in exactly ten minutes they were ready, and listening for the applause which would mark the termination of VB's performance. At the very first clap they ran down the passage; then, restraining their impatience, waited until their predecessors had made their due exit from the lecture-hall. It was with pardonable pride that they stepped on to the platform and watched the look of amazement which spread over the audience. Nobody had expected them to be in costume—that was evident. The Sixth were looking particularly astonished, indeed almost annoyed. There was a discomfited expression on their faces, highly gratifying to the conspirators. Even Miss Cartwright seemed surprised. The little German play had afforded good opportunity for dressing up, and the girls had certainly risen to the occasion.

Bess Harrison, as "Else, the daughter of the Schloss", wore a charming mediaeval robe, with velvet bodice and slashed sleeves; her long fair hair was plaited in two orthodox braids, and she held a distaff and spindle at which she worked industriously. Mildred, her betrothed, was arrayed as a baron of the Lohengrin type, in a short robe of peacock-blue emblazoned with an heraldic dragon in scarlet. Her golden hair which thoroughly supported the part, was surmounted by a small ducal coronet. She had a heavy chain round her neck, and armlets on her bare arms. Kitty Fletcher made a stately mediaeval grandmother, in silken gown, stiff ruffle, coif and wimple, and rattled the keys of the Schloss with great effect as she said her lines. Eve Mitchell as the serving-maid had a cap of real muslin, copied from on old German picture, a green-and-black-striped skirt, cherry-coloured stockings, and buckled shoes; while Maudie Stearne, in her capacity of seneschal, almost surpassed the rest in the gorgeousness of her embroidered cloak, chain armour, and winged helmet.

The girls were on their mettle to do well, and played up most successfully. The whole dialogue went without a single hitch, and the actors threw enough scorn, grief, jealousy, alarm, and devotion into their parts to have sufficed for a longer play. As finally, quite flushed with their efforts, they made their bows to the audience, the appreciative school broke into thunderous applause. The Sixth, nobly repressing any spasms of envy that may have assailed them, were clapping heartily, Miss Cartwright beamed approval, and Fräulein Schulte was all congratulations and smiles.

"Really, this afternoon's dialogues have been a delightful innovation," said the Principal. "The addition of costumes makes an immense improvement. It was a coincidence that the two Forms should have thought of it quite independently of each other. You must have been mutually surprised. I am very pleased indeed, girls. It is a step in the right direction when you organize these things on your own account."

"It isn't quite such a coincidence as Miss Cartwright imagines," chuckled Kitty, as she and her confederates disrobed in the practising room. "She doesn't know who peeped through the skylight."

"And we certainly shan't tell her," laughed Mona.

"We've stolen a march on the Sixth," said Mildred.

"Yes, they had to give us the palm this afternoon," agreed Maudie. "I think we may decidedly feel we've scored."

CHAPTER V

An Advertisement Competition

THOUGH the general census at St. Cyprian's had docketed Mildred emphatically as "musical", she was not on that account entirely debarred from joining other societies. True, she was expected to concentrate her energies on her violin, and win credit with it for the school, but so long as she did not claim a leading part in any of the alliance contests, there was no objection to her being an ordinary member. All the girls were strongly encouraged to play games, so she practised tennis in the dinner hour, and took her turn with the rank and file at cricket. She had not the essential characteristics of a champion—her physique was not vigorous enough, and she lacked perseverance—but the exercise was good for her, and as the term wore on she began to exhibit improvement. Kitty Fletcher was in hard training, and had inspired a select number of suitable votaries with a like enthusiasm.

"We shall have a hard fight presently with the High School, so we must show that St. Cyprian's is capable of something," she said. "They shan't have it all their own way. I'm sorry we can't put you in the team, Mildred."

"I don't want to be in the team. I'd much

rather look on when it's a question of matches. At present I'm thoroughly enjoying dabbling in all the societies. I've joined the sketching club, and I'm taking a turn at the Literary."

"That's more in your line than mine. I'd rather spend an afternoon at cricket than compose an essay."

"Oh, I'm not doing any real solid writing. I leave that to Phillis Garnett and Laura Kirby. They're hard at work making a magazine number that's to rival the very best on the market at the moment. My contributions are of a very light character. I sent one in the other day, and—isn't it sad?—it was rejected 'with the editor's compliments'. I tackled Phillis about it, and she said the mag. was meant to be serious, not comic. I thought my poem might have livened things up a little, but she'd have none of it."

"Have you got it here?"

"Yes; like the orthodox unsuccessful minor poet, I have it in my pocket."

"Oh, do let me see it!"

"It has the advantage of shortness, and if brevity is the soul of wit, that ought to be a point in its favour," said Mildred, producing her maiden effort. "I call it a 'compressed novelette'. Perhaps I'd better read it aloud to do it full justice. My writing isn't very clear.

"All ringed and bangled,
At me you angled;
With ways newfangled
The bait you dangled.
Yet ere bells jangled
We two had wrangled,

Our love was tangled,
My heart was mangled!"

"Not half-bad!" laughed Kitty. "I'm afraid it's hardly the style, though, to impress Phillis or Laura. If you could have written it in Greek it might have suited them. What did the others say to it?"

"Haven't had time to show it to them yet."

"Some of them will like it. They're not all as deep as Phillis and Laura. Why don't you get up a little fun among the more frivolous end?"

"It might be worth thinking of if I find an opportunity."

Mildred, who had a strong vein of humour in her composition, treasured up Kitty's suggestion. She knew the bulk of the members could not rise to the height of the learned essay which their leaders considered worthy of the magazine, but they would be quite ready to amuse themselves with work of a less exacting character. Several schemes occurred to her and were put aside, but one day she hit upon something really appropriate, and came to school with visible triumph on her face. At eleven-o'clock break she cajoled the lesser lights of the literary society to a private corner of the playground, and propounded her scheme.

"Look here," she began. "I saw this advertisement in yesterday's *Herald*, and cut it out:

"LITERARY.—Wanted, short poems to advertise a famous brand of tea. Prize of three guineas offered for best effort, and ten shillings each for any others selected. Cracker mottoes and comic verses for Christmas cards also considered. Last date for receiving, May 20th.—No. 201 X, *Kirkton Herald* Office.

Well, now, my idea is this. Let's all try and write some verses, put them together, and send them in. It would be such a joke!"

"Could we write verses about tea?" hazarded Maggie Orton doubtfully.

"Of course we can. It rhymes with heaps of things—agree, and free, and quali*tee*; it shouldn't be hard at all."

"I rather incline towards cracker mottoes," said Clarice Mayfield. "Most that one gets at Christmas parties are such drivel. I've often felt I could make better."

"Then do try. And, Margaret, you ought to be able to turn out some Christmas-card verses. Let's make a syndicate, and pool all our contributions. Everybody to send in not less than one, and more if possible."

"How about the prize, if one of the poems got it? Should we pool that?"

"We could divide it," suggested Myrtle Robinson.

"No, I've a better idea than that," said Mildred. "We'd be public-spirited, and devote any proceeds we got to the school library. We've the most rubbishy set of old books at St. Cyprian's, and want some new ones badly. Who votes for this?"

"Aye! Aye!" came quite unanimously from the girls, though Maggie Orton qualified her assent with a cautious "If we get it".

"Well, that goes without saying, of course. Naturally it's a case of 'first catch your hare'. But there's no harm in trying, so we must all set our wits to work and see what we can manage. It ought to be rather sport."

"Especially if we see the verses in print afterwards," giggled the girls.

"You'd better not tell Phillis," added Myrtle.

"I don't intend to," laughed Mildred.

The various members of the syndicate were rather taken with the idea of the competition, and exercised their brains to the utmost in evolving eulogies of the unknown brand of tea. Some of their effusions they tore up, and some they kept. In the end, after being carefully read aloud and voted on, three only were judged worthy of being submitted. These were by Maggie Orton, Myrtle Robinson, and Mildred herself. They ran as follows:—

OUR BRAND

"If a good tea you would buy,
You can always quite rely
  On our excellent and justly famous blend.
'T is a most delicious cup,
That will tone and cheer you up,
  And one that we can safely recommend.

"If you want good honest tea,
That will rich in flavour be,
  So fragrant, so refreshing, and so pure,
Just try our special brand
Of young leaves picked by hand,
  'T will give you satisfaction, we are sure.

"Let the water be fresh boiled,
Or the tea 'll perchance be spoiled,
  And brewed for just three minutes let it be.
Then we think you 'll never tire
Of sitting by the fire,
  And enjoying our delicious brand of tea."

A FAMOUS BLEND

"All those who try
Good tea to buy,
And oft have found
The price too high,
We recommend
That you should try
Our famous blend.

"By careful choice
All crops among,
We mix a blend
That can't go wrong;
For flavour rare
Housewives declare
'T is past compare.

"The huge demand
On every hand
Shows to the wise
It takes the prize.
We can rely,
If once you try,
You 'll always buy."

WORLD-FAMOUS TEA

"If a tea you would find that is just to your mind,
Yet that won't be too dear for your pocket,
Try our world-famous blend, when your money you spend
And remember our branches all stock it.
So come to our shop for your tea,
Our famous, rich, syrupy tea;
If once you will get it, you 'll never regret it,
But join in the praise of our tea.

"Home 's a glad happy place, with a smile on each face,
If our world-famous brand you will sample;
'T is the tea ladies love, as the large demands prove,
And three spoons in the pot will be ample.
So come to our shop for your tea,
Our famous, rich, syrupy tea;
Mansion, cottage, or hall, it is suited to all,
The best that can possibly be."

A few cracker mottoes and Christmas-card verses were also selected, and the whole set put together. Mildred, as the originator of the scheme, took charge of them, and promised to send them off in good time for the competition. It seemed no use forwarding them too soon, as they would probably only lie waiting at the *Herald* offices, so she put them by in a drawer to post when the right date arrived. Now, unfortunately, though Mildred could be extremely keen upon a thing at the moment, once the first excitement of it was over it was apt to slip from her memory. She had enjoyed trying her 'prentice muse at tea verses, but, having finished them, she turned her thoughts to something else. Music was at present absorbing most of her time, and in the interest of her violin the papers lay in her drawer forgotten. On the afternoon of May 20th she was sitting in the studio working at her drawing copy, with no more idea of advertisements for tea in her thoughts than if that beverage had never existed. At three o'clock she was due for her music lesson from Herr Hoffmann, and she was putting in time rather languidly at her chalk head of Venus, and wondering whether the Professor would be in a good temper, or whether he would scold her for faulty rendering of her study. Myrtle Robinson was sitting at the desk behind, and presently contrived, without attracting the attention of the teacher, to hand her a slip of paper. She opened it carelessly enough, and read:

"I suppose you posted the competitions all right? M. R."

Mildred dropped her pencil and broke its point in

her agitation. Posted the competitions? She had done nothing of the sort. They were still lying in her drawer at home, though to-day was the last date for receiving them.

"Oh, what a lunatic I am!" she groaned to herself, "I, who suggested the whole thing, and made the others write, to be the one to forget all about it! Something has to be done, that's clear. And it must be done at once, too. I mustn't on any account let the girls know I failed them."

Mildred was impulsive to a fault. At this moment the one business in life seemed to be to get the competitions to their destination, even at the eleventh hour. It was futile to post them, but they might still be delivered at the offices of the *Kirkton Herald*. There was nothing else for it, she must take them herself, and that immediately. It was almost three o'clock, and the art mistress knew that she had to go to her music lesson. She rose, therefore, received the nod of dismissal, and, ignoring Myrtle's signal demanding an answer to her question, put away her drawing-board, and hurried from the studio. Instead, however, of fetching her violin, and going straight to No. 6 practising room, where Herr Hoffmann would just be finishing Mary Hutton's lesson, she walked to the dressing-room, and put on her hat and coat. She knew she was going to do a most dreadfully unauthorized and unorthodox act, and she shivered to think of the consequences, but she did not hesitate for one moment.

"That competition's got to go in time," she told herself, "even though the Professor rages, and Miss Cartwright storms, and I get myself into the biggest pickle I've ever been in, in all my life. I can't fail the girls now. I couldn't look them in the face again. It would be too ignominious. No, I've a pressing engagement elsewhere this afternoon, and can't keep my appointment with Herr Hoffmann, though I shan't write a note and tell him so!"

At three o'clock it was extremely easy to leave the school unobserved. Nobody was about, so Mildred simply walked out through the gate. She took the tram-car home, and was rather relieved to find that neither her uncle nor her aunt was in the house. She felt she would rather not enter into any explanations just at present. The papers were quite ready in an envelope, and duly addressed, so she took them from her drawer, and caught the next tram-car into Kirkton. The *Herald* offices were in Corporation Street, a business part of the city she did not know at all, but she thought she could find it. She felt rather adventurous and decidedly naughty, for she was not supposed to go on expeditions by herself without first asking leave at home, to say nothing of having run away from St. Cyprian's.

She left the tram at the High Street corner, and turned down Corporation Street. The town was very crowded, and she was almost jostled off the pavement by the numbers of people who were passing to and fro. By dint of asking a policeman she at last found the offices of the *Kirkton Herald*. She did not know whether she was expected to ring, knock, or walk in, but she could see no bell, and as business men kept passing in and out by a large swinging door, she plucked up her courage, and followed in the wake of a new-comer. She had done the right thing, for she found herself in a big room, having a counter like a bank to divide clerks from customers. She handed in her envelope with a timid enquiry as to whether it was in time.

"Just in time," was the reply. "We close the box-office department at four-thirty."

With a sigh of intense relief, Mildred watched the clerk place her communication in a pigeonhole. So it was safe, and she had not betrayed her trust after all. She felt the satisfaction was worth almost any amount of scolding. She turned leisurely to leave the office, when the big door swung open, and she found herself face to face with no less a person than Herr Hoffmann. Most egregiously caught, Mildred turned crimson, and would have beaten a swift retreat had not the Professor barred the way.

"So, Miss Lancaster! I find you here! Are you then having a violin lesson from ze newspaper? I wait half an hour for you at ze school, and you not come! How is it you fail to-day to be at your lesson?"

Mildred blushed still redder, tried to stammer an excuse, then seeing a twinkle of amusement gleaming under Herr Hoffmann's bushy eyebrows, she took a sudden resolution, and blurted out the truth. She made her little story as short as possible, and the Professor nodded his head with German gravity at the principal points. When she had finished, he chuckled softly.

"So you would turn poets at St. Cyprian's, and write songs in praise of tea? You shall show me ze verses? Yes, some day. But while you write ze poetry, ze violin does not make progress.

To-day we were to have taken ze concerto and ze 'Frühlingslied'. Is it not so?"

"Yes," murmured Mildred, much abashed.

"I like not that you miss your lesson. You shall come to me to-morrow at my house, No. 50 Basil Street, and I will hear you play ze concerto. Yes, at four-thirty. You will be there?"

"Oh, thank you!" said Mildred. "Yes, of course I'll come. It's very good of you to make up the lesson."

"Some day you shall read me ze tea verses. Miss Cartwright, is she also satisfied for you to miss school?" said Herr Hoffmann, with a friendly nod, as he dismissed his pupil and turned to the counter.

Mildred hurried home, feeling that she had not only Miss Cartwright to reckon with, but her aunt as well. She had a very open, truthful disposition, and did not dream of concealing her escapade. She told Mrs. Graham the exact facts as they had occurred.

"I just had to do it, Tantie dear! I don't see how I could possibly have done anything else."

Fortunately for Mildred, though Mrs. Graham shook her head, she did not take a severe view of the matter.

"It's extremely good of Herr Hoffmann to make up the lesson," she remarked. "You must try to get in an extra half-hour's practice to-day, so as to have the concerto better prepared. You really don't deserve that he should give up his time to you."

"I'm rather scared at the prospect of going to his house," confessed Mildred. "But I will have

an extra tussle with the concerto to-night. I hop
he won't ask to see the tea verses."

At five minutes to nine on the following morning
Mildred walked into Miss Cartwright's study, an
tendered an explanation of her absence the after
noon before, together with an apology for he
behaviour.

"It was a hard case, I own," said the Principal
"But why did you not come at once to me, and ask
leave? If I pass over it, you must not let this prov
a precedent, Mildred. It would never do for girl
to walk out of school just when they like."

"I know. I ought to have come and asked
But somehow I never thought of it. I was in
such a hurry, I could do nothing but rush hom
for the papers. I'll never do it again, Miss Cart
wright, on my honour."

"Very well; as you have told me of it yourself
and apologized, I'll say no more about it. You
can go."

Mildred passed from the study, congratulating
herself that she had escaped so easily. She tol
her thrilling story to the other members of th
syndicate, and they rejoiced together that the competition was received in time.

"When shall we hear the result?" asked Myrtle

"Not for weeks, I expect. Besides, I don't really
suppose that anything will come of it," returne
Mildred.

CHAPTER VI

A Chance Meeting

WHEN afternoon school was over, Mildred, carrying her violin in its neat leather case, set off for No. 50 Basil Street. It was not very far away from St. Cyprian's, so she arrived in good time—too early, in fact, for the church clock opposite was only chiming a quarter-past four as she pushed open the gate. There was no mistake about the house, for on the door was a brass plate inscribed "Professor Franz Hoffmann, Teacher of Music", and she could hear from within the halting performance of a violoncellist.

She rang the bell, and after a servant had ushered her in, she was met in the hall by Mrs. Hoffmann, who asked her to come and wait in the dining-room until her teacher should be ready for her. Mrs. Hoffmann was a thin, worried-looking little woman, most palpably English. She knew no language but her own, and had no desire to acquire any other, regarding German as the tongue into which her husband relapsed when more than usually annoyed, and therefore better to be ignored than understood. Perhaps she wished sometimes that such a thing as music did not exist, since from morning till night the strains of violin or piano seemed to echo through the house. The wearying monotony of scales played by leaden-fingered learners, or the excruciating sounds produced by beginners on the violin, were, as a rule, punctuated by shouts from the exasperated master, who, being of a naturally excitable disposition, was liable to let his impatience get the better of him, and would storm at his pupils in a mixture of German and English calculated to reduce them to utter subjection.

"Young Mr. Hardcastle is having his lesson," explained the Professor's wife. "I'm afraid he hasn't come very well prepared," she added nervously, as a specially badly-rendered shake provoked a perfect explosion of wrath, quite audible through the thin wall. Mildred was left alone to wait, so she sat down by the window, listening to the performance of the pupil in the next room. She groaned as she marked his wolf notes and his lagging time, fearing that his sins might afterwards be visited on her head. She was doubtful about her own concerto, and wished she had had more time to practise one particularly-difficult phrase. She tried to amuse herself by turning over some piles of music that lay on the table, or staring aimlessly out at the sparrows in the front garden.

A smart motor-car stopping at the Professor's gate presently attracted her notice, and she looked on with interest as a handsomely-dressed lady got out, walked hastily up the path, and rang the bell with a lusty peal. There seemed to be a short colloquy in the hall, then the dining-room door was flung open, and the servant ushered in a stranger, who, it appeared, must also wait until Herr Hoffmann should be at leisure to attend to her. She seated herself in an arm-chair, and for some minutes there was dead silence, broken only by the ticking of the clock and the rasping notes of Mr. Hardcastle's violoncello.

Probably finding the situation rather oppressive, the lady, after looking several times at Mildred, seemed anxious to open a conversation.

"I suppose you're one of Herr Hoffmann's pupils," she began, with a glance at the violin-case which lay on the table. "May I ask if you've learnt from him for some time?"

"About five years," replied Mildred, wishing the Professor would hurry, for she always felt shy with strangers.

"Indeed! Then you must have begun young. How old were you when you took your first lesson?"

"Not quite seven; but I learnt from a lady to begin with," said Mildred, listening to Mrs. Hoffmann's step in the passage, and wondering if she were coming to the rescue.

"My little girl's much older than that—she's nearly eleven. I'm sure she ought to commence her lessons at once. I should have sent her to Herr Hoffmann long ago, but she's such a nervous child, and I've always heard he's so very severe. Now, as you've learnt from him for so many years, you'll be able to tell me exactly what he's like. Do you find him a kind teacher or not?"

Poor Mildred scarcely knew what to reply.

"He makes you work," she stammered, hoping, for the Professor's sake, that the remainder of the unlucky Mr. Hardcastle's lesson might go with sufficient smoothness not to give rise to any more expressions of noisy indignation from the adjacent room, and looking anxiously at the clock.

"So I expect. And how long do you practise every day?"

"Two hours at my violin, and one at the piano.'

"I should never persuade Dorothea to do that!" cried the lady. "But perhaps just at first an hour would be sufficient for her. Is this some of your music? May I look at it?"

Without waiting for permission, she took up the pieces which Mildred had laid on the table by the side of her case, and was beginning to turn them over when she stopped, evidently struck by the name "Mildred Lorraine Lancaster" written on the covers.

"Excuse my asking," she said, looking up quickly, "but Lorraine is such an unusual name that I wonder if you are any relation of the Lorraines of Castleford Towers?"

"Sir Darcy Lorraine is my uncle," replied Mildred rather stiffly, for she thought the question inquisitive.

"How very interesting! I frequently visit Lady Lorraine; my sister's home is in that neighbourhood. Isn't the Towers a beautiful old place?"

"I believe so," said Mildred briefly.

"I suppose you often stay there, though I don't remember having seen you before?"

"I've never been there at all," returned Mildred, wondering how she could stop the conversation.

"Really! And yet you must be just about the same age as Violet, and Sir Darcy is always regretting that she has no companions. Are you older or younger than she is?"

"I'm not sure," murmured Mildred, much embarrassed.

"Now I look at you," continued the lady, "I notice a most distinct likeness, though your eyes are brown, and Violet is so very fair, isn't she?"

"I don't know."

"You don't know? Why, surely you've seen your own cousin?"

"No, I haven't," said Mildred, getting quite desperate, "I've never met any of them in my life."

"How very strange!" exclaimed the lady. "Surely Sir Darcy and Lady Lorraine——"

But here, to Mildred's intense relief, the door opened, and the Professor entered, bland, smiling, and full of apologies. Patting his pupil's shoulder with the fatherly air that generally impressed parents, he asked her to wait for him in his study for a few minutes. She caught up her violin, and retired thankfully, wondering whether she had said too much. Until now it had not occurred to her to think at all about her mother's relations; but she saw how curious it must appear to a stranger that she should never have seen either them or their home, and for the first time she experienced a feeling of something like anger at their neglect. It had been humiliating to be obliged to confess that she knew nothing of a cousin whose existence indeed she had scarcely been aware of till to-day. Though her aunt had told her a few details about the Lorraines, the subject had been so closely connected with her father's sad story that she had not liked to reopen it by asking further questions. She had been quite content to regard herself as the adopted daughter of the Grahams, and had not identified herself in any way with her more aristocratic connections in the north.

She considered that the lady had taken rather a liberty in asking her so many questions, and heartily wished her full name had not been written upon her music, thus giving an opening for the enquiries.

"Well, after all, it doesn't much matter. I don't suppose I shall ever see her again," she mused.

It was, however, a strange coincidence which had brought about that afternoon's meeting, and it was to be fraught with more consequences than she suspected. It is seldom we realize the small beginnings that often determine great changes; and as Mildred dismissed the matter from her mind, she little foresaw that from a ten-minutes' conversation might issue events that were to form a crisis in her life.

Meantime Herr Hoffmann, having escorted his visitor to the waiting motor, entered his study once more, and the lesson began. The prospect of a new pupil had perhaps soothed the Professor's mind, for he was in a far better humour than Mildred had dared to expect. The eyes behind the big spectacles beamed upon her quite amiably, and the large collar, which he had a habit of crumpling up when annoyed, was stiff and immaculate. Mildred generally regarded her master's collar as a storm-signal, and could gauge his temper by its condition the moment she caught sight of it. As she was sure it must have suffered very much during Mr. Hardcastle's lesson, she could only conclude that he must have donned a fresh one before interviewing his caller, and hoped devoutly that her own playing would not cause him to disarrange its spotless expanse.

She went through her exercises and study to-day without any mishaps, and with a few misgivings began the concerto. But here she did not fare so badly as she had feared. To her surprise the troublesome bars came quite easily, and catching the spirit of the music, she played it with such vigour and expression that the Professor nodded his head in stately approval.

"So! You have worked!" he said. "It is not yet perfect, but it make progress. You take more pains since these last weeks? Yes? Oh, I can tell! I do know when a pupil does her sehr best. Sometimes you come to me and do say you have practise two hours each day. But I find you not improved. Why? Because it is practice without ze mind. Of what avail is it, I ask, for ze fingers to play if ze attention is not there? If you would a musician be, you must have both ze body and ze soul of your piece. Ze right notes, ze true time, ze correct position of your bow, they are ze flesh without which ze composition cannot at all exist, and need your altogether utmost care. But there are many people who know nothing beyond. Himmel! Any mechanical instrument can grind out a tune. True music is to give ze world what it cannot make for itself. Ze great composers leave to you indeed ze score of their works, but it is ze beautiful body without life, and it is you who must put into it a soul!"

Herr Hoffmann so seldom gave any words of encouragement that Mildred flushed with pleasure, and ventured to tell him that she had made an effort to conquer the difficulties in the "Frühlingslied", which she had thought before it was quite impossible ever to accomplish.

"That is good! We will hear what you can do," declared the Professor, opening out the music, and tuning his own violin, ready to accompany her. "Begin gently. Wait! Imagine ze 'cello which is here introducing ze motif. Now you come in and take up ze melody. Let it sing, for it is like a joyous bird, carolling on ze topmost bough. It is a 'Frühlingslied'—ze song of spring—and you must make your instrument to tell of ze blossom time. Quick! That shake is too slow. Remember it is ze bird that is trilling. Now softly! Softly! Let it die away, before all ze orchestra burst into ze chorus. Das ist sehr gut, mein Kindlein! We will rehearse it again, and if you can master ze staccato passage, you shall perform it at my students' concert."

"Oh, I couldn't! I couldn't!" cried Mildred in alarm. "Please don't ask me. I should break down. I know I should."

"Unsinn!" (which is German for "stuff and nonsense") cried the Professor. "You will do what I say. Am I your teacher, and you refuse to play when I tell you? Nein! You shall work at ze 'Frühlingslied', and each Saturday afternoon you shall come to rehearse it with my students' orchestra at ze Philharmonic Hall. Yes, I have said it!"

Mildred went home completely overwhelmed by her master's suggestion. The public recital given every year in the Town Hall by Herr Hoffmann's best pupils was a great event, at which many of the most critical music lovers in the city were generally present. It was well known that only students of unusual talent were allowed to take solo parts. The Professor was a very celebrated teacher, and had a reputation to keep up. So far, though St. Cyprian's made a particular cult of music, and Herr Hoffmann had taught there for many years, no girl had ever been judged worthy to play at this special annual concert. It was an honour to which even their wildest ambition had not aspired. To be thus chosen out, over the heads of Ella Martin and Elizabeth Chalmers, who were considered the "show" music pupils of the school, was a prospect calculated to agitate the most sober brains. But there was another side to it. To play such an important piece as the "Frühlingslied", which needed to be accompanied by a full orchestra, was indeed an ordeal for a girl hardly sixteen years of age. A public audience in the Town Hall was a different matter from the comparatively small gatherings of parents and friends at St. Cyprian's. The mere thought of it filled Mildred with nervous horror.

"I don't believe I could ever do it, Tantie," she shivered, as she discussed the project with her aunt. "I should turn tail and run away when I saw all the people. Need I? Can't I tell the Professor I won't?"

"It would be a sad pity to do that, and would be wasting a great opportunity. When Herr Hoffmann has shown such a special interest in you, it would be most ungrateful to refuse at least to try your hardest to please him. He is the best judge of what you can do, and you may be sure that he will not allow you to play at the concert unless you have given satisfaction at the rehearsals. Both he and Miss Cartwright have taken great pains with your music, and I think you owe it to St. Cyprian's to show that their trouble has not been thrown away. You must speak about it to Miss Cartwright to-morrow, and ask her opinion."

When Mildred broached the idea next morning, she found that the Principal heartily sided with Herr Hoffmann, and even made arrangements for her to have extra time at school for violin practice. She was to be allowed to omit certain classes, and to be excused various weekly essays, and her piano studies were for the next few weeks to yield place to the instrument upon which she showed the greater talent.

"Remember you will be playing for the credit of St. Cyprian's," said Miss Cartwright. "You must work both for yourself and for the sake of the school."

When the news leaked out of the honour that was in store for Mildred, the girls received it in various ways. Ella Martin and Elizabeth Chalmers congratulated her, and urged her to do her best. Correct players themselves, they were above any narrow feelings of jealousy, and were glad to see Mildred, whom they had hitherto thought inclined to be lazy, pushed forward and made to take pains. The general opinion of her own Form was divided. Music was so decidedly of first importance at St. Cyprian's that the matter naturally made a little stir. A number of the girls did not appreciate Mildred's real talent, and gave all their admiration to Lottie Lowman's more superficial performances.

"It's absurd," said Eve Mitchell. "Why should Mildred Lancaster be chosen above everyone else? I can't see that she's so musical. She missed three questions in the harmony yesterday. Her theory's dreadfully shaky. Why isn't Lottie asked to play?"

"Well, you see, it's violin," ventured Nell Hayward.

"Then Ella Martin's our crack player. It's very unpleasant for Ella to be passed over."

"I suppose that's Professor Hoffmann's affair," said Bess Harrison, taking up the cudgels on Mildred's behalf. "He'd have asked Ella if he'd wanted her."

"Think how tremendously it will make us score in the Alliance," urged Maudie Stearne. "I don't for a moment suppose that even the High School or the Manor House will have a girl playing at the Professor's concert. We'll beat them there, even if they take it out of us at games."

"Lottie may be our delegate, but Mildred's our music champion just now," declared Clarice Mayfield.

"We've got to keep her at it, though," added Bess.

It was a new thing to Mildred to work diligently and painstakingly as she had done for the last few weeks. It was quite against her natural inclination, and I fear if it had not been for the thought of what St. Cyprian's expected from her, she would never have kept it up. As it was, she felt almost astonished at her own perseverance. Time after time she was tempted not to trouble about the

"Frühlingslied", but to play instead the tunes that came into her mind, and enjoy herself.

"After all, why should one fag so terribly at a thing? I hate slogging," she confided to her chum, Kitty Fletcher.

"Why? Because you owe it to yourself and the school," exclaimed Kitty. "If I'd your talent, I'd be slaving. Do you think I'd do anything in games if I didn't train? Mildred Lancaster, you've just got to try. Some day I'm going to see your name painted on the board in the lecture hall, so please don't disappoint me."

There was a large board at St. Cyprian's on which were recorded the successes of former pupils who had gained distinction either by taking university or musical degrees. To find, some time, "Mildred Lancaster" emblazoned thereon in gold letters was an attractive goal of ambition. But between the present and that rosy prospect lay a long, dreary expanse of continual effort—effort which Mildred's artistic temperament hated and shrank from, the drudgery upon which every solid achievement must be built, and without which even the cleverest of people can accomplish little.

CHAPTER VII

A School Eisteddfod

AFTER the founding of the United Alliance, the six schools composing the league had been allowed a certain amount of time in which to organize their separate departments, but now that the various societies were going concerns it was judged expedient to hold a central meeting of delegates, so that arrangements might be made for the contests and competitions which were to form the principal feature of the movement. The conference was to take place at the High School on a Wednesday afternoon, and due notice of the event had been sent to the branch secretaries. The ten delegates from St. Cyprian's were naturally much elated at the prospect, and anxious to do their best on behalf of their College. They were armed with full authority from Miss Cartwright, and prepared with a list of vacant dates when matches could be played. Wearing their school hats, ties, and badges, they started off together, under the leadership of Phillis Garnett, the head girl, and presented themselves at the High School at the time named on the general secretary's post card.

Wednesday was a half-holiday at the High School, so the delegates had the place to them selves. Ten smiling hostesses were waiting to receive the representatives of the other schools, and gave them a hearty welcome. When the first introductions were over, Ethel Edwards, the head girl of the High School, was voted to the chair, and, having made a few general remarks upon the object of the Alliance, proposed that each branch should withdraw to a separate classroom to discuss details for half an hour, after which they would all meet again in the lecture hall. So the schools split up their forces, and marched away in groups of twelve, representing the Musical, Literary, Dramatic, Arts, and Athletics subdivisions of the league. The delegates had all come prepared to be courteous, businesslike, and accommodating, so the thirty minutes passed in good-tempered discussion, and by the time they took their places once more in the big hall they seemed on excellent terms with one another. The results of their consultations, with probable dates, were handed to Ethel Edwards, who rapidly compared them, and drew up a final table which she put to the general vote.

"I am glad we have been able to make our arrangements fit in so well," she said, "and I hope we shall have many competitions and matches as the result of this afternoon's work. I am sure we all agree that the Alliance is an excellent movement, and that a spirit of co-operation among the principal Kirkton schools is highly desirable. Though each delegate represents her own school, all are united in representing the city, and some time in the future we may, as a body, enter into competition with similar Alliances in other towns. It certainly opens up a vista of very interesting work on our part, and should prevent those evils of narrowness and cliquishness which a too-exclusive policy is apt to develop in a school. Let us determine that our *entente cordiale* is for the general good, and each try our utmost to make the Alliance a huge success. I need hardly say with what pleasure the High School has to-day welcomed the other delegates, and am glad to note that our first Eisteddfod of the season is to be held here shortly. Our general secretary will forward copies of the programme to each branch secretary as speedily as possible, and due notice will of course be given of the next committee meeting."

The delegates dispersed, feeling that they had had a very satisfactory conference. Each department was pledged to something definite. The "Games" had arranged a list of cricket matches and tennis tournaments, and had even discussed plans for next autumn's hockey; the "Dramatic" had undertaken to produce a united performance in aid of the Kirkton Children's Hospital; the "Literary" was to publish a joint magazine three times a year, under the title of *The Alliance Journal*; the "Arts and Handicrafts" was to hold a grand exhibition in the forthcoming November, charging a small admission so as to be able to send a donation to the "Guild of Play", an organization for the children of the slums; while the "Musical", to test its capabilities, was to have an immediate general festival. In addition, the schools had promised to form a Guild of Needlework, to make garments for charities; a Christmas Santa Claus Club, to distribute toys among the various poor families in the city; and a Scrap Book League, the results of which were to be sent to the Children's Ward at the Royal Infirmary.

It was part of the scheme of the Alliance that the mistresses, while reviewing and sanctioning the arrangements, should keep in the background and allow affairs to be managed as far as possible by the girls themselves. Miss Cartwright, therefore, after hearing the report of the St. Cyprian's delegates, gave full permission to the Musical Society to prepare its own programme for the forthcoming concert, which was to be in no way a public affair, but merely a friendly trial of skill amongst the six schools. Thirty members from each were to meet and compete at the High School, which possessed the largest hall. Owing to limited space it was impossible to accommodate a very big audience, but fifty guests were to be invited from each school, so as to make a fairly representative body of listeners.

The St. Cyprian's Musical Committee assembled at once under the leadership of its delegates to arrange for the important event.

"Please tell us, first of all, why the thing's to be called an Eisteddfod," begged Nora Whitehead.

Ella Martin laughed.

"You've evidently not been in Wales. Have you never heard of the great Welsh Eisteddfods, where all the famous choirs go and sing against each other for prizes?"

"Oh, a choral festival!"

"No, not quite that, because there are solos besides. In a real genuine big national Eisteddfod there are departments for painting and for poetry. They make bards, you know, and give them Bardic chairs. Well, we can't do all that in one afternoon; we have to take each branch separately, so the music's to come first. We decided that each school is to learn the part song, 'Now Cheerful Spring Returns', and to sing it one after another. Mr. Jordan, from the Crawford College of Music, is to be asked to judge; he will give so many marks to each choir, for correctness, tone, general expression, &c. Then each school is to give a ten-minutes' concert, consisting of a few pieces by its brightest stars. These will also be judged and marked, so much for each performer. The totals will be added to the choir scores, and then we shall have the excitement of seeing which school comes out top."

"St. Cyprian's will! It must!"

"We'd better not make too sure. There are some clever girls at the Manor House, I hear, and the Templeton 'Choral' is good."

"What we've got to do," said Lottie Lowman, "is to learn our part song, and practise it for all we're worth. Hadn't we better decide first who's to be choir-mistress? Shall we put it to the vote?"

There was little hesitation amongst the girls. They voted almost solidly for Lottie. Since her election as delegate for the Alliance she had taken such a principal part in the musical society that everybody was ready to follow her lead. There were a few dissenting voices, who ventured to suggest that her style was not of the best, nor truly representative of the musical standard of St. Cyprian's, but these were completely overwhelmed by the majority. Lottie, who had already on her own initiative organized a choir, was surely the most fitted to look after the laurels of the school, and might be trusted to undertake the teaching of the part song. There now remained the programme of the ten-minutes' concert to be discussed.

"It's such a fearfully short time!" growled Elizabeth Chalmers.

"Of course it is," returned Lottie, "but you see six schools with ten minutes each make an hour. The part songs will take half an hour, and allowing another half-hour for judging and intervals between pieces, we get two hours, and that's the limit. No, each school has promised on its honour not to exceed the ten minutes. Indeed, we arranged that to do so would mean to be disqualified from the competition. It seemed the only fair way."

"Then we must cram all the best talent of the school into those precious ten minutes."

"That's the real state of affairs," said Ella Martin, "and we've got to make up our minds which is the best talent. I myself propose a violin solo from Mildred Lancaster."

"And I beg to object strongly!" returned Lottie Lowman. "Mildred may be a good player—I don't say she isn't—but everyone at the Coll. knows she's not to be depended upon. If she gets a nervous fit, ten to one she'll break down altogether, like she did last speech day, and then St. Cyprian's would look silly! Unless she's exactly in the right mood she doesn't do herself justice, and is the honour of the Coll. to depend on her whim of the moment? No, most emphatically, I beg you to choose a steadier, more reliable player. Who could be more suitable than Ella, who is already your musical delegate, and ought surely to represent you?"

Lottie's arguments swayed the committee so entirely that Ella was immediately chosen for the violin solo, and her name placed first on the programme.

"I shall only play a very short Prelude," she announced, "so we ought to have a piano solo and a song to make up our ten minutes. That would give a good all-round idea of the musical work at St. Cyprian's, quite as all-round as the other schools will have the opportunity for, at any rate."

After a short discussion upon the relative merits of several names which were submitted, the committee decided upon Elizabeth Chalmers for the piano solo and Lottie Lowman for the song. There was not much time to be lost, as the Eisteddfod had been fixed for a date only ten days ahead. The choir must be carefully selected and trained, and special practices arranged for. Miss Cartwright had promised to allow a short time daily during school hours for this purpose, and extra work could be done during the midday interval by those girls who stayed for dinner at the College.

"Who are your soloists?" asked Kitty Fletcher as, the meeting over, the committee sought the playground.

"Ella, Elizabeth, and your humble servant," replied Lottie.

"Do you mean to tell me Mildred Lancaster's not to play for St. Cyprian's?"

"No, Mildred's out of it altogether."

"Then all I can say is, I'm heartily sorry for the credit of the old Coll. I think you're a set of duffers!"

"Thanks! Perhaps you'll allow us to arrange

your teams in the Games department, as you're so anxious to meddle in ours? We'll choose your captains and champions if you choose our soloists. It would be an admirably suitable division of labour."

Kitty turned away, for there was justice in Lottie's sarcasm. She would not have been prepared to admit any interference in the cricket or tennis programme, and she knew that she had no right to criticize the decisions of the other committees. And yet her whole sense of justice rebelled against Mildred's exclusion.

"It's monstrous!" she confided to Bess Harrison. "Here they're actually discarding their trump card! And it's nothing but Lottie's jealousy! She's green with envy because Mildred's to play at Herr Hoffmann's Students' Concert. I thought we were urged to put aside all petty feelings and spites in the interests of the Coll., and just aim to bring St. Cyprian's out top!"

"That was rubbed into us as our motto."

"We keep to it in Games, thank goodness! For some reasons I wish Miss Cartwright hadn't left the Alliance so entirely in our own hands."

"It's the same as the other schools. Neither principals nor mistresses are to regulate matters. Remember, it's a self-governing institution."

"Well, this branch of it hasn't the wit to know its own best asset," grumbled Kitty.

Mildred felt decidedly hurt to be so entirely left out of the Eisteddfod. She was not even asked to join in the part song, for Lottie, as choir-mistress, had the selection of the chorus. There was perhaps reason in this, for Mildred, though she always sang in tune, did not possess a very strong voice. All the same, it was a marked omission, and an intentional slight.

Lottie, as grand vizier of the proceedings, was now in her element. She assumed such complete direction of everything that she even took precedence of Ella Martin. Ella, though a monitress, never pushed her authority, and indeed was sometimes hardly self-assertive enough for her post. On the present occasion she allowed Lottie to seize the reins rather too easily. The matter was discussed by her fellow monitresses.

"A Fifth Form girl ought not to be allowed to run the whole show," said Hilda Smith. "Ella ought to put her foot down!"

"Lottie's getting swollen head!" agreed Gertie Raeburn.

If Lottie's motives were mixed, to do her justice she certainly worked very hard in her new capacity as choir-mistress. She was as zealous as a Parliamentary whip in making her chorus attend practices, and drilling them while they were there. Most of the girls found her a harder taskmaster than Mr. Hiller, the singing teacher, and she indulged in a running fire of comments on their performance completely at variance with his suave suggestions.

"Now then, heads up!" she would say. "You all stand with your noses in your books like a set of dolls that have lost their saw-dust! We'll take that verse again, and put a little more spirit into it. Can't you sing louder? I suppose you've learnt that *cres.* stands for crescendo? Then please remember that the signs mean something, and don't drone away like a set of Buddhist lamas intoning a chant!"

And the girls would laugh, for they rather enjoyed her racy remarks, even though they were delivered at their expense. Lottie, in the flush of her popularity, could not resist pressing her triumph over Mildred. She invited her to a practice one day, and enjoyed showing her authority over her pupils before her rival. Having exhibited their docility to her utmost satisfaction, she dismissed them, and turned carelessly to Mildred.

"Not such a bad little business for a beginning!" she remarked. "The Coll. will take its right place at the Eisteddfod, I fancy."

"I hope so, I'm sure," returned Mildred, without enthusiasm.

"Oh, you'll see it'll come out top side! Now tell me candidly what you think of this part song."

"Do you really want my candid opinion?"

"Of course I do!"

"Then I think everything's wrong with it. In the first place, the second sopranos are out of tune continually. You hurry the time too much in the middle, and drag it towards the end, and when you urge the girls to sing crescendo, you let them shout in the most atrocious fashion—like street-singers! There's nothing artistic about it at all."

"I might have known you'd be sure to find fault!" sneered Lottie. "It's very easy to pick holes in other folk's work. No doubt the high and mighty Mildred Lancaster would have made a most superior business of it! People always think if they'd had the reins they could have driven the kicking horse!"

"You asked for my candid opinion!" retorted Mildred.

"I didn't say I'd follow it, though. Fortunately I'm the choir-mistress, and not you."

It happened that Ella Martin and a few more Sixth Form girls had come into the room during this colloquy, and Ella now put in her oar.

"There's a good deal in what Mildred says, Lottie," she observed. "I noticed yesterday that the second sopranos were out of tune; and you certainly let them shout too loud. They're not using their voices properly. It's dreadfully second-rate style. I was going to speak to you about it. It doesn't do credit to the Coll."

"We've all noticed it," urged Dorrie Barlow.

"The quality of the voices will be a point before the judge," said Kathleen Hodson. "Mr. Hiller is so particular on that score."

"Well, if this is all the thanks I get for my trouble, I wish I'd kept out of the musical society," responded Lottie, with a red patch in each cheek and a gleam of temper in her hazel eyes. "No doubt you'd all have done it better yourselves."

"No, don't say that," replied Ella. "You must allow that I, at any rate, have the right to criticize. We all appreciate your hard work, only we want it to be in the right direction, and not thrown away. St. Cyprian's has a big reputation to keep up. Suppose you just think over what we've suggested."

Lottie turned away rather huffily. She could not help acknowledging Ella's right to interfere, but she was annoyed that the rebuke should be given in Mildred's presence. She was at first inclined to stick to her guns, then apparently she thought better of it, took her chorus in hand, and remedied their very palpable shortcomings. Ella, realizing her responsibilities, made opportunity to drop in during rehearsals, so as to keep a check upon things, and thanks to her influence the part song soon began to show marked improvement, and to be more worthy of St. Cyprian's musical reputation.

Though Mildred was not included among the performers, she at least received an invitation to the Eisteddfod. The guests were to start all together from the College, and they looked forward to the event with considerable keenness. On the day of the festival those who stayed to dinner at school spent the interval discussing the occasion. Olwen and Megan Roberts, who boasted Welsh ancestry, and had been present at a real Eisteddfod in the Principality, scored by their superior knowledge.

"Of course it can't be anything like what we had at Llanfairdisiliogoch!" they bragged.

"Oh, no! Nothing's right out of Welsh Wales!" laughed Maggie Orton. "You've often told us that!"

"I know a lovely song about an Eisteddfod," chirruped Bess Harrison, and to the tune of "The Ash Grove" she began:

> "I wass go to Pwlleli,
> Where I mingled in the dreadful mêlée,
> And was very nearly squashed to a jelly
> With the peoples treading on my toes:
> The Welshies they wass there by millions,
> All sitting in the big pavilions
> To listen to the sweet cantilions
> As you wass suppose!"

At that point she wisely dodged away; and Olwen and Megan, giving chase, pursued her round the playground, where she ran, still chanting tauntingly:

> "There wass Owenses and Hugheses,
> And Robertses and Joneses,
> All singing in their native toneses
> All over the ground!"

till the twins at length caught her up, and administered summary justice in revenge for the slight on their nationality.

Punctually at two o'clock those who had been chosen to attend the Eisteddfod set out for the High School. The performers were ushered into special rooms reserved for them, and the others were given seats with the rest of the audience in the large hall. Miss Stewart, the Head-mistress, took her place on the platform, together with the Principals of the other five schools and Mr. Jordan, from the Crawford College of Music, who was to act as judge. No time was to be lost if the whole of the programme was to be carried through, so the choral competition began at once. Lots had to be drawn as to the order in which the schools should sing, and the Manor House had secured the first innings. Their chorus accordingly took its place on the platform and commenced the test piece. They did well, and as they retired to make room for Newington Green, the second on the list, the St. Cyprian's contingent acknowledged to themselves that the Alliance contained formidable rivals. To anybody unaccustomed to festival singing it was extremely confusing to hear one choir after another render the same part song, but Mr. Jordan was no novice at his task, and well knew how to appraise their merits. He sat with paper and pencil, jotting down their respective points as to time, tune, tone and quality of voice, expression and general spirit, so many marks to each, and appeared as calm and collected and unmoved as if he were valuing goods for an auction.

"He doesn't show the least enthusiasm," whispered Mildred to Kitty, who sat next to her. "If it had been the Professor who was judging, he'd have been hopping about the platform."

"I suppose it's Mr. Jordan's rôle to look quite disinterested and impartial," returned Kitty.

St. Cyprian's was last on the list, and perhaps even Lottie congratulated herself that she had taken Ella's advice and improved the standard of her chorus, for the other schools had sung so well that the College would have to look to its laurels. She hastily whispered a few last directions as they took their places, and perhaps for the first time in her life felt a tremor of nervousness as they broke into the opening bars of "Now Cheerful Spring Returns". Fortunately the girls had remembered their instructions; the second sopranos kept well up to pitch, the time did not drag, and the crescendo passage was rendered with due regard to tone. Lottie breathed more freely when it was over. She cast an enquiring look at Mr. Jordan, but his expression was inscrutable. He merely jotted down some figures, and gave the signal of dismissal.

After this followed the series of ten-minutes' concerts, in which each school exhibited its best stars. It was of course an extremely short limit, but it was wonderful how much was accomplished in the time. The Manor House had concentrated all its energies on two brilliant pianoforte pieces, Marston Grove High School boasted a girl with a remarkably rich and strong contralto voice, Templeton had quite a fair violin solo, the High School scored at a piano duet, and Newington Green School had for champion a girl of about fourteen who played the violoncello. St. Cyprian's, with its piano, violin, and vocal solos, was felt to have given a very all-sided performance. Ella played brilliantly, if coldly; Elizabeth Chalmers's nocturne was correct to a note; and Lottie sang the rather sentimental ballad she had chosen with much expression and display of feeling. Her confidence stood her in good stead, for the Marston Grove contralto had been palpably nervous, and had almost broken down at one point.

Mr. Jordan rapidly added up the marks gained by each school, putting chorus and concert scores both together. Then, rising, he announced the results:

Out of a maximum of 280 marks:

St. Cyprian's College, ...	230 marks
The Manor House School, ...	220 ,,
The Templeton School, ...	195 ,,
The Kirkton High School, ...	190 ,,
The Newington Green School, ...	180 ,,
The Marston Grove High School, ...	165 ,,

The St. Cyprian's girls felt just a little crestfallen. They had won, to be sure, but it was by a very narrow majority. They had not scored quite the signal success which, considering the amount of time that the College devoted to music study, might reasonably have been anticipated. There were no prizes given for the competition, so as it was now long past four o'clock, the Eisteddfod broke up, and the audience was dismissed. As the girls filed from the hall, the various schools mingled in the corridor. Kitty Fletcher and Bess Harrison happened to be walking behind two Newington Green girls, and overheard an interesting scrap of conversation.

"Well, what did you think of the famous St. Cyprian's?"

"Nothing up to what I'd expected. I'd heard they were so A1."

"So had I, but after all they weren't much better than the rest of us. That fair girl played the piano like a pianola! She put no expression into it."

"And the one who sang was vibrato all the time. I thought her rather claptrap!"

"As for the violin, it was brilliant, and good bowing, but it didn't appeal to me like Althea's 'cello."

"I thought they were supposed to have such a crack violin player at St. Cyprian's—Herr Hoffmann's pet pupil at present, so they say."

"Well, if this was the girl, I don't admire her. I should say she's very much overrated."

Kitty clutched Bess Harrison's arm close in her indignation. As soon as they were outside the school she exploded.

"Oh, to think they never heard Mildred! And they actually imagine Ella Martin's our crack player! It's wicked! It was suicidal for

St. Cyprian's not to put Mildred on. I can't imagine what the committee was doing."

"The committee was swayed by Lottie," returned Bess, "and I don't think it has altogether good reason to congratulate itself on the results. Undoubtedly St. Cyprian's ought to have done better, and it will have to look hard after its reputation in future."

"I shall play up at the cricket match, or I'll never touch a bat again!" vowed Kitty. "Nulli secundus—second to none! We've got to live up to our school motto."

CHAPTER VIII

St. Cyprian's versus Templeton

It was now more than three weeks since Mildred and the other members of the literary syndicate had sent in their poetical effusions in praise of tea. So far they had heard nothing of the matter, and they were beginning to grow anxious as to the fate of their verses.

"Perhaps it was just humbug," speculated Myrtle Robinson.

"Surely nobody would go to the expense of putting an advertisement in the *Herald* just for humbug!" objected Mildred.

"It may be a cheat, though," suggested Maggie Orton. "Suppose they use our poetry and never tell us?"

"If we saw it in print we'd prosecute them for breach of copyright!"

"I'm afraid it's all found its way into the waste-paper basket."

"That's more than likely."

Mildred had put her own address on the manuscripts as secretary of the syndicate, and every day she looked hopefully at the letters which were delivered at Meredith Terrace. One morning she arrived at school in a state of unusual excitement, and, rushing into the dressing-room, hailed her fellow poetesses.

"Oh, jubilate! Just look here! This came only five minutes before I started. Isn't it ripping?"

"You don't mean to say we've won the prize?" gasped Maggie Orton.

"No—not the prize! But we've got something. Quite enough to cock-a-doodle about. Here, read what they say!"

A cluster of heads immediately collected over the letter. It was typed, and appeared strictly business-like. It ran thus:—

"60 KING STREET,
KIRKTON.

"DEAR MADAM,

"We are in receipt of your verses in respect of our competition for advertising our brand of tea. Though they do not attain the level of first prize offered, they are not bad on the whole, and we think we might be able to use them. We are therefore willing to give you £5, 5*s*. for the three, and would add a further sum for the Christmas-card verses and cracker mottoes, making £10 for the lot. We retain your verses pending your consideration of this offer, and will forward cheque and copyright agreement should you accept it.

"Yours faithfully,
"JONES & JACKSON, LTD."

The successful authoresses turned to one another with almost incredulous delight, and broke into open rejoicings.

"Goody! How stunning!"

"What a joke!"

"Accept it? Ra-ther!"

"Hi-cockalorum! We're in luck!"

"I never dreamt we'd really win anything."

"We shall have to sample this tea now. We praised it up enough!"

"Write to-day, Mildred, and say 'Done!'"

"Oh, we have scored!"

Mildred received the cheque by return of post, and as her uncle kindly cashed it for her at once, she brought all the money to school to exhibit to her proud co-operators. The syndicate marched at once to the Principal's study, and, after a brief explanation, handed over the amount for the College library. Miss Cartwright was very much astonished, and laughed heartily as she tendered her congratulations.

"I didn't know we had so much talent at St. Cyprian's," she remarked. "We must keep a copy of the verses. It is a very nice idea to devote the money to the library, and I think you, who have gained it, ought to have the choosing of the books."

"Oh, may we?" said the girls.

"Most certainly. Bring me a list of what you would like, and I will order them from Bartholomew's."

The members of the syndicate felt themselves public benefactresses as they consulted the rest of the Form upon the drawing up of the list. There was naturally plenty of discussion, but in the end a dozen volumes were selected, and made quite a valuable addition to the not-too-well-stocked library. The incident drew attention to the scantiness of the collection on the shelves, the monitresses took the matter up, and it was put to the vote and carried unanimously that in future every girl, on leaving the College, should be asked to present two books—one for the senior and one for the junior branch—as a parting gift to St. Cyprian's. By this method the number of volumes would be annually increased; and though it was not compulsory, it was thought that nobody would be likely to refuse to offer her contribution.

The Alliance had brought many new interests to the school, and now that the Eisteddfod was over, the pendulum of excitement swung round from music to games. It was the turn of the Athletic branch of the league, and a cricket match had been fixed for the following Saturday afternoon between St. Cyprian's and Templeton. It was to be held at Haselwell, a suburb a few miles out of Kirkton, where the county matches were always played. The Alliance, of course, could not aspire to the county ground, but they were able to hire a very good pitch, which was often let out for school matches, and which afforded plenty of accommodation for spectators, including a covered stand.

Naturally St. Cyprian's team had been doing its utmost in the way of training; and Joan Richards as captain, and Kitty Fletcher as chief organizer of the Games department held many anxious consultations. They congratulated themselves that they had been drawn to play their first match against Templeton, and not against either the High School or the Marston Grove School, both of which had acquired a well-justified reputation in the cricket field. Of Templeton's play they knew little. Like themselves, it had not before contested with other schools, and beyond the fact (which Kitty had heard at the High School) that its captain, Marjorie Rawlins, was an excellent bowler, its points were problematical.

Joan was making her eleven concentrate its final energies on fielding, especially on catching and throwing in, which she regarded as half the battle.

"Some girls muff the ball, and some throw it about twenty yards, and the next fielder has to go for it while the other side's making runs," she affirmed. "I know you don't like fielding, but, if we want to score, we've got to practise it."

To Joan and Kitty, as "Athletics" delegates, the success or failure of this their first match meant much. The idea had got about at St. Cyprian's that the College was no good at games, and they were very anxious to correct so mistaken a notion. Once establish a precedent, and the girls would have more confidence, and be far more strenuous at their practices. They had never forgotten a certain rosy era of prowess under the tuition of a former mistress, and if they could once more be brought to the pitch of enthusiasm they had reached with Miss Pritchard, all would surely be well for the future.

The Alliance, having taken the cricket pitch for the afternoon, issued tickets of admission to any of its members who wished to go as spectators, and about sixty girls from St. Cyprian's availed themselves of the opportunity, Mildred among the number. The match was to begin at two o'clock, so after an early lunch they went by tram-car to the city, and caught the 1.25 train to Haselwell. Some of the girls had been there before to see county matches, and pointed out the famous ground, with its tiers upon tiers of wooden seats, the modern counterpart of an ancient Roman circus. Their own pitch was not far away from the station, and turned out to be quite well kept and satisfactory. Mildred took her place next to Maudie Stearne on one of the benches, and looked about her. There was a good gathering of spectators, for not only had St. Cyprian's and Templeton girls come to watch, but a fair number from the other schools had also turned up.

"The Coll.'s on appro. to-day," said Maudie. "I hope we shan't disgrace ourselves before all that set from the High School."

"Joan's in a flutter!" said Mildred.

"But Kitty's as cool as a cucumber. She might be going to play her little brothers in her own garden!"

"Good old Kitcat! She'll do her level best, I know."

"Has Miss Harris come with Templeton?"

"No, I don't see her. I'm glad Miss Cartwright's here, though. One likes one's Principal to see one's first match."

"They're going to toss!" exclaimed Bess Harrison excitedly.

The two captains now came forward, exchanged a few civilities, and the orthodox penny went spinning into the air.

"Tails!" cried Marjorie Rawlins. "Tails it is! We'll bat!"

Joan lost no time in placing her field, and presently the two first bats sallied forth from the pavilion, and St. Cyprian's scanned them narrowly.

One was short and squat, with an air of general strength about her, and used her bat as a walking-stick as she came; the other, tall and slim, carried her bat under her arm, and leisurely put on her batting gloves as she walked up to the pitch.

"Gladys Fuller and Beryl Norton," volunteered Bess Harrison, who knew something of the Templeton strength.

Beryl was to take first ball, and seemed rather nervous as the umpire gave her her centre; then, glancing round to take a last look at the position of the field, she prepared to face the bowling. Kitty was no "duffer" with the leather, having been assiduously coached by a critical brother who was in the Kirkton Grammar School eleven, and tolerated neither lobs nor half-volleys. A moderately long run with a swinging step brought her to the wicket; with a high overhand action she sent the ball down the pitch at a good pace. Luckily for Beryl it was off the wicket, as it beat her entirely. The next ball was dead straight, but Beryl was prepared for the pace this time, and played it respectfully back to the bowler. In fact, she was evidently not out to take risks, and the first over proved a maiden.

Who was going to take the next over was in everyone's mind. The point was soon settled, for Joan rolled the ball gently in the direction of Daisy Holt. Daisy's bowling was not quite orthodox according to modern ideas: she bowled lobs, hence her pseudonym with the team of "Lobster". But she knew how to vary both her pace and pitch, so that her bowling was quite dangerous. Her first ball pitched a little to the onside and had an artful break; but Gladys, to show her contempt for "underhand", swept round to leg, and missed it. She had failed to allow for the break, but, luckily for her, her skirts entangled the ball, and Daisy's instant appeal for l.b.w. was refused. Rendered wary by experience, Gladys played her next ball more carefully, and scored a single. This brought Beryl to the other end. It is strange how a long course of overhand bowling induces contempt of lobs. Daisy's next ball was a splendid one—straight, swift, and of good length; but Beryl, who seemed to have lost all her caution, mis-timed the blind swipe she made at it, and the next moment was walking off rather crestfallen towards the pavilion, amid uproarious applause from St. Cyprian's, and shouts of "Good old Lobster!"

Maggie Lowe, the next bat, was well known as a good player. She handled her bat with a freedom and precision which augured ill for loose bowling, and the first half-volley that Daisy sent down she promptly sent to the boundary. After this the score mounted slowly, runs coming in twos and singles, and both girls seemed to gain in confidence, and played more freely. Kitty had all this time been bowling well and keeping a good length, though she had met with no luck as yet. Her turn was soon to come, however. A swift rising ball slightly to the off tempted Gladys to her destruction, and away glanced the ball to long slip. But Jessie Hudson was ready, having profited by her training. Would she reach it? The whole field held its breath. She's got it! No! The ball rebounds from her hands, but she has it again before it reaches the ground, thus bringing off a brilliant catch at the second time of asking. Thirty one for two, last player fifteen, went up on the board—not such a bad score after all! Templeton's captain, Marjorie Rawlins, now came forth with a look of determination on her face. She played with extreme care at first, but soon seemed to get her eye in, and runs came more quickly. Forty went up, and then fifty, to a great round of applause from Templeton. Joan now went on to bowl herself, instead of Daisy. She bowled a good medium-pace overhand, with a very tricky break from the off. Alas for Maggie Lowe! A well-pitched ball to the off tempted her to step out, but she had misjudged the length and ignored the break. The next moment her bails were flying, and she returned to the pavilion amid hearty applause for a useful innings of fourteen.

The next player was one of those happy-go-lucky, slashing hitters who are always a great accession of strength to a team when their batting comes off. She commenced hitting about her with great freedom, showing small respect for the bowling at either end. Fortunately for St. Cyprian's, Joan's careful training in fielding told its tale, and runs came less freely than might have been expected. Still, the score was mounting up steadily, and Miss Slasher seemed to be greatly enjoying herself when a really good catch at long-on put an end to her innings.

Sixty-seven for four now went up, and St. Cyprian's began to pull rather long faces, and wondered what Joan would do next. Joan had evidently made up her mind, for at the next over Edna Carson appeared at the wicket. St. Cyprian's took heart of grace, for Edna's bowling was very peculiar. It was a sort of compromise between roundhand and underhand, and where she had learned it nobody knew. However, it was swift and straight, kept very low, and was by no means easy to play, and, coming as it did after bowling which rose sharply from the pitch, it took the batters quite by surprise. Her first ball was dead on the middle stump. Marjorie Rawlins, who appeared to be expecting a slow, struck too late, and the next moment Peggie Potter, the wicket-keeper, threw the ball gleefully in the air, while the umpire sedately walked up to replace the bails.

The next player was no more successful. She spooned an easy catch to point, and was followed after a short interval by a fine strapping girl who came striding up to the wicket like a boy.

"Janet Armstrong," remarked the knowing Bess Harrison; and at the very sight of her powerful form the fielders all moved outwards, not even waiting for the signals which Joan was so plentifully bestowing upon them.

Janet took her block composedly, and waited with her bat slightly raised. "Now," thought Edna "if I can only drop the ball just under that bat, out goes the champion!" It was the third ball of the over, and St. Cyprian's maintain that it was the swiftest Edna had ever been known to bowl. Janet made a powerful stroke at it, apparently thinking it was a half-volley. But Edna's aim was true. She had sent down a deadly "yorker" which got under Janet's bat and spread-eagled her wicket.

"Well bowled! Well bowled!" shouted St. Cyprian's. "Why, she's done the hat trick!" and for several minutes delight and excitement reigned supreme.

"You shall choose it at Liberty's!" cried Joan, oblivious in her enthusiasm of the depleted state of the club exchequer.

The next player was already taking her centre from the umpire before order was restored. After this Templeton seemed to lose heart, their batting quite collapsed, and the innings closed for seventy-nine, two of the remaining three wickets falling to Joan, while Edna captured the last by an amazingly swift full pitch.

The Templeton captain was not long in arranging her field, and Joan, after some delay caused by a prolonged search for batting gloves, sent in Kitty Fletcher and Clarice Mayfield to face the bowling of Janet Armstrong at one end, Marjorie Rawlins herself taking the ball at the other.

Things started none too well for St. Cyprian's. The bowling was decidedly difficult. Marjorie Rawlins's slow overhand twisters needed constant watching, while Janet Armstrong was evidently trying all she knew to get her own back again. She was showing very fine form, and her easy, graceful style and capital pace and length struck St. Cyprian's at once with admiration and dread. Kitty and Clarice were both steady bats, however, and faced the bowling with a courage which did them credit, though runs came very slowly, and it was not until the third over that Kitty managed to score a single off Janet. This brought Clarice to the other end, and the first ball she received, a lovely bailer, proved too much for her. Peggie Potter came in next, with instructions from Joan to "stonewall everything" and wear the bowling down. These she communicated to Kitty in a mysterious conclave between the wickets before taking her centre, and both girls carried them out to the letter, playing a very careful and cautious game for several overs.

Kitty was by this time beginning to bat with more confidence and freedom, when, in playing back to an awkward ball from Marjorie Rawlins, she managed to hit her own wicket. With two wickets down, the score still under ten, and the bowling what it was, things looked rather black for St. Cyprian's. The buzz of cheerful girlish chatter died down, and a taciturn gloom took its place. Joan herself was going in next. Would she and Peggie manage to make a stand and wear down this terrible bowling? was the thought in each girl's mind as they saw her walk up to the wicket, take her centre, and prepare to receive her first ball from Marjorie Rawlins. It was on the off side, and slightly overpitched, and Joan sent it straight to the boundary for three, amid rounds of applause from her delighted supporters. Over was now called, and Joan faced the bowling of Janet Armstrong. Having broken her duck, however, she was breathing more freely, and soon found that the bowling, though good and accurate, was by no means unplayable. After a few overs of careful play she began to get her eye in, and with Peggie stonewalling with dogged persistence at the other end, and now and then making a single, the score crept up, at first gradually, and then more rapidly, till twenty, thirty, and then forty appeared on the board. At this point a sad mishap befell poor Peggie. She was getting so keen on backing up Joan's free and frequent drives that she was tempted out of her ground before the ball was actually delivered. Janet noticed this, and the next time it occurred, instead of delivering the ball she turned round and put down the wicket. Greatly disgusted with herself for having given her wicket away in such a silly manner, Peggie walked back to the pavilion, where, to her great relief, instead of the chaff and upbraiding she expected, she received quite an ovation. For had not she and Joan made a great stand at a critical point in the game, and saved a situation which might easily have led to a complete collapse?

Edna Carson, who went in next, obviously meant to continue Peggie's policy of keeping her end up and letting Joan do the scoring. She stolidly blocked everything that came her way, to the great disgust of Janet, who was evidently thirsting for her wicket, and was sending down some astonishingly good balls. But with swift balls, even if only blocked, you can often steal a run, and as the Templeton fielding was not nearly so good as St. Cyprian's, Edna frequently managed to make a single, and thus give Joan the opportunity of which she was not slow to avail herself. Gradually the score increased until fifty went up amid much rejoicing. At this point Edna, who had never seemed at her ease, though she had been batting freely for nearly half an hour, gave Janet her revenge by returning an easy catch. Grace Ashworth was the next bat, but did not stay long, being clean bowled by Janet Armstrong; and a similar fate befell Winifred Barbour, without adding to the score. Just as Sophy Manners, the next player, was coming out of the pavilion, Joan heard the neighbouring clock chime the first quarter. "A quarter-past four," she thought complacently, but moving a few paces from the pitch, she took a glance at the clock to make sure. To her horror and dismay the hands pointed to a quarter-past five!

"Hit out for all you're worth!" she whispered to Sophy as she came up. "Thirty to win, and only a quarter of an hour to make them in!"

Sophy, who was both bold and handy with the bat, and, as the girls all declared, "simply had no nerves", was nothing loath to take this advice, and for the next few minutes both she and Joan were scoring merrily. Sixty for six—that did not look so bad; but only nine minutes remained, and twenty runs were wanted to win. Joan glances uneasily at the clock, and hits out harder than ever.

But the bowlers still keep a good length, and runs are coming more slowly; for Joan knows that if either of the present wickets falls she has no one left to rely upon in an emergency like this, so she plays with more caution, only lashing out when opportunity offers. Seventy goes up, with only four minutes left! Sophy gets one round to leg for three, and a moment later has one to the boundary for four. Three runs wanted to win, and Joan has the bowling. She sends one to the on for two. Now for the winning hit, and only a minute to make it in! Marjorie Rawlins artfully sends down the ball a trifle slower and shorter pitched than before. St. Cyprian's hold their breath. A moment later they are gasping in agony, for Joan has misjudged the ball, and up it goes like a rocket between cover-point and bowler.

Both girls make a dash for it, but realizing the imminence of a collision, each suddenly stops short, thinking it is the other's catch, and the ball drops harmlessly between them, just as Joan arrives at the other end with the run to her credit, and the match won for St. Cyprian's by four wickets.

CHAPTER IX

The Students' Concert

THE time was drawing very near now for Herr Hoffmann's Students' Concert, and whenever Mildred thought about it her heart descended somewhere into the region of her shoes. The Professor had been giving her lessons at his own house in addition to those she took at St. Cyprian's, and with the one exception of the day of the cricket match, she had attended every Saturday afternoon at the Philharmonic Hall to practise the "Frühlingslied" with the students' orchestra. For the first time in her life she was really working hard, and sometimes she almost astonished herself at the progress she made. Technical difficulties, which before had seemed impossibilities, smoothed themselves away, and her supple fingers began to acquire a new mastery over her instrument. That she needed all her best efforts she knew well. The fear lest she should fail in her piece haunted her like a bad dream. The Professor was not easy to satisfy. His ideal was so high that she continually fell short of it, and in spite of incessant practising and extra music lessons, so hard seemed the task which she was attempting that she sometimes felt inclined to fling down her violin in despair, and give up the concert altogether.

The one thing that upheld her was the remembrance of the story of her father's life which her aunt had told her. The unknown father, whom she had lost when she was still only a baby, had left her his Stradivarius as a legacy, with his dying injunction to make the good use of it which he had once hoped to do himself. The violin was her one link with him. Often now, when she practised it, she thought how his fingers had played on it before, and what beautiful music they must have brought from it. To respect his last wish seemed to her a solemn obligation. What he could not accomplish himself he had charged her to perform, and it was a trust which she must strive faithfully to fulfil. She felt as if her success might compensate for his failure. The talent which he had trifled with she must foster to the utmost of her power. The Comte's secret (solved, alas, too late!) should be her watchword for the future. Her father's neglected genius was like a debt left owing to the general good of the world, and on her shoulders must fall the burden of paying it.

Added to this was the knowledge that she had a duty to the uncle and aunt who had already spent much on her music lessons, and to the college where she was receiving her education. Her playing at this concert was an important point for St. Cyprian's, and she must think not only of her own personal successes, but of winning laurels for the school. She knew that Miss Cartwright had been disappointed in the result of the Eisteddfod, and this was a golden opportunity of upholding the reputation which that festival had slightly undermined. St. Cyprian's must show to all Kirkton that its special system of music culture was of real value, and that its training could produce a pupil worthy of its high aims. Yet the very thought of how much depended upon her efforts brought its own penalty.

"I wonder if everybody else is as nervous as I am?" she said, as she talked the matter over with her aunt. "I've heard all the other students now, down at the Philharmonic. We took a full rehearsal last Saturday. I don't believe Mr. Frith, who plays the 'cello, minds at all. He never cares in the least when the Professor's angry, he simply laughs and shrugs his shoulders. Miss Buchanan, the pianist, told me she couldn't sleep at night for thinking about the concert. It means so much to her, because she hopes to get pupils of her own by and by. The orchestra will manage best. The audience won't notice if one of them plays a wrong note, though Herr Hoffmann's sure to hear it, and scold afterwards. I hope the room won't be very hot, or I know I shall break a string. If I did, it would upset me so dreadfully, I don't believe I should be able to go on, even if the Professor handed me his own violin instead."

"We'll hope you may have a better fate than that," returned Mrs. Graham. "Your little Strad. doesn't often treat you so unkindly. It's generally a most faithful servant."

"I'm glad I've such a splendid instrument," continued Mildred. "It makes the most enormous difference to one's playing. When I try some of the other students' violins, they sound like banjos. I believe the Professor likes my 'Strad.' far better than his own Amati. He often catches it up and plays on it, just out of sheer enjoyment. It is a beauty, with its lovely old Cremona varnish, and the wonderful label inside: 'Antonius Stradivarius Cremonensis fecit'. There's no mistake about its genuineness. By the by, Tantie, do you know the Mayor and Mayoress are coming to the concert? Isn't it terrible?"

"I don't think you need mind them very much. They're probably kindly people who will have nothing but praise for all the performers. I should be much more afraid of the newspaper critics, who really know the points of good playing, and will judge you by a musician's standard."

"If only there could be no audience!" groaned Mildred. "It's the feeling that everyone will be looking at me that's so dreadful. We rehearsed in the Town Hall last Saturday, and I quite enjoyed playing to rows of empty benches!"

"Try to forget that anybody is there. Just think of your piece, and imagine you're playing it at school, or in Herr Hoffmann's study. It will be time enough to remember the audience when people begin to clap. Have you anything prepared for an encore?"

"I don't suppose I shall get one, but the Professor's making me practise the D minor Polonaise, so that I could be ready. It's a bright little thing, and not too long. Oh, how glad I shall be when it's all over! And yet I don't want the day to come!"

The brief week left before the concert seemed to Mildred to run away only too quickly. The date had been fixed for 16th July, for Herr Hoffmann liked his recital to form a winding-up of his year of musical tuition, which had commenced in

September. It was probably as anxious a time for him as for his quaking pupils, and he certainly spared no trouble in coaching them for their performance, though he lost his temper so often in the attempt that some of the students declared he would never find it again.

At length the great day arrived. Mildred had had her final lesson from her Professor, and a last word of encouragement from Miss Cartwright, who, with many of St. Cyprian's teachers and music pupils, was to be at the concert. Poor Mildred, who grew hourly more and more nervous, was almost sick with apprehension as her aunt helped her to put on her white evening dress before the long mirror in the spare bedroom, and to arrange her wavy gold hair.

"Cheer up! You look like a little ghost!" said Mrs. Graham, pinching her niece's pale cheeks. "It won't be half so bad as you expect. You make it far worse by thinking too much about it. All the other performers are in the same case as yourself. You'll have plenty of companions in misfortune."

"I don't want to break down and disgrace you," said Mildred, gulping back something in her throat that threatened to rise up and choke her.

"You won't do that. You've worked really hard, and if there's any truth in the Comte's secret, I believe the Stradivarius knows it, and will make you play well in spite of yourself. You've one great advantage over the piano students, that you can bring your own instrument. Try to think that though this is your first recital, your little violin is very well accustomed to appear in public, and will feel so at home in the concert hall that when you take the bow in your hand it will almost talk of its own accord. It has been a long time in retirement, and to-night it's anxious to show every one what it can do."

"I hope I shan't disappoint it!" said Mildred, laughing a little. "It's rather hard on it to belong to a beginner, as it's accustomed to such laurels. Tantie, I'm so glad you're sitting in the front row, so that I know you're near me. I believe if I feel very bad, it will just help me to see you there. I shan't think so much about other people if I can look at your face."

The car arriving at the door put an end to all further conversation. Mrs. Graham wrapped Mildred in an evening cloak, Uncle Colin was ready and waiting downstairs, and together they drove to the Town Hall.

"Good luck to you, lassie!" said Dr. Graham, kissing his trembling little niece as he left her at the performers' entrance. "Don't you worry yourself! You'll play quite well enough to please me, and a great many other people besides. We don't expect a Paganini at fifteen. Do your best, and you'll get through all right. Here comes Herr Hoffmann to encourage you."

It was indeed the Professor himself, so resplendent in evening dress, so bland and gracious, so overflowing with genial smiles and good humour, that Mildred hardly knew him.

"Ach! you have got a fit of ze nerves!" he declared, leading his pupil to a room at the back of the platform. where most of the students were already assembled. "Take it not so to heart, lieb

Kindlein! You will be a good Mädchen, and play just as I have taught you. Frisch! Wohlan! Here is a cup of coffee, very strong. Drink! It will give you courage. Himmel! Did I not suffer myself like this once? But now it make me to smile."

He patted her kindly on the shoulder as he handed her the cup of black coffee. It was not nice, but Mildred felt better when she had swallowed it, and, recovering her spirits a little, began to look round her, and take some notice of her fellow performers. Some were anxiously tuning their instruments, and some were chatting with affected carelessness. A few of them she knew already, for she had spoken to them at the orchestra rehearsals, and several came forward now to give her a word of welcome. She was the youngest in the room. Most of the other students were practised players, some of whom indeed were training for a musical career. The Professor, anxious to keep up his deservedly high reputation as a teacher, would allow none but his best pupils to appear at his recitals.

"You get used to it in time," said one of the piano students, a tall, pretty girl with chestnut hair, just out of her teens, who stood working her fingers about as if to keep her joints supple. "I thought I should have died at my first concert, and now I don't really care very much."

"I think a good audience is rather inspiring," said a violoncellist, a self-conscious young fellow whose long waving hair and artistic necktie proclaimed him a budding professional. "I can always play better from a platform. A little applause seems to spur one on."

"Yes, if you get it," said another, nervously rubbing resin on his bow. "That generally remains to be seen."

"I've never missed an encore at any concert I've played at," returned the first confidently. "I shall be astonished if my Barcarolle is not a success, though one can't expect much real musical appreciation from town councillors and an ignorant public. I believe they'd applaud a jazz band!"

"Not so ignorant as you seem to think," said a third student, coming up to join the group. "I don't know any audience that can tell good music from bad better than a Kirkton one. It needs your best work to give satisfaction, and there's always a full and most intelligent criticism in the *Herald* next day."

"I suppose the old Professor's exploiting you," said the violoncellist, turning to Mildred. "He isn't keen on juvenile prodigies as a rule. The last he had was little Mathilde Zimmermann, and she did nothing after all! Do you go out to 'At Homes'?"

"Oh, no!" replied Mildred. "This is the first concert I've ever played at—except just at school. I don't want to now, only Herr Hoffmann says I must."

"They aren't running her professionally, so she won't interfere with you or your engagements," put in the piano student. "She's the Professor's pet pupil at present, that's all. But if you don't wake up, she'll take the shine out of you some day, so look to your laurels!" Then, speaking to Mildred, she added kindly: "Don't mind him, dear! You'll find when you begin to play in public that you'll meet with a good deal of jealousy from other performers, but you mustn't let it worry you. The music's the only thing to care about, and if one can interpret that, one feels it's something to live for, in spite of all."

"Are you ready, ladies and gentlemen?" cried the Professor, entering in a perfect whirlwind of excitement. "Ze hall is already full! It is ze hour! Ze audience await us. Come, we commence!"

The first selection on the programme was an "Overture to Lucretius", and as nearly all of the company were members of the students' orchestra, Mildred found herself left alone with the few piano pupils. She had often attended concerts, but so far had always been numbered among the audience. This was her first peep behind the scenes, and it seemed strange to listen to the music from the back of the platform. She could hear the applause at the conclusion of the overture, and the duet for violin and violoncello which followed.

"It will be my turn next," said her friend of the chestnut locks. "There's one comfort in coming on early, you get it over,—though I always find the audience cold at first. I suppose they think if they call for encores too soon, they'll never get through the programme. I see you're three-quarters down. That's the best place you could possibly have, just when everyone has got enthusiastic, and before it's time to begin and think about catching trains. You couldn't have been more lucky. There's the last bar! Now for my ordeal! Good-bye!"

Sitting waiting with her violin in her hand, poor Mildred felt as if no concert had ever dragged along so slowly. She wished she could take a peep into the hall, and see where her uncle and aunt were sitting. That the room was very full she knew from the remarks of the other students, but so far the audience, though fairly appreciative, could hardly be described as warm. Piece followed piece, then came the ten minutes' interval; the second part of the programme commenced, and at length the "Frühlingslied" drew near. As the finale of the orchestral movement which preceded it died away, Mildred took her violin, and summoning all her courage went with a beating heart up the steep little staircase which led to the platform. The Professor stood at the top, his broad face beaming encouragement.

"So far it goes sehr gut," he announced. "No one have break down or spoil anything. Remember, mein Kind, not to hurry ze time in ze legato passage, and to wait in ze allegretto till ze 'cello begin."

He tested her Stradivarius himself to see that it was in tune with the other instruments, then handed her between the rows of violin stands to her place in front of the piano, and taking up his baton rapped smartly on the conductor's desk, as a signal for the orchestra to be in readiness. For the first time in her life Mildred found herself face to face with a public audience. She stood there for a moment, such a childish little figure in her white dress, with her golden hair shining under the lights, and a frightened look in her dark eyes, that a wave of sympathy seemed to pass through the hall, and a few people began to clap. She started at the sound, and so great a panic of fear seized her that she felt as though she could scarcely draw her breath; but at that instant, looking down in front, she caught her aunt's eyes fixed upon her with a hope and confidence in them which calmed her, notwithstanding the knowledge that hundreds of listeners were waiting for her first notes. Suddenly the remembrance of Mrs. Graham's words came back to her—the Stradivarius had been in public before, and could make her succeed in spite of herself. It was the bird of the "Frühlingslied". She had only to draw the bow, and it would surely sing.

"Are you ready? Now!" whispered the Professor. He waved his baton, and the piece began.

Once the ice was broken, Mildred forgot the hall and the rows of people. There was something inspiring in the subdued accompaniment of the orchestra, her violin was like a living creature that thrilled under her fingers, and so well did it respond to her touch that all the springtime seemed to ring in the full, clear tones. She had got at the heart of the musician's meaning, and those who listened felt that throb of pure delight which comes to us sometimes with the sight of the dawn or the early song of a thrush, that sense of freshness, of oneness with Nature at her gladdest, that can raise our commonplace lives for the moment to the level of the skies above.

It was an astounding performance for a girl of scarcely sixteen. The piece not only demanded extreme facility of execution, but the maturest thought and feeling, and to many it appeared incredible that so young a player could have assimilated so much of the life and the mystery of things as to enable her thus to interpret the mind of a great composer. The audience seemed to hold its breath as the last crisp chord resounded and died away; then it broke into a perfect storm of applause. There was no mistaking the warmth of the reception, for instead of subsiding, the clapping grew louder, and shouts of "Brava!" and "Encore!" echoed through the hall. Suddenly realizing that she was the centre of all eyes, Mildred made a frightened acknowledgment, and fled precipitately to the staircase, to be brought back by her triumphant master, who, taking her hand, led her once again to the front of the platform.

"Courage, mein Kind!" he whispered. "One little effort more! You will not fail now? Ze encore!"

How Mildred played the "Polonaise" she never quite knew. She only afterwards retained a confused remembrance of glaring light, a sea of faces before her, and a sense that the notes came of themselves, urged somehow from her fingers by the knowledge that they gave pleasure to her hearers. It seemed a dream, a strange, bewildering unreality, an exhilaration such as she had never before experienced, but which ended in so great a revulsion of feeling that as she turned from the applauding audience to leave the platform she could control herself no longer, and, breaking down utterly, burst into tears.

"There, there!" said the Professor soothingly, patting the subdued golden head; "it is finished now, and you are my very good pupil. Wait in ze anteroom till I come, for I would speak to you after ze performance."

"It was beautiful—beautiful!" cried the piano student, kissing Mildred as she helped her down the staircase. "Don't cry, dear! It was worth the effort. Such music is only granted to a few. Be thankful the talent is yours, and that you are able to give it to the world. We, who are less gifted, can only envy the future that lies before you."

The rest of the programme was soon finished, and the orchestra, returning, crowded round Mildred to congratulate her on her success, while some members of the audience, invited by Herr Hoffmann into the anteroom, added kind words of approval and praise.

"Let us go, Tantie!" said Mildred, clinging to her aunt, who had come to fetch her, and longing unspeakably for the quiet of home again; "I want to get away from all this!"

"The car's waiting, darling! We're going now," said Mrs. Graham, hastily making Mildred's adieux and her own, and trying to edge her way through the crowded room. A group of people talking together blocked their progress at the door, and as they paused for a moment to find an opportunity of passing, a lady sprang forward and shook Mildred warmly by the hand, a lady whom she recognized at once as the stranger who had spoken to her at Herr Hoffmann's on the day she had first visited his house, and had waited so long for her music lesson.

"My dear, I am charmed! Your master ought indeed to be proud of you! I should have known you the minute you came on to the platform, even without your name on the programme. I am going to Westmorland to-morrow, and I shall be sure to tell your uncle what a clever niece he has. Such music would be enchanting in a drawing-room. I hope I may see you again before long."

"Come, Mildred!" said her aunt, hurrying her away from the effusive stranger. "Here is Herr Hoffmann waiting to say good-bye."

"Mein Freundchen!" cried the Professor, holding his pupil's little hand in a bearlike grip, and relapsing into German in his excitement. "Is it not worth while to have taken trouble? Ze exercises, ze scales, you did not like them at ze time, but they are ze all-necessary foundation of true art. To-night you have shown me that you can make progress. Go on! There is much remaining to be done. Do not let one little applause cause you to think that you can yet play. It is try each time a something more difficult till you can master it, and some day you will thank ze old Professor that he has made you work. Auf Wiedersehen!"

CHAPTER X

Changes

MILDRED'S signal success at the Students' Concert was a subject of much congratulation to St. Cyprian's. Never before had a pupil at the College made so public an appearance and obtained such an ovation. The newspaper critics highly praised her playing, and several of the most prominent musical people in the city, who had been present on the occasion, congratulated Professor Hoffmann on the result of his teaching. Among these was Mr. Macmillan a Scottish gentleman of great influence in Kirkton, who was president both of the Crawford Concerts and of the College of Music, and whose opinion therefore was of considerable value. To her schoolfellows Mildred's laurels amply compensated for the low majority with which they had won the Alliance Eisteddfod. Many girls from the other schools had been at the concert, and it was a great satisfaction to feel that they had heard St. Cyprian's musical champion in such favourable circumstances.

Mildred herself was experiencing that strong reaction which often follows great effort. Now that her ordeal was over, she felt how severe had been the strain of those weeks of unaccustomed hard work. She flagged visibly, and her pale cheeks and listless manner drew comment at home.

"No, I'm not ill really, Tantie," she replied to her aunt's enquiries. "It's only that I'm tired of everything just at present. I think I want a change."

And a change was coming to her—something so utterly unexpected and unthought-of that if anyone could have told her of it beforehand she would scarcely have believed it to be possible. It began with a letter—an innocent, inoffensive-looking letter. She had brought it herself to Dr. Graham, and had noticed the crest on the envelope, and then thought no more about it than she had done of the many others which were received daily at the house, and which did not concern her in the least. That her uncle and aunt seemed to have many earnest conversations together, which they broke off abruptly when she entered the room; that they were even more affectionate to her than usual, and looked at her sometimes with a kind of wistfulness in their eyes, did not strike her particularly at the time, though she remembered it well afterwards; and it was not until Mrs. Graham broached the subject one afternoon that she had any idea of the strange new plans which were being discussed for her future.

"There's something I wish to speak to you about, Mildred. It's a question your uncle and I have been weighing very anxiously. I believe we've looked at it from every side, and I trust and hope that we've come to a right decision. I have told you before that your mother's father, Sir John Lorraine, disowned her at her marriage. He never saw her again; and although we wrote to tell him of her death and of your birth, he took no notice, and made no enquiries about you afterwards. There was no mention of you in h's will, all his property being left to his son Sir Darcy, who is the present owner of The Towers, as you know. Your uncle and I adopted you from the very first, and we have never had any communication with your mother's relations, who for nearly sixteen years have given no sign that they wished to remember you. You can imagine, then, our astonishment at receiving a letter from Sir Darcy Lorraine. It contained what seemed to us a very startling offer, which at first we thought it impossible to accept, until, after talking the matter over, we think it ought at least to be considered. But before you can understand me, I must read you the letter. It is dated from The Towers, Castleford, and addressed to your uncle:

"DEAR SIR,

"There has recently been brought to my notice a sense of my responsibility in regard to the upbringing of my late sister's child, Mildred Lancaster. I find on enquiry that so far you have undertaken her full guardianship, and have provided for her entirely. As it seems only right that she should both know her other relations and give them the opportunity of performing their fair part in her education and maintenance, I now offer her a home at The Towers, where she could share my daughter's studies, and afterwards take that position in society which she would occupy as my niece. Should you feel disposed to agree to this proposal

I should be ready to make arrangements to receive her without further delay.

"I much regret that unfortunate family misunderstandings should have caused this apparent neglect of one to whom I feel I owe a duty, and I would endeavour to atone for past omissions by affording her every advantage which is within my power.

"Trusting that our negotiations in this matter may prove of a satisfactory character.

"I remain, dear sir,

"Faithfully yours,

"DARCY LORRAINE."

"He surely doesn't mean I should leave you and Uncle Colin and go and live with him?" gasped Mildred incredulously.

"That's exactly what he proposes."

"But it's quite impossible!"

"Is it? Well, we'll talk about that later on. You don't want to leave us?"

"Of course not! All the Sir Darcys and Lady Lorraines in the world wouldn't make up! Tantie! How can you even speak of it?" said Mildred reproachfully, getting up and flinging her arms round her aunt. Mrs. Graham held her very close for a moment or two.

"You've been our little daughter for so many years that we could ill spare you, sweetheart. What we think, however, is that you ought to go there for the summer holidays at any rate. We wish you to pay them a seven weeks' visit. Sir Darcy is your relation after all, just as much as we are, and it's only fair that you should have an opportunity of getting to know him and your aunt and cousin. Your uncle and I feel that if, for our own selfish love of your company, we were to refuse to part with you, you might some day justly reproach us for having kept you from social advantages which we cannot give you. You are young, Mildred, and have never known any place but Kirkton, and we think you ought to make a trial of this other home before you finally choose between the two. It has always been my dearest wish that you should study music; but if after visiting Westmorland you find the life there is really more congenial to you than our plain workaday existence here, we would not allow the affection you feel for us to interfere in any way with your prospects. You would be perfectly free to cast your lot with whichever relations you believe could make you the happier. Do you quite understand me? It's our very love for you that makes us willing to part with you."

"I understand, but I don't want to go, all the same. I feel the Lorraines have forgotten me so long that it's rather late suddenly to remember my existence. You and Uncle Colin have been caring for me all this time. Can't you say I won't go?"

"We've already arranged to send you. As it happens, it fits in most curiously with an offer which arrived by the same post, inviting your uncle to go out to Canada for the Medical Congress, as representative of the Kirkton Public Health Association. He has not been well for some time, and the voyage would do him good, while very fortunately Dr. Holt would be able to look after both the practice and his appointments until his return. He is most anxious that I should go with him, and as the opportunity occurs for you to pay this visit while we are away, I feel we might leave with a free mind."

"Tantie, I can't take it in! You and Uncle going to Canada!"

"Only for a six weeks' holiday. It is a great honour for your uncle to be chosen to represent Kirkton at the Congress, and one he can hardly refuse; while it seems such an excellent arrangement for you to spend the time of our absence at The Towers that I feel we can't do better than accept Sir Darcy's offer."

"What will the Professor say? He had decided that I might be allowed three weeks' rest, and after that I was to go to his house for lessons twice a week until school began again. He wouldn't hear of my spending the whole of the holidays just practising by myself. He said I should get into bad habits, and undo all the progress I had made lately. He was most determined about it."

"That's the unfortunate part. I'm sorry beyond words for you to miss your lessons, but, after all, a few weeks is not a very large slice out of your life. You need a change for your health's sake, and if you really decide that you wish to study music, you will be able to make up for lost ground afterwards."

"The time will seem ages to me," declared Mildred. "I shall count every day till I'm home again."

"You mustn't say that, dear. I want you to promise to try to like Sir Darcy and Lady Lorraine.

I think they are anxious to make up now for having overlooked you so long, so don't be ungracious, or allow any unforgiving remembrances about the past to creep in and spoil the good feeling they seem willing to show to you. Just let bygones be bygones, and be ready to make friends."

The change which awaited Mildred seemed an earthquake in her hitherto uneventful life. The more she thought about it the less she liked it. Although she was nearly sixteen she had never been away from home alone before, and she shrank from the prospect of spending seven weeks with those unknown relations. Naturally of a nervous and sensitive disposition, she was shy with strangers, so what to many girls would have appeared an attractive invitation, to her meant a species of exile.

"I don't know whether we're wise," said Dr. Graham to his wife. "The child's fretting already. Can't we take her with us to Canada? Is it really right, when we've brought her up so carefully, to be willing to hand her over to those who probably have very different standards from ours? She's just at an age when she will be led most easily. If she sees social success and amusement put as the great aims of existence, will she still hold to what we believe to be the higher ideal in life? I'm a little afraid for her, I confess. One side of her disposition is so ready to take the easier path and shirk difficulties that I feel as if removing our influence were a throwing away of our responsibility."

"I don't think you need have any fears," replied Mrs. Graham. "This will certainly be a great trial of Mildred's character, but I believe she'll stand the test, and will come back to us infinitely more our own, if she has chosen us voluntarily, than if she had never had the chance of a different life. Surely some of the seed we have sown for fifteen years must have taken root, and if we only have the patience to stand by and wait, we shall see the harvest blossoming by and by."

It was decided that Mildred was to start for The Towers directly the holidays commenced. There were many preparations to be made before her departure—new clothes to be bought, and a selection made of articles which she wished to take with her. Among other treasures she did not forget to pack her diary.

"Dear little book, I wonder what I shall find to write in you?" she said. "Tantie, don't you wish we could take a tiny peep into the future, and see beforehand what's going to happen?"

"No, I think it's often better to have it hidden. I hope you will find the next seven weeks pleasant ones, and whatever choice you make at the end of them, you must always remember that your uncle and I have acted for what we believe to be the best."

Mrs. Graham had acquainted Herr Hoffmann with the facts of the case, and when Mildred went to say good-bye to her teacher, she found that he took the parting badly.

"It is what you call 'hard luck'," he declared. "I have taught you all these years, and to no other pupil have I given more attention and trouble. I tell you even in Vienna Conservatoire no professor could have laid you a better foundation in bowing.

At one time you were idle. You did not like to work. Then, just when you wake up, and begin to make real progress, you leave me! And all my labour is for nothing! You say you will come back, but that I cannot tell. I hear other relations want to keep you. If you have any true love for your art, any desire to master your instrument and to give your life to music, you will return. Practise by yourself, but do not let anybody give you what they call 'lessons on ze violin'. Lessons! I am the only one who can teach you, in all England! All others would spoil what you have already learnt. I understand you go to a very great and rich house. I wish you well; yet do not quite forget ze old Professor, and think too of the music, which is a gift of Almighty God, more to be esteemed and held in honour than gold or high name."

"I won't forget, I won't indeed!" cried Mildred, her eyes moist at the Professor's emotion. "You know I love the music. I did like it all the time, even when I slacked, except the scales and arpeggios. But I'll practise even those to please you, and I'll work just as hard as you want at everything—when I come back."

. . . . . .

One morning at the beginning of August found Mildred ensconced in a corner of a ladies' compartment in the northern express, steaming out of Kirkton station on her journey to Westmorland. Her grief at parting from her uncle and aunt had been keen, and at present she felt somewhat like a small boat suddenly cut loose from its moorings, and drifting on a swift current towards an unknown land. It is a great event in our lives when we first leave the safe shelter of home, where constant familiarity has made everything dear to us, and even our faults have been judged by the tolerant standard of those who love us, to be plunged into a world where we know we shall be taken at a different estimate, and where, to a certain extent, that absolute reliance on another's judgment must give way to a sense of duty and responsibility on our own account. Hitherto Mrs. Graham had been Mildred's conscience, the one being in the world to whom she could take each trouble and difficulty, and could lay bare every part of her soul; and there had existed between the two that entire confidence which is only possible with those who have known us from our first years, and who also have that rare gift of absolute sympathy which makes them able to understand our innermost mind.

We seldom question our earliest friends. They have grown dear to us long before we are at an age to criticize them, our love afterwards blurs our sight to what failings they possess, and consciously or unconsciously we are apt to measure all others by their standard. Mildred felt that her new relations, however kind they might prove, would never be the same as those who had stood to her in the place of father and mother. This separation must necessarily cast her on her own self-reliance; it was the break between childhood and womanhood, the parting of the ways, when she must loose the hand that had guided her so carefully, and take her life into her own keeping. That it would be extremely good for her, Mrs. Graham had no doubt. Mildred was so childish for her age, so dependent and lacking in initiative, that it was time indeed she should begin to think for herself, and gain greater confidence. She needed to be shaken out of her dreamy ways, and given a wider knowledge of the world. Seven weeks among entirely fresh surroundings would be a wholesome probation, and at the end of the holiday she would be in a position to decide whether the new or the old régime was the more congenial.

CHAPTER XI

The Towers

MILDRED meantime was speeding northward, and once the wrench of parting from home was over, she could not be altogether unattracted by the novelty of the change in store for her, and the prospect of seeing fresh places and faces. The dingy bricks and mortar of the town had given place to green fields, woods, and streams, and these in their turn yielded to bare moorland slopes, with stone walls instead of hedges, till presently in the distance she could catch her first glimpse of the hills, their grey peaks outlined against a pale-blue sky. The train ran on for fully an hour more, between craggy heights and thickly-wooded glens, the scenery growing in beauty with every mile, till at length the engine plunged with a whistle into a long tunnel, and finally emerged at the little station of Whiterigg.

"Here you are, Miss!" cried the guard, flinging open the carriage door, and helping her out in a hurry. "Your luggage is at the end of the platform. We're a bit late to-day. Right away!"

And waving his flag, he jumped into his van as it passed him, leaving Mildred with her violin case in one hand and a suit-case in the other, almost bewildered at this sudden termination of her journey. As the retreating train rumbled away in the distance she heard the hoot of a motor-horn, and a car came rapidly along the road and drew up at the gate below. A tall, handsome man jumped out, and ran up the station steps on to the platform.

"Why, here you are at last!" he cried, shaking hands heartily with Mildred. "I'm glad you've found your way here safely. Is that your luggage? We're sending for it later. These light things can go in with us."

Mildred followed her new uncle shyly. His face was pleasant, and his manner was kind as he helped her into the car. To her great relief, after his first greeting was over, he did not trouble her with much conversation, but left her to enjoy the scenery. The road wound up and down in a gorge between two ranges of hills, sometimes passing through woods, and sometimes crossing a noisy stream, overshadowed by brambles and hazel bushes.

"That's Helvellyn!" said Sir Darcy, pointing to a tall peak so far off that it was difficult to distinguish it from the cloud banks in the sky. "It's not often we can see it from here, there's generally a mist rolling over; but when we do, it foretells fine weather. That stream marks the boundary of the property. As soon as we enter the wood we shall be out of Whiterigg and in Castleford, and in a few minutes you'll get your first peep of the lake."

They had at last reached the end of the valley, and, rounding the spur of the hill, went through a thick pine wood, where the tall red stems of the trees stood upright as the masts of a ship. Then, climbing a short incline, they came into an open road above, from which there suddenly burst upon Mildred's eyes such a view as she had never hitherto even imagined. Below her lay the lake, an outstretched shining mass of shimmering brightness in the afternoon light, enfolded by wooded slopes like a jewel in a setting. Here and there a rocky promontory, jutting out into the water, broke the line with its dark reflections, while at the farther end rose a precipice of wild splintered crags, leading up to the tall rigs and fells beyond.

Nestled in a hollow, where it could receive some shelter from the woods and yet command a full view of the water, rose the ivy-covered turrets of a fine old house, the many windows of which were flashing back the light from the lake. Surrounded by beautiful gardens and pleasure grounds, it was indeed a stately home, man's best handiwork set amongst Nature's grandest surroundings, and it was with a thrill of perhaps pardonable pride in his voice that Sir Darcy turned to Mildred and said: "That is The Towers."

The great wrought-iron gates were open, and they entered the park, where a herd of deer and some Highland cattle, which were grazing under the trees, ran off in a mad stampede at their approach. Through a long avenue of beeches and under a carved stone gateway they passed, then into a paved courtyard, and drew up at last before the broad steps of the front entrance.

Sir Darcy took Mildred into the hall, the panelled walls of which were hung with stags' heads, antlers, armour and weapons, well in keeping with the carved oak of the antique furniture. A splendid white deerhound sprang forward, barking a tempestuous greeting to its master. The sound seemed to announce their arrival, for from a room beyond a tall, graceful lady came hastily, followed by a girl who might perhaps be six months younger than Mildred herself—a very pretty girl, whose slender figure, fair face, and light flaxen hair made a charming picture against the background of old oak.

Lady Lorraine welcomed her niece kindly, and was so gentle and encouraging that Mildred's shyness began slightly to thaw. Violet also made smiling overtures of friendship.

"We hear you are very musical, my dear," said Lady Lorraine. "I'm afraid Violet cares nothing about it, though she practises every day. Perhaps you will be able to spur her on a little."

"I'd never open the piano if I weren't obliged," declared Violet. "I hate lessons of any sort, so it's no use pretending I like them. When I'm grown up, I'm just going to hunt and play tennis. They're the only things worth bothering about."

"She's a true Lorraine!" laughed Sir Darcy, patting his daughter on the shoulder. "We all like outdoor sports better than books. We shall have to see how Mildred takes to the saddle. A good gallop across country would soon bring the roses into her cheeks. Can you ride, Mildred? Well, well, we'll soon teach you. Never too late to learn, is it?—though the younger you begin, the firmer your seat. Violet could manage her little Shetland by the time she was five."

"Mildred must get accustomed to country life by degrees," said her aunt. "We will not frighten her with too many things just at first."

When Sir Darcy and Lady Lorraine discussed their niece afterwards, they both decided that she had made a favourable impression upon them.

"A pretty, lady-like girl, though painfully shy," was her uncle's verdict. "I'm much relieved to notice that she has such nice manners. I was afraid we might find her lacking in many ways. I see a strong look of the Lorraines in her face, and no doubt, now she is separated from her other relations, she'll soon get used to us, and in time will forget even to think about her early surroundings, and will not wish to remember that she has ever known anything different from The Towers. I am glad we sent for her. It was certainly rather a venture, but I think the experiment seems likely to prove a success."

The wheels of life, well oiled by a handsome income, ran very smoothly at The Towers. Sir Darcy Lorraine was a fine specimen of an English country gentleman—a splendid shot, a hard rider, interested in the improvement of his estates, and to a certain degree in the welfare of his tenants. He entertained well, subscribed liberally to local charities, supported the Church, and, as a magistrate and guardian of the poor, took what part he could in the affairs of the district without allowing the ensuing duties to monopolize too much of his time. Neither public school nor college had been able to endow him with any love for learning.

"My fly-book and my cheque-book are all the literature I want," he often declared; and though he occasionally sat in his well-furnished library, he rarely, if ever, took down the handsomely bound volumes from their shelves. With other ways of life than his own he had scant sympathy, regarding the arts and sciences as harmless diversions for amateurs who might like them, and a means of livelihood for those who were obliged to take up professions to earn their bread. A good landlord and a kind master, he liked to have everybody bright and cheerful around him, but did not care to be distressed by social problems or tales of outside misery. Always in easy circumstances himself, and never having experienced any reverses, he had a vague idea that misfortunes were mostly caused by people's own fault, and that lack of success was due to lack of merit.

Lady Lorraine had been a society beauty in her girlhood, and still retained enough of her former good looks to attract a considerable amount of attention at hunt balls and garden fêtes. In her way she really worked quite hard at local duties, being always ready to open bazaars, attend flower-shows, distribute prizes, and organize charity dances. She was mildly interested in the village school, where the little boys all respectfully touched their forelocks, and the little girls smiled shyly at her whenever she looked at them. She occasionally visited at some of the cleanest cottages, and could never resist putting her hand in her pocket; though the Vicar, who did not approve of indiscriminate charity, complained that she pauperized those of his parishioners who knew how to whine, while the deserving went unhelped.

Both Sir Darcy and Lady Lorraine idolized their only child. To dress Violet prettily, to take her to garden parties and flower-shows, to see her admired, and finally to bring her out successfully into society, was her mother's chief ambition; and her father, though he would have preferred a boy who could inherit his title, gloried in his little daughter's fearless riding and her achievements in the hunting field.

To Mildred the beauty and novelty of her surroundings at The Towers were a source of great pleasure. As the weeks went on, and her first shyness and homesickness wore away, she began thoroughly to enjoy herself. The motoring, the riding, the many tennis parties and other festivities made an ideal holiday time, and everything seemed new and entertaining. She had soon formed a friendship with the Somervilles at the Vicarage, an amusing family, consisting of three sons and a girl of her own age. Rhoda was pleasant and companionable; and with Rodney, the second boy, Mildred found a strong bond of sympathy, for he was to go to Kirkton in the autumn to study engineering at a large motor works, and was glad to hear all that she could tell him about the city.

Though Mildred thoroughly appreciated the advantages of her new life at The Towers, she nevertheless missed the Grahams continually. Generous as the Lorraines were to her in many respects, their conduct was sometimes lacking in thoughtfulness. They were people who could only be kind in their own way. They considered they had done her an immense service by taking her away from Kirkton, and they would refer to her past surroundings with a contempt which she found it very difficult to bear. Her cousin treated her with a kindly patronage. Violet was glad to have Mildred as a companion, but made her quite understand that she was to occupy a second place. Mildred, accustomed to the "give and take" of a big school, found this attitude decidedly trying, and often longed for the congenial society of Kitty Fletcher, Bess Harrison, Maudie Stearne, or other St. Cyprian's girls, whose friendships were conducted on terms of strictest equality.

In the midst of all the pleasant arrangements at The Towers Mildred found it very difficult to get in even the hour's daily work at the violin which she had faithfully promised Professor Hoffmann not to neglect. Practising by herself seemed so different from learning from her enthusiastic teacher. Away from his watchful eye, she felt as if all kinds of faults were creeping into her playing, and she had not sufficient courage to wrestle with hard passages when she knew there was no one to appreciate her exertions. She set herself with grim determination to master certain new studies; but it was only by constant effort, and the remembrance of what the Professor would expect from her, that she could keep up to anything like the mark of his high standard.

Towards the end of August Miss Ward, Violet's governess, returned from her holidays. She was a pleasant, amiable lady, not clever, but with a general smattering of a good many subjects. She was much appreciated by Lady Lorraine, as she did not attempt to work Violet too hard, and was extremely useful at arranging flowers, writing letters and addressing invitations, and keeping the accounts of local charities. As Miss Ward was considered to be musical, Violet one day asked Mildred to bring her violin into the schoolroom.

"Is this your fiddle?" said Miss Ward, catching it up. "It looks rather a nice one. Give me the bow and let me try it."

To hear her beautiful and priceless Stradivarius called a "fiddle" was a shock to Mildred's ears, but it was nothing to the sounds which followed when the governess began to play. Such scraping and rasping notes it had never before been her misfortune to hear, even from the very worst of Herr Hoffmann's pupils, and she could not have believed that her dear violin could give vent to those harsh and discordant tones. It was playing that would have caused the Professor to tear his hair; everything about it was wrong, from the bowing to the way the instrument was held. The Stradivarius seemed to be shrieking in an agonized protest at the indignity of its treatment, and so painful was the effect on Mildred's sensitive nerves that it was all she could do to sit still with a semblance of politeness.

"Really quite a nice one! Where did you get it?" asked Miss Ward, having complacently arrived at the end of her piece, and handing back the violin to its outraged owner.

Mildred took her treasure somewhat as a mother rescues her crying child from strangers, feeling as if she owed it an apology for having entrusted it to such a 'prentice hand.

"It was my father's," she answered quietly. "It's a genuine Stradivarius, and I value it very much. I wouldn't part with it for anything else in the world."

"Can you remember a tune?" asked Miss Ward, to whom the magic name of Stradivarius appeared to imply very little. "I should like to hear how you can play."

"Yes, do, Mildred!" added Violet. "I've only heard sounds from your bedroom before breakfast, when I was much too sleepy to listen to them."

Mildred paused a moment. She longed to plunge into the "Frühlingslied", but knew it was impossible to do it justice when the orchestra was lacking, so she began instead the Polonaise which she had given as an encore at the Students' Concert. Violet listened in amazement to the true, clear notes. She had never before heard such playing, and though she was quite unmusical, she fully recognized the difference between a good performance and a bad one.

"You did score a triumph over Miss Ward!" she remarked to Mildred afterwards, when the two girls were alone. "I dared not laugh, but it was too funny to watch her face while you were fiddling. You took all the spirit out of her. She had been anxious to teach me her scraping, squeaking instrument, but I declined with thanks. I can't bear the sound of it. Gelert always howls dreadfully the moment she begins, and I feel as if I want to howl too! I'm made to strum on the piano for an hour every day, but I hate it. It's all nonsense! What's the use of learning a thing you don't care about? The only music I really like to hear is a view halloo or a good tally-ho!"

As the summer went on, Mildred thought the scenery at Castleford seemed to grow more and more beautiful. The ripened corn gave a golden touch to the fields, the moorlands were ablaze with purple heather, and on the hillside slopes the bracken was beginning to turn to gorgeous shades of ochre and sienna brown. She and Violet took many walks with Sir Darcy round the estate, and she was beginning now to know the neighbourhood quite well. One day Sir Darcy, who was busy talking with a keeper, left the two girls to rest on a stone at the head of the precipice which bounded the lake.

"How lovely it looks!" said Mildred. "I think it is the most exquisite view I've ever seen in my life."

Violet gazed thoughtfully at the purple-grey lake lying below them, the encircling woods in all the glory of their summer green seeming richer in contrast with the peaks of the craggy hills behind. By the water's edge stretched lush meadows, the village and the church could be seen in the blue distance, and close at hand rose the turrets and chimneys of The Towers. Violet did not very often think about such things, but just then a verse came into her head which she had sung in the psalms at church the Sunday before, and which had caught her attention at the time—

> "The lot is fallen unto me in a fair ground: yea, I have a goodly heritage."

"Yes," she replied with a long breath; "it's the dearest place on earth to me. There's no other like it anywhere. And it's our own, as far as you can see it—that's the best of it! The Lorraines have held it ever since the Conquest. It's Father's, and some day I suppose it will come to me. I can't take the title, but luckily the land is not entailed now. It's grand to think of possessing all this.

Mildred, you shall live here with me as long as you like. I want you to enjoy it too. I'm most dreadfully sorry for you. It's hard luck to have absolutely nothing of your own."

Mildred looked down where her cousin's beautiful inheritance lay stretched before her. Her heart was too full to answer. Perhaps for a moment a shade of envy crossed her mind. It was indeed a fortunate lot to be heiress to such broad acres and so old a name. Some of the best things that life could offer had fallen to Violet's share. And what had she herself? An old violin, and the skill to play it—that was all! A possession utterly valueless in Violet's eyes, yet in those of Dr. and Mrs. Graham and the Professor a rare and special talent such as God gives to but very few in this world—a talent to be taken humbly, and rejoiced in, and treasured zealously, and cultivated carefully, and which might bring more joy and beauty into the lives of others than even these glorious woods and waters; for music can lift the soul to the very summit of earthly ecstasy, and in some of its divinest strains we can almost catch an echo of the chorus of the "choir invisible" above. She could not explain—it was quite impossible to put into words what she only felt deep down in her heart; but as she quietly thanked Violet for her offer, it seemed to her that, in spite of her lack of lands, she was not quite portionless. God's gifts to His children were not all alike. To one the estates handed down by a long line of ancestors from the past; to another the genius that has the power to create for itself. Which was the nobler bequest she could not tell, but she knew that after all she, too, had an inheritance.

CHAPTER XII

At Tiverton Keep

SINCE Miss Ward's return to The Towers Violet had begun lessons again, and was occupied each morning with her governess in the schoolroom. Mildred, who was still enjoying holidays, was therefore left for several hours every day to her own devices. She found it no hardship, for it was easy enough to amuse herself. Sometimes she sat with a book in the garden, sometimes sauntered round the grounds, or explored the beautiful borders of the lake. She had brought her camera from home, and the taking and developing of photographs gave her plenty of occupation. She was making a little collection of views of Castleford, and meant to paste them in an album as a reminiscence of the lovely scenery. One glorious warm morning it occurred to her that she would like to take snapshots of Tiverton Keep, an old border turret which stood on a hill a mile and a half above The Towers. So far, while Violet and Miss Ward were busy, she had kept strictly to the private grounds of the Castle, but to-day she thought there would surely be no harm in venturing farther afield. She would have asked permission, but Sir Darcy was out, Lady Lorraine was in bed with a headache, and Miss Ward was giving Violet a music lesson; so

Mildred decided that she might very well make the expedition on her own authority. Down the road through the wood she started, therefore, rounding the corner of the lake and turning up through the village. As she passed the Vicarage she met Diccon, the youngest boy, wheeling his motor bicycle out at the gate.

"Hello, Mildred!" he cried. "Where are you off to? You told me you never stirred out of the garden till the thermometer dropped. Whence this thusness?"

"I'm going to take some snapshots of Tiverton Keep. It's such a glorious morning for photographing. The light and shade will be just perfect."

"Wish I could have gone with you! I'm obliged to ride over to Whiterigg to send off a parcel by train to London. By the by, if you're going to Tiverton, keep a look-out for the lunatic!"

"What do you mean?"

"What I say. Someone of unsound mind has been haunting the place lately, and he might, perhaps, give you a fright."

"I haven't heard of anybody."

"He's been there, though. He's quite a young chap, so I'm told (that's the pity of it!), but he's been overworking at classics, and gone clean dotty. His relations have brought him here to recruit, and generally they keep a good eye over his movements, but sometimes he dodges them and scoots off by himself. Then he's apt to play some uncommonly queer pranks. He's taken a tremendous fancy to the Keep, goes poking about, filling his pockets with pebbles and things, and insists that the place is still in the mediaeval condition, and inhabited by people who lived in the days of the Plantagenets. He gets violently excited and dangerous if anyone ventures to contradict him. They have to pretend all sorts of nonsense to humour him. The family are staying at Lowood Farm."

"I heard that some people are there for the summer," replied Mildred, "and I certainly saw two girls in the lane with a young man of about twenty. He didn't look insane. What a most fearful affliction!"

"Yes, it's a warning against overworking oneself," said Diccon. "Shall you venture to the Keep?"

"I must go and take those photographs. I don't suppose I shall meet this unfortunate young fellow. If I do, I'll be careful to give him a wide berth. His family ought to have an attendant for him, if they can't look after him properly themselves."

Tiverton Keep was still a mile away—a beautiful walk up a rocky glen, and then over the open fell. It was much cooler on the moorland than in the village; quite a pleasant breeze was stirring, there was a refreshing bubbling sound of small brooklets trickling between clumps of heather and lady fern, while below lay the silver gleam of the lake. The old castle stood on a slight eminence, commanding an excellent view of the surrounding country, and in former days it must have been a useful factor in border warfare. Only a portion of the Keep was still standing, but the ancient guard-room remained intact, and a winding staircase led to the battlements. The day was an ideal one for using the camera. The light was perfect, and Mildred congratulated herself that she would be able to take a splendid series of snapshots.

"How delightful it is to have the place to oneself, without any tourists about!" she thought.

She did not spare her films, and after photographing the exterior and the ground floor, she toiled up the winding stairs till she reached the broad walk that ran round the top of the tower. Here she took several pictures, and finally climbed a few remaining steps which led to a little turret at the extreme summit of the Keep. From this crow's-nest she had a grand bird's-eye prospect of the whole landscape. How small everything looked! The windmill at the other side of the glen was like a child's toy, and the sheep grazing on the moor seemed white dots. She leaned her arms on the railing, and peered down into the castle courtyard below. Someone was walking about there, for she heard the sound of footsteps, and presently the intruder came in sight. Mildred's heart gave a sudden uncomfortable jump. She recognized in an instant the tall figure of the classical student who was staying at Lowood Farm. He moved slowly, with his eyes fixed on the ground, as if he were searching for something, and every now and then he dived among the piles of loose stones, apparently picking up small objects which he placed in his pockets.

"So Diccon was right!" thought Mildred. "How fearfully sad! He looks such a fine young fellow physically, one wouldn't imagine he'd lost his mental balance. Poor creature! Filling his pockets with rubbish! I hope he's not here all alone. Where are his sisters?"

She looked around anxiously to see if a feminine petticoat were fluttering in the vicinity, but there was no sign of anyone.

"He must have escaped again, and run from them, I suppose," she soliloquized. "I hope he won't notice me on the tower, for I certainly don't want to encounter him."

After a little consideration she decided to stay where she was, to give the intruder time to go away before she ventured from the battlements. He soon disappeared out of the courtyard, but whether to enter the guard-room, or to take his departure, Mildred had no means of ascertaining. She lingered for what seemed an immense while, and heard no sound of further footsteps.

"I've been here for ages; I'm sure it must be nearly half-past twelve," she thought. "I wish I had put on my watch. I can't wait for ever. I expect he's gone, so I'm going to risk it," and she sallied down from the turret.

She had walked half-way round the battlements, and was just gaining confidence, when she suddenly saw a head appearing up the winding staircase, and before she could beat a retreat a tall figure in tennis flannels stepped on to the parapet. He glanced at Mildred with a mixture of confusion and consternation in his face, hesitated, seemed for a moment inclined to retrace his steps, then walked forward with a determined air.

"Good morning! Admiring the view here?" he remarked politely.

Mildred was shivering with alarm, but she had the presence of mind to assent calmly.

"Whatever I do, I mustn't let him see that I

notice anything unusual about him; I believe lunatics are very sensitive on that score. If I behave in an ordinary manner, perhaps he'll go away soon," she thought.

"I'm particularly fond of the battlements, they seem such a great height up," she added aloud, leaning over the wooden railing which guarded the parapet.

He glanced hurriedly down, as if measuring the distance to the courtyard beneath, then turned to her with a marked uneasiness in his gaze.

"It's really nicer below on the grass," he urged. "Won't you come down and try the difference?"

"No, thanks, I prefer remaining here," replied Mildred, hoping that her unwelcome companion would depart by himself to test the superior merits of the courtyard.

To leave her, however, did not seem to enter his calculations. He stared at her again, with a queer look, almost of apprehension, fidgeted a little, coughed, turned rather red, and finally remarked shyly:

"They're waiting for you in the hall."

"Who?" asked Mildred.

"Why, the seneschal and the Baron, and the retainers, and—er—the jester, and all the rest of them."

"There! He's begun on the mediaeval topic!" thought poor Mildred. "He's evidently as mad as a hatter. I mustn't irritate him. Diccon said he grew very violent if contradicted. I must try and humour him."

"The Baron may wait my pleasure," she replied, with an attempt at what she hoped was the hauteur of a *grande dame* of the Plantagenet period. "As for the rest, they are but vassals and serfs."

"True, lady, but they long for the sunshine of your presence. Will it not please you to show yourself to them on the dais?"

"The dinner is not yet ready," faltered Mildred, trying to conjure up any plausible excuse, though she could not frame it in mediaeval language.

"My lady mistakes. The scullions are even now removing the wild geese from the spits, the boar's head is placed on the trencher, the venison pasties are baked, and the ale is broached."

"He knows far too much about old customs," thought Mildred ruefully. "How shall I get out of it? I must put him on another track." Holding her hand to shade her eyes, she gazed at the distant horizon. "Methinks there is a rumour that the Scots are abroad. Tell me if you see aught that looks like a body of armed men on yonder fell."

Her companion scanned the hillside seriously and earnestly, as if he really expected to find flashing pikes and helmets, though nothing more dangerous than a flock of sheep was to be seen.

"It will perchance be the Black Douglas," he answered in solemn tones. "Lady, your position here is one of danger! You are a mark for every arrow. I pray you descend to the safety of the guard-room."

"They are not near enough yet to shoot," said Mildred quickly. "Indeed, I am not certain whether it is the foe, or merely a band of peaceful pilgrims. If you would mount into yonder watch-tower, you could call to me if you recognize the banner of the Black Douglas."

Mildred hoped by this suggestion to send her companion up into the little turret, and the moment his back was turned she intended to bolt down the winding staircase. Apparently he saw through her design, for he replied at once in the negative. He moved a step nearer to her, and a watchful look came into his eyes.

"How atrociously clever lunatics are!" thought Mildred. "It seems impossible to outwit him. Yet I simply daren't walk down the stairs with him. He might give me a sudden push. What can I possibly say to him next? I'll try flattery."

Looking him over coolly from head to foot, she announced:

"Methinks I like not my lord's attire. 'Tis unworthy of so handsome a knight. I would have you put on fresh bravery, and present yourself to me in your velvet doublet and the trunk-hose which even the Baron envies. They would do justice to your comely person."

Her companion glanced at his tennis flannels and blushed—yes, actually blushed. He gazed at her for a moment almost despairingly, then took a hasty walk up and down the parapet, twisting and untwisting his hands with a nervous action.

"I hope he's not getting excited and violent," thought Mildred.

He returned at last, as if for a final appeal. "It my lady will come and review my poor wardrobe, perchance she may find something to her taste, and I will don it at her command."

He held out his arm, awkwardly enough, and not at all with the grace of a mediaeval courtier, as if to lead her from the battlements. Mildred edged away from him, holding on to the railing. Would no one come to the rescue? She thought she heard a footstep, and glanced down anxiously into the courtyard below, hoping that one of his sisters had arrived in search of him. To her horror he immediately rushed at her and grasped her firmly by the arm.

"You shan't take your life if I can prevent it!" he exclaimed.

To find herself thus in his clutch was more than Mildred's self-command could stand. She shrieked with terror, trying to tear herself away, but the more she pulled the more tightly and determinedly he gripped her.

"There! There! That'll do, Chorlton. Let her go; she's all right," shouted a familiar voice; and loosed as suddenly as she had been seized, Mildred turned and saw the grinning face of Diccon appearing from the doorway of the staircase. He advanced along the parapet in explosions of laughter, which were certainly not shared by either Mildred or the stranger, both of whom stood regarding him with amazement.

"Oh, you simpletons! You credulous pair of infants! I never imagined you'd both swallow it whole. Oh, it's too ripping for anything! It's absolutely killing me! I've been listening to the whole interview. Oh, let me get my breath!"

In a flash Mildred comprehended.

"Diccon! You odious boy! Do you mean it's all a hoax?"

"Of course it is! Poor old Chorlton's as sane as you are! Oh, I say, Chorlton! Don't look so deliciously blank, or I shall have a fit!"

"This wretched boy told me you were mad," faltered Mildred apologetically to her companion.

"And he told me that you were mad, with a suicidal tendency," replied Mr. Chorlton.

"The whole thing worked out so neatly," chuckled naughty Diccon. "Please allow me to recount my own joke. I told Mildred that you were violent unless humoured on the subject of mediaevalism, and I told you that she might fling herself over the battlements if she were contradicted in supposing herself a lady of the Plantagenet period."

"You thoroughly deserve a thrashing, you young imp!" declared Mr. Chorlton.

"No, I don't. I've afforded you each a most exciting adventure. You didn't know Chorlton was a college friend of Eric's, Mildred? We only discovered last night that he's staying at Lowood Farm. I stuffed you about him for a lark, and then when I met him in the village just after you started, I couldn't resist the fun of playing a trick on you both. Chorlton was going to the Keep, too, so I told him a yarn about an unfortunate demented girl who occasionally escaped there and tried to commit suicide. He went up the battlements on purpose to cajole you down to safety. Oh, it was great to hear you fencing with each other!" and Diccon rubbed his hands in his glee.

"I think you've treated Mr. Chorlton abominably," said Mildred.

"Then you'll consent to descend the staircase with me now?" said Mr. Chorlton, smiling.

"Yes, if you promise not to don trunk-hose and a velvet doublet."

"Trust me! I was racking my brains all the time for mediaeval terms. I must have appeared an awful lunatic!"

"But may I ask why you were picking up pebbles in the courtyard? That did look rather peculiar, I own."

"They weren't pebbles. They're land-snail shells. I'm collecting them. Mad on conchology, if you like!"

"I had to sprint to Whiterigg and back, so as to be able to follow you," chuckled Diccon. "I was so afraid I might be too late for the fun. It was luck to get here just in time."

Mildred had much to tell on her return to lunch at The Towers. Violet, to whom Diccon's practical jokes were well known, was immensely amused, though Sir Darcy and Lady Lorraine were not inclined to treat the episode so humorously.

"Mildred must not take solitary walks again," said her aunt. "I should never have given her permission to go out alone, and she must remember that in future."

"I won't forget," promised Mildred. "I was horribly scared at the time."

"Oh, it was funny!" laughed Violet. "That wretch Diccon deserves to be paid back in his own coin, though. I wonder if we couldn't manage to play a trick upon him? I'm going to cudgel my brains till I think of something."

CHAPTER XIII

Third Cousin

VIOLET, who was herself extremely fond of practical jokes, was determined to turn the tables upon Diccon.

"I owe him one or two little things, for he often plays tricks on Rhoda and me at the Vicarage," she said to Mildred. "The difficulty is to hit upon anything really good. It won't be easy to take him in. I shall have to think and think. Oh, I verily believe I've got it! Enid's the very girl! She'd love it! Oh, it fits in capitally!"

"Who's Enid?"

"She's a distant relation from New Zealand—a kind of second cousin, once removed. She and her people are in England for a year, and we met them in town last June. They're staying with the Harcourts at present, only twenty miles away, and I'll persuade Mother to let me invite Enid for the day on Saturday. The car can fetch her and take her back. We'll ask Diccon to come to make up a set at tennis, and then spring a surprise on him. Father and Mother were out in New Zealand five years ago, and they brought home Maori costumes and all sorts of beads. Yes, I see my way splendidly! I believe he'll really swallow it whole.

Mildred, can you keep your face absolutely, in an emergency, and not laugh?"

"I'll do my best," returned Mildred.

Violet laid her plans carefully, and after Enid had accepted the invitation for Saturday she sent a note to the Vicarage asking Diccon to tennis. The members of the Somerville family often came to The Towers to make up sets, and as Diccon was a better player than his brothers, it occasioned no particular surprise that he should be invited alone. He arrived therefore about three o'clock, quite unsuspiciously. Violet and Mildred were waiting for him in the garden.

"I want to introduce you to a friend of ours," began Violet; "a third cousin, in fact. She only came this morning. She's over from New Zealand."

"I'd forgotten you had any overseas relations," observed Diccon.

"Oh, yes! A great-uncle of Mother's went out to Auckland years and years ago, and married a native. I had just a peep at this cousin when we were in London. Of course she's very peculiar-looking, but we like her, don't we, Mildred? I rather admire her dark complexion."

"She's absolutely ripping!" affirmed Mildred cordially.

"I thought I'd better prepare you for the fact that she's a real New Zealander," continued Violet. "Come along and see her. She's sitting in the gun-room. She seems to like it better than anywhere else in the house."

"Queer taste for a girl," commented Diccon.

"She enjoys being amongst weapons," explained

Violet. "I suppose it's a savage instinct. It takes a long time to eradicate the old Adam. Her New Zealand grandfather was a very warlike character."

"Swung a tomahawk, did he?"

"They're not called tomahawks in New Zealand. You're thinking of Fenimore Cooper's American Indians. But never mind, come and be introduced to Rata."

"Is that her name?"

"Yes; don't you think it's pretty?"

"Oh, well enough! Look here, what am I to say? Does she speak English?"

"Quite decently. You'll have no difficulty in understanding her. I shall just introduce you."

"And what then?"

"Why, you must shake hands. She'll expect it. She's given up rubbing noses since she came to England."

"Oh, I say!" murmured Diccon faintly. "I don't think I feel quite well. My head aches."

But Violet ignored his plaintive excuse, and firmly led the way to the gun-room. Squatting on a low stool near the window, reading a New Zealand paper, was a decidedly queer-looking figure—odd, at any rate, to English eyes. The face and hands were very dark, and both cheeks and forehead were tattooed all over with an intricate pattern in red and blue. A magenta silk scarf was tied over the head, completely hiding the hair, and a huge pair of ear-rings drooped over the dusky neck. The girl was dressed in a bright skirt, with a striped rug flung round her shoulders; her wrists were loaded with native-looking bangles, and she wore slippers of plaited grass. She took no notice at all when the door opened, but simply went on reading.

"I'm glad you warned me beforehand," whispered Diccon. "Isn't she pleased to see us?"

"Oh, yes! But she's not used yet to our customs. Remember, she has been brought up in New Zealand ways. Rata, here's a visitor to see you," continued Violet aloud. "Won't you speak to him?"

At this direct appeal, the strange cousin rose from her stool, and bowed with a certain stately dignity. She did not offer to shake hands, and Diccon, fearful that she might relapse into her old habit of rubbing noses, kept cautiously in the background.

"You must be awfully glad to come to England," he stammered, for want of anything else to say.

"It is a great pleasure for me to see my father's country," she replied in a decidedly foreign accent, "and to meet the relations who are so kind to me. Lady Lorraine promises to take me everywhere. To-day I go to tennis and to a dance."

Diccon looked hastily at Violet, who nodded in confirmation.

"The Tracys 'phoned asking us to go to tennis at The Chase this afternoon, and wouldn't take a refusal. They said we must bring you and Rata with us, and that we must all stay to supper, and they would have a little dancing afterwards; just May's and Frank's friends."

"I believe I ought to show up at a village meeting at six o'clock," declared Diccon desperately.

"What rubbish! You certainly won't be needed there. We've told the Tracy's you're coming with us; they'll be offended if you don't. Father and Mother are getting ready now. We've ordered the car for half-past three. I wonder how the sets will be arranged this afternoon? You're a good player, Diccon, so you'd better take Rata. She hasn't had much practice in English courts, so you must look after her and teach her."

Diccon's face was a study.

"Wouldn't your cousin have learnt better on the lawn here?" he urged eagerly.

"Oh, no! She'll enjoy going to the Tracys, and I'm sure you'll be able to give her hints. By the by, we want her to have a nice time at the dance afterwards, and plenty of partners. Will you ask her for the first waltz? It's always well to fill up one's programme beforehand."

"I'm—I'm afraid really I shan't be able to stay for the dance," stammered Diccon. "Shan't have any togs with me, you see."

"That's all right," returned the inexorable Violet. "We've sent Fletcher to the Vicarage to ask your mother to pack your bag with anything you'll need. Rata, this is your partner for the first waltz. You won't forget?"

"No, no, I not forget," replied the soft foreign voice.

"Run and get ready now, dear! We mustn't be long. Mildred and I are going to put on our hats and coats. You'll wait here for us, Diccon, won't you?"

The girls walked away with their extraordinary foreign guest, and Diccon remained in the gun-room in a very dejected and disconsolate frame of mind. He would have "done a bolt", but he did not care to risk offending the Lorraines. He was accustomed to Violet's autocratic ways, and knew that she would not forgive him if he refused to fall in with her wishes. Yet his very hair rose on end at the idea of going out for the afternoon and evening in the company of this New Zealand damsel, to whom he was expected to pay so much attention.

"I don't know how the Lorraines can stand it," he thought. "If I had such a cousin thrust on me, I'd die of shame."

So far from seeming ashamed of her outlandish relation, Violet evidently regarded her with the utmost complacency. Rata herself did not seem to realize that her appearance was singular; perhaps, indeed, she considered it more pleasing than that of her European friends, and was longing to suggest tattooing as an aid to beauty. Nevertheless, that Diccon, a member of his school cricket team and the winner of three silver cups, should be required to play tennis and to dance with this indescribable girl was an outrage on his feelings. Why, he would be a laughing-stock! If anyone else would take the first turn with her, he would not mind quite so much, but to make a start! Oh, it was sickening! He would have shammed illness if there had been the slightest chance of being believed. If he did not look pale, he looked decidedly sulky as Violet came downstairs into the hall.

"Here we are!" she said sweetly. "I'm afraid we've kept you waiting a little. You see, it took rather a long time to change Rata's dress. She decided, after all, that she wouldn't go to the Tracys in Maori costume."

Diccon turned, and could not restrain a gasp of surprise. Instead of the extraordinary native, Violet and Mildred were accompanied by a very pretty and elegantly-dressed girl of their own age, whose brown eyes were gazing at him with politely restrained amusement. Not a trace of tattoo marks upon that white forehead or those rose-leaf cheeks. The ear-rings were gone, also the magenta scarf, and her brown hair had been most beautifully coiffured by an expert hairdresser.

"Good night!" exclaimed Diccon, subsiding weakly into a chair.

Then the three girls exploded, and laughed till they grew almost hysterical.

"It serves you right, Diccon!" gurgled Violet. "We've paid you out for the trick you played on Mildred at the Keep. Oh, I never thought we'd take you in so well. You believed every word, and looked so deliciously dumbfounded."

"Well, I'd heard before that Lady Lorraine's uncle had married a New Zealander," retorted Diccon.

"So he did, but she was a settler, not a Maori. Aunt Margaret Fowler was a daughter of General Berkeley, who distinguished himself very much in the native wars, on the British side, please! Our cousins are still out there, some of them at least, you know. By the by, Rata is only a pet name, and not often used. I must introduce Enid properly —Miss Fowler!"

"I hope you liked my get-up?" enquired Enid, without a trace of the foreign accent. "It was rather elaborate, but we flatter ourselves it repaid our trouble."

"How did you do it?"

"We evolved it amongst us. I rubbed my face

and hands with glycerine, and then powdered them with cocoa. It gave just the right Maori complexion. As for the tattooing, Mildred painted it. She copied it from a picture of a Maori woman in this New Zealand magazine, and I told her what colours to use. She did it splendidly. I felt loath to wash it off. We tied on the ear-rings with silk thread, and a few shawls and scarves and bangles did the rest."

"We might have had more fun out of it," said Violet regretfully. "I wanted to ask you to lunch, and for Rata to come to table in Maori costume. We'd planned that she was to talk about all sorts of old savage native customs. I did so hope you'd ask if she were still a heathen! But Mother said she and Father would never keep their faces, and the servants would have fits, so she wouldn't let me try the experiment. Admit now, Diccon, that it's 'the biter bit', and that you were just as much taken in as Mildred was at Tiverton Keep. Here's the car! Don't forget, by the by, that you've asked Enid for the first waltz."

CHAPTER XIV

Mildred's Choice

AMONG the new friends whom Mildred had made at Castleford none proved more congenial than the Somervilles. They were a decidedly musical family: Rhoda and Rodney both played the piano well, and the Vicar himself had considerable skill on the violoncello. The Chorltons, who were staying at a farm near the village, were also fond of music, so many pleasant little gatherings were held in the Vicarage drawing-room. Young Mr. Chorlton was possessed of a capital voice, and played his own accompaniments on the guitar in what Diccon called "true mediaeval style, worthy of Tiverton Keep"; and his sisters sang pretty duets with admirable taste. Violet, who cared for nothing but outdoor sports, did not often join these parties, but Lady Lorraine allowed Mildred to visit the Somervilles as frequently as she wished. Mildred thoroughly enjoyed the pleasant, unconventional home, so simple yet so refined, so full of many interests and much work—a home in which the general atmosphere was stimulating to a degree, for the Vicar loved to discuss both literature and the current topics of the day with his children, and generally had some intellectual subject on hand

He was an ardent botanist, and with Rhoda's help had made a splendid collection of dried plants, which were kept on special shelves in his study. He was at present engaged in writing a book upon the flora of the Lake district, and it was Rhoda's immense pride and privilege to be allowed to help in the compiling of lists or the copying of certain pages. To be her father's amanuensis was her greatest ambition, and she treasured every hour she spent with him at their favourite hobby, whether writing in the study or hunting for specimens on the hillsides.

Eric, the eldest son, was at Cambridge, in the same college, though not in the same year, as Mr. Chorlton. Rodney, who had just left school, was looking forward to learning motor engineering at Kirkton. He was an ingenious young fellow, and had made many clever contrivances at the Vicarage: a windmill that pumped water from the well, an electric motor that turned either his mother's sewing-machine or the churn in the dairy, and numerous handy little achievements in the way of carpentry. Mildred liked him by far the best of the three boys. Eric was rather inclined to be superior and conceited, and to wish to lay down the law to the rest of the family; and Diccon, who was still at school, was too fond of mischief to be taken seriously; but Rodney was perfectly frank and unaffected in his manners, in spite of his undoubted cleverness, and quite the most satisfactory at home.

Rhoda, so far, had been taught by her father, but she was hoping to go to school for a year or two to finish her education, and have the advantage of mixing with other girls. She questioned Mildred eagerly about St. Cyprian's, and was anxious to hear every detail of the life there: the lessons, the teachers, the games, and the Alliance which had lately been formed with so much success. As reminiscences of Kirkton were strongly discouraged at The Towers, Mildred found it a great relief to talk to Rhoda about the many interests of her school. She would descant upon the joys of St. Cyprian's, the fun of cricket matches or Eisteddfods, and of the various plans that had been made for the autumn term, till her friend was filled with a longing to go and taste the joyful experiences for herself. Rodney also asked many questions about Kirkton; and to these two confidants Mildred by degrees described all her home life at Meredith Terrace, the concerts she attended, her lessons with Professor Hoffmann, and the hopes he entertained that she should follow a musical career. She did not forget to enumerate the many advantages of Kirkton, and sang the city's praises with the utmost enthusiasm, setting it down next to London itself in the variety of opportunities of every sort which it afforded.

Mildred sometimes took her Stradivarius to the Vicarage, and her friends there were both surprised and charmed with her playing, the Vicar, who was a good judge of the violin, thinking even more highly of it than he deemed it discreet to tell her.

"The child's quite a genius," he said to his wife privately, having listened to Mildred improvising one afternoon. "The music's in her. You can see it in her sensitive little face and her big dark eyes. She's an artist to her finger tips, full of emotion and poetical imagination. I have rarely heard such playing in a concert room, and to find both the technique and the spirit of such a subtle work as the 'Frühlingslied' grasped by a girl of only sixteen is simply marvellous. Her own compositions are full of merit, though naturally still immature; they have the right ring about them, somehow—they're original, and not a mere reflection of what she has heard elsewhere. If she goes on with her training, she ought to have a great career before her, and make a name for herself. I don't suppose they appreciate her talent in the least at The Towers, and I can only hope, for the sake of the musical world at large, that she may go back to the relations who value her gift, and who have cultivated it so carefully."

As September arrived, and the time drew near for Dr. and Mrs. Graham to come back from Canada, Mildred naturally began to feel some anxiety about the subject of her return to Meredith Terrace. The Lorraines seemed to have taken it for granted that she was to remain permanently at The Towers. They scarcely ever alluded to the Grahams, and though they knew that she corresponded with them, they never asked for any news of them, and appeared to take not the slightest interest in their affairs, evidently regarding Mildred's life at Kirkton as a past episode, to be ignored as much as possible, and certainly never to be revived. How she was to break to them that she wished to return, now that her visit was over, Mildred could not imagine. She had really been happy at Castleford, and could not bear to seem ungrateful for all the kindness she had received, and she could only hope that some way might be found out of the difficulty by which she could leave without giving offence.

September was a busy month at The Towers; not only was the house full of visitors, but people were continually riding or motoring over, and luncheon and dinner parties were of almost everyday occurrence. Violet and Mildred were allowed to spend a short time in the drawing-room each evening, and the latter thus had her first little peep at society, and into that gay world which her cousin looked forward so much to entering when she should be old enough to "come out". Sir Darcy and Lady Lorraine were going away soon to join a shooting party on a beautiful estate in Scotland, and as a last effort of hospitality before their guests departed, they decided to give a large "At Home", to which all their friends in the neighbourhood were to be invited.

"Everybody will be here," said Violet in much excitement; "the Rochesters and the Markmans, and Lady Dorothy and Admiral Newson. Colonel Thorpe is bringing quite a big party, and the Musgraves have that beautiful cousin with them who made such a sensation this season. Mrs. Dent says she sings, and we must be sure to ask her."

"Are you going to have music, then?" enquired Mildred, who was dressing in her cousin's bedroom that night.

"Yes, a little, I expect," answered Violet, sitting down to allow the maid to arrange her fair hair. "And there'll be dancing afterwards in the hall. Most of the people seem just to like to sit and talk to each other. I think it's a pleasure to them to meet. Do you like my pearls or my corals?"

"Your corals, I think," said Mildred. "Will anybody else sing, besides the Musgraves' cousin?"

"Mrs. Cavendish has rather a good voice, and so has Colonel Thorpe. One of the Dents plays the piano; she always brings some pieces with her when she comes. I'm afraid people don't listen very much, they're generally talking so hard all the time; but they seem to like to hear it going on, and they always say 'Thank you!' at the end."

"How funny!" said Mildred, who could not reconcile the ideas of combined music and conversation.

She had not before been present at a large party, and she was curious as to what would take place. She went into the drawing-room rather shyly with her cousin and Miss Ward. They were only to be allowed downstairs for an hour, as Lady Lorraine did not wish to bring Violet forward too much while she was still in the schoolroom, and had told Miss Ward to send both the girls to bed at half-past nine. Mildred knew very few of the people present, and she was glad to slip into a retired corner behind the piano, where she could watch the gay scene without being noticed herself. The room was full, and, as Violet had prophesied, conversation seemed so entirely to constitute the chief enjoyment that the music contributed by some of the guests was scarcely appreciated as much as it deserved.

"How do you do, my dear? I'm very pleased indeed to meet you here," said a voice in Mildred's ear; and, turning round, she found herself face to face with Mrs. Trevor, the lady whom she had first met at the Professor's, and through whose instrumentality it was that she had come at all to The Towers.

"I expect you will have nearly forgotten Kirkton by now," said Mrs. Trevor. "No? Well, at any rate I hope you have not forgotten your beautiful playing. Are we to have the pleasure of listening to you to-night?"

"Oh, no!" said Mildred, horror-stricken at the suggestion. "I never play here, only practise."

"But we are all longing to hear you," said Mrs. Trevor. "I was telling Mrs. Dent about you only the other day, and she said she would like to see your Stradivarius. Lady Lorraine! Is not your little niece going to bring down her violin? Either Miss Dent or myself would be charmed to play her accompaniment. Please ask her to let us have some of her delightful music. It would be quite a treat."

"Fetch your instrument, then, Mildred, if Mrs. Trevor wishes to hear you, and will be so kind as to accompany you," said Lady Lorraine promptly, but without much enthusiasm; adding, as Mildred blushed and hesitated: "Go at once, my dear."

Mildred had not expected in the least that she would be asked to perform on such an occasion, and her natural shyness made her more than usually diffident. The guests looked up with interest as she took her place by the piano, and, allowing Mrs. Trevor to choose a piece from among her music, began a "Fantasia" on some old Hungarian melodies. All the conversation was hushed, and those who had talked the loudest before now listened intently, attracted at once by the little violinist and her talented playing, and asking themselves who she could be. Mildred was very warmly thanked and congratulated at the conclusion of her piece; many people examined her violin and spoke kindly to her, and both Mrs. Trevor and Miss Dent questioned her about her practising, and whether she still continued to take lessons.

She had put the Stradivarius away, and had returned into the hall, where she was standing half-hidden by the curtain of the dining-room door, wondering whether she could find either Violet or Miss Ward, when she suddenly became aware of a conversation which was taking place between two ladies sitting on low chairs behind a group of palms close by her. As she did not realize at first that she herself was the subject of their remarks, and as, too, the hall was so crowded that she could not have moved away just then without pushing quite rudely amongst the guests, she was obliged to overhear what she felt afterwards had certainly not been intended for her ears.

"It was wonderful playing," said the first lady. "She's as good as any of those prodigies one hears in town, and a very pretty, graceful girl too. Where did they pick her up?"

"Hush!" said the second. "She's Sir Darcy's niece. I'd never seen her before. She's really marvellously clever."

"His niece! Why, it's most unusual to find such talent in an amateur. She's equal to any professional."

"Well, I hear that she has been a professional.

I certainly know for a fact that she has appeared in public."

"But you told me that she is Sir Darcy's niece. I shouldn't have thought the Lorraines would allow that."

"It's an old story," said the second speaker, lowering her voice still more. "Sir Darcy's sister made a disgraceful match. She actually ran away with her music master. It caused a terrible scandal at the time, and Sir John never forgave her. I believe he was a very clever man, and played divinely, but of course nobody would have anything to do with her afterwards. I heard they were both dead. This is their child, and no doubt it's only natural she should have been trained in this manner, as she's been living among her father's relations. Sir Darcy has taken her now, and intends to provide for her, but I really am astonished that he should allow her to play here to-night, when everybody must know the circumstances of the case."

Growing quite desperate, Mildred felt that she simply must move away, and, at the risk of being rude, managed to slip between a group of talking people. As she did so, she caught a glimpse, at the other side of the curtain, of Sir Darcy, who had also been standing in the shelter of the dining-room door, and she knew instantly, by his face, that he, too, must have overheard the conversation. Threading her way amongst the groups of visitors, she at last reached the staircase, and rushing up to her bedroom she locked the door, and flung herself on to her bed in a passion of hot, angry tears.

Why should they talk thus of her father? she

asked herself bitterly. Was his genius not equal, nay superior, to rank and wealth? Did they class her, too, as infinitely beneath them? Which was the higher aim in life, to glory in the things that had been given you through no merit or toil of your own, and to scorn all those who did not possess them, or to make the very utmost of your talents, and let them be of some use to your fellow creatures, and by working your hardest feel that you had at least tried to take your share in the world's burden?

"I shall have to tell Uncle Darcy I'm going back to Kirkton," thought Mildred. "I don't know how to do it, but it's got to come somehow I daren't leave it any longer, or Uncle Colin and Aunt Alice may begin to think I want to stay. It's most beautiful here, and I get ever so many things I shan't have at Meredith Terrace, but it's not home. They're very kind to me, but they don't love me in the least, and I'm sure they won't miss me when I'm gone. I'm nothing to them, and though it may be very grand to live at The Towers, it's a hundred times happier in my own dear home, and among my own people who really care for me."

After all, it was not so difficult as she had imagined, for the very next day the occasion arrived. The guests who had been staying in the house had gone away by the midday train, Miss Ward and Violet were at lessons, and Sir Darcy, Lady Lorraine, and Mildred were by themselves in the morning-room. The talk fell on the "At Home" of the night before, and Lady Lorraine made some comments on the singing of Miss Beresford, the Musgraves' cousin.

"By the by, speaking of music, I should like to take the opportunity, when we are alone," said Sir Darcy, "of mentioning that in future I should much prefer that Mildred should not play her violin in public. There are several reasons which render it most undesirable that she should do so. I don't know whether Miss Ward is giving her lessons, but if so, they had better be discontinued, and she must confine herself to the piano. A little music is a nice accomplishment for any girl, but I do not consider it quite ladylike when it begins to rival professional playing; and as Mildred will not have to earn her living by her instrument, I wish her to put her violin entirely aside, and turn her attention to other things. Do you hear what I say, Mildred?"

"Yes, Uncle Darcy," answered Mildred, trembling all over, and feeling that the moment had come. "But oh, please, I can't give it up, because Uncle Colin and Aunt Alice want me to go on learning."

"Dr. Graham is no longer your guardian, and has nothing further to do with the matter," replied Sir Darcy, frowning slightly.

"But he will when I go back," faltered Mildred.

"When you go back! Why, I thought you quite understood that I had taken the entire responsibility of you. I offered you a home at The Towers, and I always keep my word."

"You've been very kind—please don't think I've not been happy," said Mildred, speaking in little gasps; "but I only came for the holidays—my visit's over now—and I think I had better be going soon."

"Do I understand from what you say that you choose to return to Dr. and Mrs. Graham in preference to staying here at The Towers?" asked Sir Darcy, as if he could scarcely believe the evidence of his own ears.

"They want me," said Mildred, bursting into tears. "It's my own home, and oh, I must go back!"

"I can't discuss the question with you now," said Sir Darcy. "I must talk it over with your aunt. I'm certainly very much surprised to hear that you should wish to leave us, but I consider you too young to settle your own affairs, and I shall arrange the matter in whatever way I consider best for your welfare. In the meantime you must attend to what I have said as regards your music, and I don't expect to hear your violin again in the house."

Poor Mildred left the room, feeling that she was in dire disgrace. She knew that she had not explained herself properly, and that both her uncle and aunt would think that she was making a very poor return for their kindness to her. She could tell from the coldness of their manner during the next few days that they considered her both unreasonable and ungrateful, and the knowledge added to her unhappiness. She put the Stradivarius safely away inside her wardrobe; she did not dare to practise now, and only hoped that Sir Darcy would not take her violin away from her altogether.

"I can't give it up, and I won't!" she said to herself. "No more than I mean to give up Uncle Colin and Aunt Alice. I'd rather have my music than anything they can offer me instead, and I shall go back to Kirkton, if I have to run away."

She wondered what Sir Darcy intended to arrange for her future, and whether he would be able to keep her at The Towers against her will. Would Uncle Colin be willing to resign her? And would she perhaps never see either him or her aunt again? The misery of the prospect seemed almost more than she could bear to contemplate, and she went about in a state of such dejection that Violet, to whom the whole affair was incomprehensible, rallied her continually on her low spirits.

Matters were at this crisis when Mildred one morning received a letter in Mrs. Graham's handwriting—not in the thin envelope with the foreign stamp that she had been in the habit of looking out for lately, but a stout English one, bearing the familiar Kirkton postmark.

"Oh! They're back at last!" she cried with delight as she tore it open.

Dr. and Mrs. Graham had indeed returned to Meredith Terrace, and they now wrote to Mildred to tell her that the time had come when she must make her choice between their home and the Lorraines'.

"We do not wish to influence you in any way, darling," wrote her aunt. "You must act entirely for your own happiness. If you feel that you would rather remain at The Towers, it is our earnest desire that you should do so; but if, on the other hand, you still cling to us, you will find the very biggest welcome waiting for you here. Your uncle is writing to Sir Darcy by this post, so no doubt he will speak to you about the matter."

"As if I could want to give them up!" cried Mildred, kissing the signature. "I'm so glad they are at Kirkton again, for they feel so much nearer to me now. I wonder what Uncle Colin has written to Uncle Darcy, and what he'll say to me?"

Mildred had not long to wait, for after breakfast that morning Sir Darcy called her into the library, where he and Lady Lorraine had evidently been consulting over a letter which he held in his hand.

"I wish to have a little talk with you, Mildred," he said, rather stiffly. "I have here a communication from Dr. Graham, in which he states that, as representing your father's family, he considers himself to be your joint guardian. He is equally willing with myself to be responsible for you, and it appears ne is anxious that you should receive a special musical training. I have talked the matter over with your aunt, and we have come to the conclusion that it will be better to allow you to decide for yourself whether you make your home with us or with the Grahams. If you wish to stay here, you will have the benefit of many social advantages which you would certainly not find at Kirkton; but, on the other hand, I cannot undertake to encourage your study of the violin. We are willing on our part to do our best for you, to give you a good general education, to introduce you into society when you are at an age to leave the schoolroom, and to make such provision for you as to ensure that you should never be in want. More than this I cannot say, and it only remains for you, therefore, to take your choice between your two guardians."

"You've been very good to me, and so has Aunt Geraldine," said Mildred, summoning up all her courage. "I can never forget your kindness, or thank you enough for it; but Uncle Colin and Aunt Alice are just like my father and mother. I've lived with them ever since I was a baby, and I can't help loving them the best. I don't want to give up my violin either; I feel as if it would be giving up my birthright. So please don't think me ungrateful, but I feel that my home's at Kirkton. It's where I've been brought up, and I'm really happier there. I know you would have been very kind indeed to me if I had stayed at The Towers, but as I may have my choice, I should like to go back to Meredith Terrace."

Mildred had felt some apprehension as to how Sir Darcy and Lady Lorraine would receive her decision, but much to her relief it seemed to be only what they had expected, and they at once began to make arrangements for her return.

"We shall not lose sight of you altogether," said Lady Lorraine kindly. "Both Violet and I shall expect to hear from you sometimes, and you must pay us a visit every now and then. I should be sorry if, after having made an effort to be friends, we were to become estranged from one another again, and I want you always to feel that if you like to come and see us you will be welcome here."

Though she did not repent her choice, Mildred certainly felt a pang at leaving all the many beauties of Castleford behind her. She had grown so used to the ever-changing aspect of the lake, the calm of the silent woods, the glory of the rugged fells and the rushing streams, that she should miss them like old friends; they had inspired the poetical side of her nature, and she owed a debt to them in increased powers of imagination which she would some day realize. Coming at this period of her life, the time spent at The Towers had been to her of untold benefit; it had enlarged her views, altered her estimation of many things, and adjusted her childish standpoint to a truer judgment of this world's affairs. Both from the Lorraines and the Somervilles she had learnt much, and it was only after she had returned to Kirkton that she felt how great a change the visit had made in her.

"We don't want to lose you, dear, but I think you're quite right," said Mrs. Somerville, as Mildred said good-bye at the Vicarage. "Rhoda will miss you dreadfully, but we shall hope to meet again, and in the meantime we wish you every possible success in your study of music. You're going to work very hard, I know, and I expect when you next play to us we shall be even more delighted than now. We shall all be anxious to hear news of you, and you must never forget your friends at Castleford."

As Mrs. Graham had said, a very big welcome awaited Mildred when she at last returned to her old home. The thought that a parting had been possible gave an added zest to their reunion, and both her uncle and aunt held her in their arms as if they could scarcely let her go again.

"You are our own little girl now," said Uncle Colin, "and we intend to keep you! We haven't very much to give you, darling, except a great deal of love, but you're sure of that, at any rate;

and if you think you'll be happier here with us, you know you'll not find anyone who'd be fonder of you than we are."

"There was never any choice about it at all," cried Mildred, distributing her kisses alternately. "I meant from the first to come back. I'd rather live here a thousand times than at The Towers. They were very kind to me, but oh! it wasn't at all the same. I'm your girl, not theirs; I always have been and always will be, so please don't try sending me away again."

"You were right," said Dr. Graham that evening to his wife. "It was a risky experiment, but I'm glad we tried it. Mildred has had her taste of society, and of everything that wealth and position can offer; she knows perfectly well what she's giving up, and if she would rather live with us, and study her violin, she has made the choice of her own free will, and there's the less likelihood of her repenting afterwards. I think, however, that she really prefers our life to theirs, and will be happier with some definite work than spending all her time in amusement. As you predicted, the seed which we planted has sprung up. I hope we may live to see great things from her in the future, and that she may never regret the step she has taken."

CHAPTER XV

Monitress Mildred

NEVER at the beginning of any term had Mildred been so delighted to return to St. Cyprian's. Owing to some rather protracted building operations the school had had unwontedly long holidays, so that her lengthy visit to Westmorland had not prevented her being in time for the reopening. There were naturally great changes at the College. Ella Martin, Phillis Garnett, Joan Richards, Dorrie Barlow, and all the other leaders had left, and the former members of VA were now raised to the Sixth Form. Laura Kirby was head of the school, and among the monitresses were Bess Harrison, Lottie Lowman, Freda Kingston, Maudie Stearne, and Mildred herself. It was quite a surprise to Mildred to find herself placed as a monitress. She knew she had done well at the July examinations, but had not realized that her success would entitle her to so great a reward. The position was one of much trust at St. Cyprian's, and carried many privileges; to attain to it was the ambition of every girl who entered the school.

Some readjustment of the Alliance committees was of course necessary in consequence of the alterations in the Forms, and a fresh election of delegates was held, the present members of VA being now eligible as candidates. This time the voting seemed almost unanimous, and the list came out as follows:

LITERARY.—Laura Kirby, Constance Muir.
MUSICAL.—Mildred Lancaster, Elizabeth Chalmers.
DRAMATIC.—Lottie Lowman, Sibyl Anderson.
ARTS AND HANDICRAFTS.—Freda Kingston, Ivy Linthwaite.
GAMES.—Kitty Fletcher, Edna Carson.

Great satisfaction was expressed at this result. It was felt that in every department a wise choice had been made. All realized that Mildred ought to represent the musical element of the school, but they were glad that Lottie Lowman's undoubted talents should be utilized in the "Dramatic", where she would really find a freer scope for her energies. The appointments of Kitty Fletcher and Edna Carson as Games delegates were immensely popular. They were known enthusiasts, and it was considered that Kitty would make an admirable successor to Joan Richards. After distinguishing itself at cricket, St. Cyprian's was now anxious to win laurels at hockey, and looked forward with great keenness to matches during the season. Freda Kingston and Ivy Linthwaite were admittedly the art "stars" of the College; the November exhibition was the next great event on the Alliance calendar, so it was well to have such trustworthy representatives to look after the school honours. In literature nobody could surpass Laura Kirby, and Constance Muir had also contributed good work.

To have at last won the Musical delegateship was to Mildred an even greater pleasure than her new post as monitress. She anticipated many interesting competitions with other schools, and had moreover a project of her own which she meant to broach at the first favourable opportunity. She thoroughly appreciated her colleague. Elizabeth Chalmers was a very pleasant girl, easy to get on with, and ready to be enthusiastic. The fact of her being a pianist was a great advantage, especially as she happened to be an excellent reader, for she would be able to play accompaniments to anything that was required.

With her fellow monitresses Mildred also hoped to keep on good terms. It was perhaps not altogether fortunate that Laura Kirby should be head of the school. Her high marks at the examination had placed her easily in that position, but she was not really fitted to be a leader of other girls. Extremely clever at any form of brainwork, she was gauche and brusque in her manners, and totally lacking in perception. She did not command any great respect among the juniors, and found difficulty in keeping order. She was upright and conscientious, and anxious to make an efficient "head", but she was incapable of taking hints, and would blunder along where a less clever but more tactful girl would have smoothed away difficulties. Lottie Lowman, Maudie Stearne, and jolly Bess Harrison were already very popular, and Freda Kingston, though quiet and retiring, was reliable, and could assert her authority when required.

None at St. Cyprian's could fail to notice the marked change in Mildred since last Easter. The summer term had been a time of transition, and now her holiday at The Towers and her new school responsibilities had completed the transformation. Instead of the dreamy, unawakened, indolent, dependent girl of heretofore, she had developed into a brisk, alert, and highly original character, anxious to take her share of the world's burden, and spur others on to do the same.

"Mildred seems years older since we said good-bye on breaking-up day," said Kitty Fletcher to Bess Harrison. "She was always rather a baby. Now she's suddenly begun to grow up!"

"And doing it quickly too," agreed Bess. "I'm as astonished as you are. I didn't think Mildred had it in her. I believe she'll make one of the best monitresses St. Cyprian's has ever had."

Professor Hoffmann's joy at the return of his favourite pupil was Teutonic in its warmth and fervour.

"Mein Freundchen, you have come again!" he cried, shaking hands with a vigour that almost made her cry out. "You remember what I tell you? Yes? Nothing in this world can compare with music. You did not wish to live at the rich and great house? So! Zou have chosen well. Now you shall study. Ach! we shall see what you will do! You have played at my Students' Concert. What if one day you have a concert of your own? But you must give people something to which it is worth their while to listen! You can do it, yes! It is in you, if you will let it come out. The power is there, but it needs training, patience, care, and again training. It knows not yet how to express itself aright. Himmel! You have a great aptitude for your instrument. Some day we shall see you an artiste, if you will only continue to work."

Hard work Mildred certainly found to be her present destiny at St. Cyprian's. The curriculum of the Sixth Form demanded extra brain exertion in addition to her increased violin study. Fortunately for her, the particular arrangements of the school, as divided into Collegiate and Musical sides, made allowance for the large amount of practising which was now daily expected from her; and Miss Cartwright, regarding her as a special case, made further concessions, and adapted her timetable so as to give the first place to her violin.

Most of the other girls in the Form were also putting their powers to the proof. Laura Kirby was working for a Girton scholarship, and several others were to take various other examinations. They were being carefully coached, and extra teachers came to the College to give them lessons in special subjects. For one or two chemistry classes they were sent to the women's department of the Kirkton University, where some of them hoped afterwards to continue their studies and obtain degrees. Even Kitty Fletcher, who was not at all clever, was preparing for the Senior Oxford and Cambridge Combined Board, an examination which it was necessary for her to pass if she were to take up the Kindergarten teaching upon which her heart was set.

There were naturally a few drones in the hive. Sheila Moore kept up a well-deserved reputation for idleness, and Eve Mitchell and Nora Whitehead were prepared to rival her, in spite of Miss Cartwright's protestations. On the whole, however, the average was high, and the girls seemed disposed to live up to the past traditions of the

Form, and set an example in strenuousness to the rest of the school.

One delightful privilege was accorded to the Sixth. They had a little sitting-room to themselves, where those who stayed for dinner could spend their spare time, or where preparation might be done in quiet at certain hours. This sitting-room was always considered the private property, for the year, of the Sixth, and the girls took a pride in making it pretty. It was the custom for every member to bring one article, which she could take away with her when leaving the school, so that the room should be free for its next occupants. Chairs and a table were provided, but the girls contributed pictures, framed photographs, cushions, a table-cover, some books, and a variety of knick-knacks, which gave the place a very homely and cosy air.

This term, by special permission from Miss Cartwright, a tea-service was added to the other possessions. The girls intended to hold committee meetings at four o'clock, and afterwards to make tea in their sanctum, taking it in turns to provide the comestibles. It had always been rather a rush to have meetings during the midday interval, as some members returned home for dinner, and could not be back until after two o'clock, so that the bell for second school was apt to ring just in the midst of the most animated discussions. Mildred's contribution to the sitting-room consisted of a tea-cloth which she had worked while at The Towers. Kitty Fletcher brought a framed photograph of last term's cricket eleven, taken just after their triumph over Templeton. Freda Kingston had some of her own water-colours framed, and these were so pretty that they were awarded the place of honour by general vote. Laura Kirby lent a well-stocked book-shelf, and Lottie Lowman placed a clock on the mantelpiece, so that by the united efforts of the whole Form the room looked quite as nice as it had done under the headship of Phillis Garnet and her set.

To Mildred this sanctum was a delightful retreat. She was a day-boarder, and she had always found that the schoolroom or the playground afforded rather cold comfort during the interval. With others of the "Needlework Guild" she could retire here to make the charity garments which the Alliance had promised for the Children's Hospital, or construct little presents for the "Santa Claus Club" that was to aid in stocking the Christmas-tree for the poor little orphans of the city. At Kitty Fletcher's instigation a Christmas Card Association was formed. The girls brought to school a large selection of their last year's cards, and set to work with paste-brush and blank paper to cover over the names which were on them, writing instead some suitable greeting. These were to be sent to the orphanage for distribution on Christmas Day, and it was to be hoped to prepare enough for each inmate to receive one. It was an occupation which most of the girls enjoyed, and proved more popular than needlework, so a large amount of snipping and pasting went on, and the pile of finished cards grew steadily.

The autumn term was only about a fortnight old when a new pupil arrived, who, in Mildred's opinion at least, was a most welcome addition to the College. Mr. Somerville had been so much interested in the descriptions he had heard of St.

Cyprian's that he had decided to send Rhoda there without further delay. She was to live at the Principal's private house, for Miss Cartwright had decided to try the experiment of taking a few boarders, and had provided accommodation for six. Rhoda was particularly anxious to come to St. Cyprian's, partly because Mildred was there, and had given her such entrancing accounts of it, and also because Rodney was commencing his engineering work at Kirkton, and was already installed in rooms on his own account. With Mildred to act as her school godmother, Rhoda very soon made friends, and began to settle down happily into her new life. Her former lessons with her father, though in some subjects she was well advanced, had left her behindhand in other respects, so she had been placed in VB, the Form to which Miss Cartwright generally relegated backward girls who were too old for the Fourth, and not capable of doing the work of VA. Here she soon began to pick up the points in which she was deficient, and made excellent progress. She found several congenial friends of her own age, and became an active supporter of all the special institutions of her Form.

With Miss Cartwright's permission Rhoda was allowed frequently to visit Meredith Terrace, where Rodney also was invited to meet her. Dr. and Mrs. Graham were delighted with both the young people, and strongly encouraged the friendship, being indeed anxious to repay the Somervilles for their hospitality to Mildred during the summer. Rodney, who was fond of science, was immensely interested in Dr. Graham's fine microscope, and delighted to help him in the preparation of slides. He became so handy in this respect, and also in connection with one or two other special hobbies of the doctor's, that he was soon at home in the house, and passed many evenings in the study trying chemical or electrical experiments. Dr. Graham was pleased with the young fellow's enthusiasm and scientific taste.

"It renews my youth to work with him," he declared. "He revives old interests and stimulates new ones. He has a decided inventive faculty, and some of his ideas are really very original and clever. We have a little scheme between us now, which, if it turns out well, may be worth patenting. We're as eager about it as two old mediaeval alchemists."

Mildred had sometimes felt the lack of companions of her own age at home, and was glad therefore that her friends received so hearty a welcome. The young people spent many pleasant evenings together at music. Rodney played well, and Rhoda was just beginning to cultivate a very good soprano voice, and to be anxious to try over every fresh song that came in her way. Mildred would often accompany her softly on the violin, so with Rodney at the piano they formed an excellent trio.

About this time Mildred found her powers of composition develop in a manner which surprised even herself. She had always been fond of improvising, but now her ideas took more definite shape, and she was able to produce short pieces, which she wrote down on paper. Her brain was full of haunting melodies, and it became her favourite recreation to weave these together into the form of waltz, polonaise, gavotte, or sonatina. The more rein she gave to her imagination the better it served her; the tunes would come as if by inspiration, and as she grew more accustomed to transcribing them, she could elaborate them at her leisure. She showed a few of them to Professor Hoffmann, and found his advice invaluable in aiding her to put her themes into proper notation. In spite of his evident appreciation of this new phase on the part of his pupil, he still remained the rigid martinet, and would not allow her to spend too much time over her own compositions, urging her to study the works of the great classical masters, and obtain a wider knowledge of general music.

"There are many who can write waltzes and drawing-room songs," he affirmed. "If you have once entered into the mind of Beethoven and Chopin, these will not content you."

Mrs. Graham often congratulated herself at this period that she had sent Mildred to St. Cyprian's. At no other school would it have been possible for her to devote so great a portion of her time to music. Her aunt felt that had she been brought up with private tuition at home, she would have suffered from the lack of the wholesome College interests and the companionship of other girls. She rejoiced that Mildred had been made a monitress, and encouraged her to do all she could for the sake of the school, as she considered the public spirit thus engendered would prevent her from becoming too narrowly engrossed in her one particular line of study.

Mildred did not need any urging to play her part

in the life of St. Cyprian's. She thoroughly appreciated being a school officer, and particularly enjoyed the committee meetings.

One afternoon at the end of October the monitresses were gathered in the sanctum for their weekly discussion. It was a particularly jolly little assembly, for they had decided to celebrate it with tea, and had each brought a contribution of some kind. A tempting display of cakes was spread on the table, and a jug of dairy cream completed the feast. It was perhaps hardly orthodox to combine the sitting of a committee with the consumption of raspberry buns, but the girls did not wish to stay too long, so they decided that for once they would discuss their business over the teacups. Laura Kirby was therefore requested both to take the chair and to wield the teapot, and performed the united office with much zeal.

"I'm sure my brains work better when they're lubricated with tea," declared Bess Harrison, tilting back her chair at a comfortable though rather dangerous angle, and accepting the queen-cake which Lottie Lowman offered her. "I wish we could represent it to Miss Cartwright, and have cups sent round during maths. It would make all the difference to one's problems."

"Don't you wish you may get it, my child!" replied Maudie Stearne. "Even pear-drops are taboo, and I was once sent out of the room for sucking a peppermint. No, it's only at our own functions that we can indulge in luxuries. Yes, I'd like some of Freda's seed-cake, if you'll pass it to me."

"I made it myself last Saturday," boasted Freda.

"Yes, I did, and sat over it while it was baking, for fear it should burn. And I iced it afterwards, and put the pieces of candied apricot on the top."

"Does you credit," murmured Maudie, sampling the delicacy in question. "You have my permission to make another for next monitresses' meeting. May I suggest a cherry-cake, as my favourite?"

"To business!" cried Laura, rapping the table. "This is most shameful 'frivol.'. Do you realize that we haven't begun our work yet? Bess Harrison, please give me your report."

"I've had a little trouble with IIIA," began Bess. "The young wretches were playing all sorts of pranks, and wouldn't walk decently downstairs. I caught Nellie Brewer sliding down the banisters, and harangued her till she blubbed. I think she won't try it on again."

"My precious kids took it into their heads to bolt into the playground while I was solemnly conducting them to the studio," remarked Maudie Stearne. "I had quite hard work to collect them and march them off. I didn't spare them, though, and stopped them all from the tennis-courts for the day. It gave them a warning."

"I find IIIB do rather outrageous things sometimes," said Mildred plaintively. "Yesterday four of them purloined clubs from the gym., and were playing Red Indians, or some such nonsense, with them in their classroom. They managed to break an inkpot and upset the black-board."

"One has to be very firm," volunteered Freda. "It doesn't do to let them think they can take the least advantage of you. Once give way, and your influence is gone."

"Yes, an easy-going monitress means a slack Form," agreed Lottie. "The juniors know the rules perfectly well, but I think it would be a good plan to write them out and pin a list up in each class-room. If they see them in black and white they've no excuse for pretending they've never heard of them."

"We can't have juniors usurping the senior tennis-courts or using the studio piano, and those are two of their chief crimes," observed Freda.

"I'll make a list of all the hitherto unwritten laws of St. Cyprian's," said Laura. "If you can all spare ten minutes for an extra committee meeting to-morrow, we can read them over and pass them."

"Carried unanimously!" replied the girls.

"If you'll offer us tea again!" murmured Bess.

"Don't be greedy! No, to-day must content you. We can't have such an upset and spread to-morrow, or Miss Cartwright may put a veto on teas altogether. By the by, this isn't of course an Alliance meeting, but a few of us delegates are here. How is the 'Dramatic' getting on, Lottie?"

"Quite tolerably," replied Lottie; "but you know I'm ambitious. We're giving a united performance at Christmas with the High School and the Manor House in aid of the Children's Hospital. It's quite a good piece, a sort of Twelfth Night revels and mummers all combined. It's to be held at the Exchange Assembly Hall. I wish it had been in the Shakespeare Theatre, then we might have had an orchestra with it. I'm afraid the piano will sound so horribly thin and inadequate in that huge room.

Somehow these things need a band to make them go. It isn't half festive without."

"Is the music written for the piano?" enquired Mildred.

"Yes, and it's really quite pretty."

"It would be fairly easy for strings, I dare say?"

"What do you mean?"

"I have an idea, but I'll think it over, and tell it to you to-morrow."

CHAPTER XVI

The Autumn Term

NEXT day the monitresses reassembled in their sanctum at four o'clock to hold the short meeting which had been proposed. Laura had drawn up a list of very sensible and necessary rules, which it was their duty to see kept, and these were read, approved, and carried unanimously.

"It's all very fine for Laura to draft rules, but will she enforce them?" whispered Maudie Stearne to Bess Harrison. "I wish we could get her to be firmer with those juniors. She lets them take liberties continually."

"We'll try and keep her up to the mark," replied Bess, "and we must do all we can ourselves. It's well to have something to go upon, at any rate. I bless Laura for this list. I shall hold it over the heads of my set of youngsters, and make a special black roll of any sinners who transgress the least fraction of it."

"Woe betide IVB if they talk in the hall or make signals to each other across the studio again!" said Lottie aloud. "I think these regulations will about fix up the juniors, and if we stick to them we'll have no more trouble. Is this all the biz, or has anybody anything else to put to the meeting?"

"I have an idea," said Mildred. "You know

you said yesterday that you wished your Twelfth Night revels could have the advantage of an orchestra. You're afraid the piano alone will sound so thin. Well, I've been thinking it over, and I believe we could get up quite a decent little band amongst the Alliance. Mary Fawcett plays the violin very well, and Lizzie Lucian, Clare Verrall, and Mary Langworthy are getting along nicely now with Herr Hoffmann. Then don't you remember the girl who played a solo for Templeton at the Eisteddfod?—Erica Newstead, I think her name was. They've a girl at the Manor House, too, who I believe is quite good, though they didn't trot her out at their concert. I'm sure, if we asked her, that Ella Martin would come and help us, and with myself that would make eight violins. Then Millicent Greenwood plays the 'cello, and we'd invite that girl who did the solo for Newington Green—Althea Ledbury. With four first violins, four second violins, two violoncellos, and the piano we should have quite a jolly band. What do you think of my project?"

"Excellent!" agreed the girls.

"It sounds splendid," said Lottie, "but there are just one or two things we ought to make clear. First, who's going to conduct? You and Ella will both be needed to play."

"I thought of Elizabeth Chalmers," replied Mildred; "she's very musical, and keeps time like a metronome. I believe she'd manage splendidly. She won't be needed for the piano, as you say one of the High School girls is to take that."

"Elizabeth's the very 'man for the job'! I hadn't thought of her. Yes, I wish the High

School hadn't commandeered the piano, but as it's a limited affair we were obliged to let them take it. There's one other objection, though, to the scheme, and rather a big one, I'm afraid. The music is only written for voices and piano."

"That shelves the band, then, I'm afraid!" said Laura.

"Not at all," returned Mildred. "If Lottie will bring me the music, I'm perfectly certain I can arrange it for first and second violin and 'cello parts. I've been doing so much quartette work lately with the Professor that it really shouldn't be very difficult."

"Good old Mildred! I'm quite sure you can!" exclaimed Bess. "I believe you'd fix it up for a whole orchestra, wind-instruments included if required, not to mention the kettle-drums!"

"Hardly that," laughed Mildred. "I'd prefer to keep to strings. However, I won't boast too soon. I'll try what I can manage, and then show you the results."

"I'll fetch the music to school to-morrow," said Lottie. "It would be lovely to have an orchestra to augment our 'Dramatic'; it would just make the thing go."

Lottie arrived next morning with several books, in which she had marked the special songs that were to be sung in the Twelfth Night revels. On taking them home, Mildred found that the airs were quite simple, and with her knowledge of harmony and recent experience in quartette playing, she was able to arrange second-violin and violoncello parts, allowing the first violin to sustain the melody. It took her a long Saturday to perform the task, but she was satisfied with the result, and brought the score to school on Monday morning. Some of the other girls volunteered to make the necessary copies during the dinner interval, and with their help the work was soon finished. The girls from the Manor House, Templeton, and Newington Green readily accepted the invitation to join the orchestra, and arranged to come to St. Cyprian's for practices. Ella Martin was quite pleased to revisit her old school, and her clear, correct playing was of great assistance. As Mildred had expected, Elizabeth Chalmers made a capital conductor. Her sense of time was excellent, she kept everybody well together, and above all things made sure that the instruments were in tune. She wielded her baton almost like an old, experienced bandmaster, rapping on her desk, if faults occurred, with a promptitude worthy of Professor Hoffmann himself.

Mildred found it the greatest relief to have Lottie for a coadjutor instead of a rival. As dramatic delegate, Lottie was responsible for the members of St. Cyprian's who were acting in the revels, and was herself to take a prominent part. She helped to train a chorus, but did not otherwise interfere with the music, confining her attentions mostly to drilling her own students in the rather elaborate dances which they had undertaken. Mildred was quite ready to appreciate Lottie's powers of administration, and often admired her diplomacy in dealing with difficult situations. Lottie, on her side, having found her true sphere in the "Dramatic", was more ready to yield Mildred the palm in music, and the friction which had formerly existed between the two girls seemed to have died away. They both made zealous and capable monitresses, and on this common ground could meet in harmony.

A subject had lately arisen upon which they were entirely agreed. They considered that Laura Kirby, as head of the school, was not nearly keen enough upon her duties. Laura was working very hard, in view of her very important scholarship examination next summer, and as Literary delegate she was also preoccupied with the number of the *Alliance Magazine* that was to be printed in time for Christmas. She did not care to be worried with too many school details, and rather than trouble to enforce her authority on the juniors, she would shut her eyes to much that was going on. Every now and then, if things got rather bad, she would seemingly wake up, and distribute punishments where they were due; but the younger girls soon found out that she preferred to keep a conveniently blind vision for some of their transgressions, and, taking advantage of this, they began to grow rather out of hand.

A particular point at present disturbing several of the monitresses was the behaviour of the juniors on their way home from the College. St. Cyprian's was situated in Lime Grove, a quiet avenue which communicated with one of the main roads connecting Kirkton and its suburbs. Many of the girls used the tram-cars, the stopping-place for which was just at the end of the Grove; they had often five minutes or more to wait until their various cars arrived, and during that interval they conducted themselves in a most unseemly fashion. Instead of standing aside and chatting quietly, they blocked up the pavement to the inconvenience of passers-by, and talked and laughed in a manner that rendered them highly conspicuous.

"The last few days it has been absolutely shameful!" said Freda Kingston, discussing the situation with Lottie and Mildred. "There they are, in their school hats and badges, so that everybody knows they belong to St. Cyprian's. They bring disgrace on the Coll.! Some of them actually won't trouble to put on their gloves, and their behaviour makes people stare."

"And when their trams come up, they make a rush and crowd on in the rudest manner, pushing past older people, and giggling, and generally making one ashamed for them," said Mildred.

"The worst of it is that the very ones who behave so shockingly go by the Carlton Hill car, and Laura is nearly always on it herself. She's there waiting at the corner, and she hears the babel of noise they're making, and sees them stampede up the steps on to the top of the tram, and she just pops inside herself, opens a book, and takes no notice," said Lottie.

"Something will have to be done, or St. Cyprian's will get quite a bad reputation."

"It's so abominably unladylike."

"It's that wretched little Katie Carter who's the ringleader. She's a horrid child, and needs suppressing. Do you know what she and half a dozen others did yesterday? Actually dared one another to run into the gardens of those nice houses half-way down the Grove, and each plucked a flower! If I had only caught them! It was Hilda Kilburn who told me."

"It's simply moral slackness on Laura's part not to interfere."

"What's to be done?"

"Convene a special monitresses' meeting, bring the subject up, and put it strongly."

"And tactfully too! We don't want exactly to take Laura to task if we can help it. We shall have to get her to summon the meeting."

The affair was arranged with due diplomacy; and when the monitresses gathered next day, during dinner interval, in the sanctum, Freda, as spokeswoman, put the case without casting any imputation upon the head girl.

"It has been urgently brought to our notice," she began, "that our juniors are conducting themselves on their way home in a manner utterly unworthy of the traditions of the Coll."

"Are we responsible for them once they're off the premises?" asked Laura, blushing slightly.

"Most certainly. It's of vital importance to keep up the credit of the school. As long as they are in the streets in St. Cyprian's hats they belong to the Coll., and either establish its reputation or brand it with disgrace. They're doing the latter at present."

"It's bad enough to have to manage the little wretches in school without tackling them outside," sighed Laura. "How can one enforce rules in the street?"

"It's got to be done somehow," said Lottie. "We don't want it to come to Miss Cartwright's ears, as it very soon will if it's not stopped at once. My proposal is this. Make a list of which girls go by tram. Place them in groups according to their separate cars, and apportion a monitress to look after each set. Laura goes by the Carlton Hill, Mildred by the Alleston, and I go by the Lincoln Street, so we could be responsible for any girls on those cars; and Bess and Maudie could take it in turns to act guard over those who are waiting at the corner, while Freda patrols the Grove to prevent a repetition of the garden outrage."

"Good! For the time we should all be acting police," agreed Mildred. "We'd give out beforehand that all juniors must leave the school premises before 4.15, and that for any breach of ladylike behaviour on the road we'll report them to Miss Cartwright. Once they know we mean business, they'll have to reform."

"I put it to the meeting, then," said Lottie, "that the monitresses in future hold themselves responsible for the good conduct of the juniors in the street and on the trams."

"And I beg to second it," said Freda.

Thus brought to a sense of her duty, Laura could not fail to agree with the proposition. The juniors were informed of the new code, and that very afternoon it was put into force. The monitresses meant to stand no nonsense, and marshalled their flocks as if they were drilling them in the gymnasium. The effect was marvellous. Instead of a chattering, loud-voiced crowd obstructing the pavement, a queue of quiet, well-conducted girls waited at the corner almost in silence, and boarded their respective trams with perfect decorum. All wore their gloves, and had been more particular than formerly that their coats were put on neatly, and their shoelaces well tucked away. Even Katie Carter was subdued, and did not dare to play tricks on her confederates.

Perhaps the matter had come to Miss Cartwright's ears after all, for in the course of about a week she congratulated the monitresses upon their vigilance. They referred to her remarks with much satisfaction at their next meeting.

"It's nice to have one's efforts appreciated," said Bess. "I vote we don't slack off, but keep up this patrol business. Of course it's a great deal of trouble——"

"But it's well worth it," agreed the others.

Now that this matter with the juniors was settled, St. Cyprian's seemed to be going on well in every respect. Kitty Fletcher and Edna Carson were zealous in looking after the Games department, and spurred on the girls to come to hockey practices. They had had a match with Newington Green, and though they had been vanquished they had shown a good fight, and, considering the excellence of the rival team, had not on the whole comported themselves badly. By increased efforts Kitty hoped that before the hockey season was over they might be able to win at least one match, and show that St. Cyprian's could take its place in athletics on a footing with other schools in the Alliance. She often regretted Joan Richards, and wished she could have asked her to join the team in an emergency; but it was against the rules for ex-pupils to play in matches, so she had to content herself with present members. One unexpected source of strength consoled her for Joan's loss. Rhoda Somerville took to hockey like a duck to water, and promised under Kitty's tuition to become a most valuable asset to the team. She seemed to have every qualification for good play, and an enthusiasm which rejoiced the heart of her captain. Rhoda's active habits in Westmorland had fitted her for sports, and in the gymnasium also she was beginning to establish a record. Her cricket capacities, of course, could not yet be tested, but Kitty hoped next summer to put her to the proof.

Rhoda found the life at St. Cyprian's most congenial. She had been placed on the Musical side of the school, and thoroughly enjoyed her piano lessons with Mr. Wellsbourne, and the classes in theory and harmony which she attended. There was a delightful series of lectures this term on the great classical composers, with illustrations from their works, and Rhoda, who had not before had the opportunity of joining such a course, found them deeply interesting. After her quiet country home at Castleford, St. Cyprian's seemed a new world, full from morning to night of fresh impressions. She had learnt German with her father, so she had the pleasure of finding herself in Fräulein Schulte's advanced class, and taking part in the monthly dialogues.

In company with the other five girls who were boarded at the Principal's house, Rhoda had an excellent time. Miss Cartwright was kindness itself, and they had so many indulgences that they were almost regarded with envy by the day scholars. As there were so few of them, it was possible to allow them more privileges than they could have had at any ordinary boarding-school, so they often congratulated themselves upon their good fortune.

In spite of these advantages, Rhoda's life was

not without troubles. She was backward in several subjects, and had to work very hard to keep up with her Form. Sometimes she was almost baffled by the difficulties which arose, but she had any amount of grit and determination, and was resolved to make headway in the school. On the whole she was a favourite with her Form, but there was one girl whom she found a perpetual "thorn in the flesh". Lottie Lowman's younger sister, Carrie, was at a rather disagreeable stage of her development. Lottie had improved very much since her appointment as monitress, but Carrie's sharp tongue was nimble in exercising itself at the expense of her class-mates. For some unexplained reason she had taken a dislike to Rhoda, and lost no opportunity of making her the butt of her wit. Carrie, though the youngest in the Form, was one of the cleverest, and prided herself on the two points. If Rhoda unfortunately made a mistake in a lesson, she would sneer: "What! You sixteen and don't know that yet? Why, we learnt it in the Upper Third!" She would visibly nudge her companions if Rhoda faltered in answering a question, thereby making her more nervous, and would come out with pointed remarks about girls whose brains ran to hockey instead of "maths.". In the gymnasium she would watch Rhoda's performances with a critical eye, and triumph openly at her failures. To be sure, these were all rather foolish things, hardly worthy of notice, but they hurt notwithstanding, and had the effect of making several girls, who might have been friendly, join in the gibes just for the mere fun of teasing.

Rhoda was subjected to many small annoyances.

One afternoon, just as everyone was off for a practice, she could not find her hockey shoes. She was perfectly certain they had been in her boot locker only an hour before, but now there was not a sign of them. She hunted vainly up and down the dressing-room, asking the girls if they had seen them, but nobody could give her any information, or seemed inclined to trouble to help her.

"How can I tell where you put your things? You should keep them in your locker!" retorted more than one irritably.

"I did put them in my locker, but somebody's taken them out!" protested Rhoda.

"Well, I didn't, at any rate! I've never even seen your shoes!"

In a violent hurry the girls rushed away, leaving Rhoda alone in the dressing-room, still searching for her missing property. It was only when she had examined every one of the long row of lockers that she discovered her shoes stowed away under the books of Mabel Pollitt, who was absent that day, and therefore could not possibly have appropriated them. Changing as quickly as she could, Rhoda ran out to the hockey ground, to find the captain in a ferment.

"We've been waiting five minutes for you, Rhoda Somerville! Why can't you be punctual? I shan't allow time to be wasted, and if you're late again you may stop away altogether, so I give you fair notice!"

"I couldn't find my shoes!" panted Rhoda.

"A very poor excuse. Have them ready next time, and then there won't be all this trouble!"

Carrie Lowman was nudging her chum, Beatrice

Blair, and the two were giggling with such open amusement that it was not difficult for Rhoda to know to whom she might attribute her loss. She taxed them with it, but they only burst into peals of laughter, and refused to answer her.

"I'm sure they did it," said Doris Brewer, who was friendly to Rhoda. "I saw them sniggering over something in the dressing-room."

"Next week I shall put my shoes inside my desk, so that no one can play tricks with them," declared Rhoda. "It's much too bad to rag me like this."

Carrie and her friends considered Rhoda, as a new-comer, fair game for any sport, and they were prepared to take advantage of her ignorance in many ways. Rhoda's mathematics were decidedly below the standard of the rest of the Form; and one morning, when she had been even less successful than usual, Carrie approached her after school.

"You've failed again hopelessly, Rhoda Somerville," scoffed Carrie. "I suppose you're aware that any girl who gets only ten per cent of her problems right three times running has to go and report herself to the monitresses?"

"I didn't know!" gasped Rhoda.

"It's a solid fact!" declared Beatrice Blair.

"They're having a meeting at one o'clock, so you'll have to turn up now, and confess your sins and cry *peccavi!*" added Carrie. "Laura Kirby's A1 at maths., so I'm afraid you won't meet with too tender a reception."

Poor Rhoda, who still had not grasped all the rules of St. Cyprian's, and was constantly encountering new ones, went off at once in a panic of compunction. It was a decided ordeal to face all the monitresses, even though Mildred was one of them, and she felt it humiliating to be obliged to confess her failure. She knocked timidly at the door of the sanctum, and entered, looking decidedly dejected, in response to Laura's "Come in!"

"Well, what do you want?" asked the head girl rather impatiently.

"I—I've come to report myself," stammered Rhoda.

"What for?"

"For failing three times running in maths."

"Why, that's no business of ours."

"But I was told to come."

"Who sent you?" asked Lottie sharply.

"Your sister—and Beatrice Blair. They said it was the rule."

Lottie coloured with annoyance.

"I shall have to speak to Carrie," she remarked. "She has no right to rag new girls. It's a stupid custom, and must be stamped out of St. Cyprian's."

"We have no such rule, Rhoda," said Mildred gently. "It was too bad to send you on a false errand."

"Then I needn't come here again and report my failures?"

"Certainly not."

"Oh, thanks!" Rhoda's face had lightened with visible relief. "I'm afraid I interrupted you."

"I don't blame you. It wasn't your fault," returned Laura, closing the interview. "I advise you in future to be careful what you believe. Ask somebody whom you can trust, before you accept anyone's statements. You can go now, and please shut the door after you."

CHAPTER XVII

The Alliance Exhibition

HALF-TERM had come and gone, and November days were closing in fast. The date fixed for the Alliance Exhibition of Arts and Handicrafts was drawing near, and it behoved St. Cyprian's delegates to be making preparations for the event. Freda Kingston and Ivy Linthwaite had not let the grass grow under their feet, and since the re-opening in September had been quietly arranging what exhibits were most likely to do credit to the College, and setting apart certain girls to work at them. A wide choice had been given, for the "show" was to include not only drawings and paintings, but clay modelling, fretwork, carpentry, répoussé brasswork, stencilling, bookbinding, basket-making, embroidery, illuminating, bent iron-work, wood-carving, poker-work, photography, sweet-making, cookery, and in fact every variety of handicraft that might be submitted.

Naturally St. Cyprian's did not hold classes of instruction for all these branches, but some of the girls took private lessons at home, or tried experiments on their own account. Miss Whitlock, the drawing-mistress, was very anxious to cultivate an artistic spirit among her pupils, and had introduced many new methods. She particularly endeavoured to encourage originality, condemning the old-fashioned course of "freehand, model, and cast" as likely to reduce all to one level of monotony. When she came as art mistress to St. Cyprian's she had astonished the girls by demanding from them a weekly portion of home work, and setting them a subject which they were to illustrate.

At first it had seemed to them an utter impossibility to draw "The Parting of Arthur and Guinevere", or "The Meeting of King John and his Barons", but with a little practice they were soon able to make the kind of design which Miss Whitlock required. She did not allow them to copy any picture outright, but they might take a horse from one, a knight from another, a lady from a third, and adapt them so as to make a fresh illustration. She knew that the skill of her pupils was not equal to evolving the figures for themselves, but she considered that in this way they would gain a far better knowledge of the requirements of composition than by a mere slavish reproduction of a drawing intact.

The girls found it quite interesting work, and as Miss Whitlock gave out the list of subjects for the whole term beforehand, they would amuse themselves in their leisure hours by searching through art books for suitable figures to act as the Lady of Shalott, Robin Hood, King Cophetua, Flora Macdonald, Lord Marmion, or other heroes and heroines of romance. Naturally many of the results were not remarkably talented, but Miss Whitlock considered that they had served their purpose by training the judgment, and that with practice would come an increased facility both in the drawing and the general arrangement of the designs.

The sketches were not confined either to any particular size or special medium—they might be executed in pencil, pen and ink, chalks, pastels, or water-colours, according to individual taste; and this latitude gave a much wider scope to the work. Freda Kingston, who loved to try new departures, had hit upon quite an original method of her own, which she pursued at home. She pinned large sheets of cartoon paper upon the wall, then, placing a strong lamp in a suitable position, would persuade one of her brothers or sisters to stand in the attitude she required, so as to throw a shadow upon the paper. She would carefully outline this, and afterwards reduce the life-size drawing to more manageable proportions. In this way she was able to get some very striking poses, which held all the freshness of the living model. She did not attempt to elaborate them too much, but would lay on flat washes of body colour, and finish with a bold outline, so that in style they much resembled advertisement posters.

It was quite a little weekly excitement for the art class to pin up these home studies in the studio, and see all the widely differing representations which had been made of the same subject. Miss Whitlock would criticize them, and class them according to ability, giving many helpful hints and suggestions for future improvement.

The lessons themselves were made as varied as possible. One day it would be the drawing of objects in a given time; on another it would be memory sketching. Sometimes only a single outline was required, and on other occasions great detail would be demanded, so that nobody had the chance of getting into a groove and cultivating only one style of expression.

Though Miss Whitlock had little time to teach the girls handicrafts, she would criticize what work they brought to school to show her, and give any hints she could on the subject, leaving them to try experiments at home. By recommending tools, manuals of instruction, and suitable materials she was able to give substantial help, and would often start a girl on a new hobby, and by judicious aid, if she got into a difficulty, tide her over the initial stages till she was able to make progress on her own account. There is always something infectious in enthusiasm, and Miss Whitlock's genuine love of her subject made her students very keen in carrying out all her ideas. One or two of them were really clever, and the general average improved quickly under her system of tuition, the imaginative girls especially finding scope for their particular talents.

With this foundation of art training to work upon, St. Cyprian's considered it ought to make as good a show as any of the other schools in the Alliance. Six members were chosen for a committee, and a very businesslike meeting was convened in the studio. Freda, as principal delegate, took the chair, and Ivy Linthwaite, as second delegate, occupied the position of secretary.

"What we've got to do," said Freda, "is to find out any individual talent in the school, and push it for all we're worth. I think we'd best each make out a list of those who, we consider, ought to do certain things, and then keep them as our special protégées. There are lots of girls who'll begin a thing, go on a little way, and then get tired of it, or be discouraged and throw it up. These are the ones we must look after. They need constantly urging on, and keeping up to the mark. Has anybody any particular person to suggest, whom she thinks likely to do anything outstanding?"

"I believe Rhoda Somerville has rather original ideas," said Nina Campion. "She was telling me about a model of a cottage which she had made at home. It sounded most ingenious."

"Then take Rhoda as your protégée, and see that she makes something equally good."

"I have my eye on Nancy Rostron," said Eleanor Duncan, "but I'd rather not say in what particular line till I've discussed the matter with her."

"Meg Croisdale's the girl for me!" declared Pauline Middleton. "Her illuminations are beautiful!"

"And I have a scheme on hand with Gertrude Spencer," announced Aveline Wilson.

"I book Cissie Milne," said Ivy Linthwaite; "we've been working together for a fortnight."

"Well, if we each have a protégée, with what we're going to do ourselves, that will make at least twelve principal contributors. I dare say we'll soon fill the one table we're to be allowed for special exhibits," said Freda. "It won't do to crowd things up too much; better have a fair amount of space, so as to show them up well."

"I rather believe twelve is the limit allowed for table exhibits," said Ivy, consulting a note-book. "Yes, that is what we arranged at the General Committee."

"Good! Then we'll soon fix that up."

As the room where the united exhibition was to be held had only limited accommodation, and the Alliance was conducted on lines of strictest fairness and equality, a certain number of feet of wall space and one table were apportioned to each school, so they were obliged to confine the number of their exhibits within specified bounds. The conditions applied equally to all, so there was no particular hardship; it was merely a question of elimination, and making the very wisest choice among the many and varied crafts from which they had to select. Freda considered that anything out of the common, and original, would probably attract the judge's attention, and also that a diversity of objects would be likely to form the most interesting table. She herself was very busy making a beautiful set of illustrations to Hans Andersen's "Goose Girl". She spared no trouble, printing the text of the story in an exquisitely neat hand, so that the little book should be perfect, and completing it with a most artistic cover. Quite early in the term she had fired her friend Natalie Masters with an enthusiasm for illustrating. Natalie could not draw well, but she was decidedly clever with the camera, and she resolved to make a series of photographic views depicting scenes from "The Babes in the Wood". She prepared for her work by arranging costumes for her two little sisters, who were to represent the babes, and for two brothers whom she induced to act as either father, wicked uncle, or ruffians, as the case might be.

The Masters possessed a country cottage in a very beautiful neighbourhood, and the whole family went there for the half-term holiday, so that Natalie was able to get backgrounds for her photographs which she could not have obtained in Kirkton. She posed her models partly in the lovely autumn woods, partly in an old castle, and, for the more domestic scenes, in an ancient farm-house that was provided with antique furniture, and therefore made an excellent fourteenth-century setting for her figures. The results were mostly very good; allowing for a few failures, where she had miscalculated the exposures, or the light had been insufficient, she got a sufficient number of negatives to be able to select a dozen as satisfactory, and with the aid of a little retouching made a series of beautifully soft sepia prints. These were mounted, three together, on long brown cards, and had a most harmonious and artistic effect. Her models had been excellent, the little sister who was dressed as the boy looking particularly charming in the wood scene, where the two babes were standing among the tall bracken, reaching up to gather the blackberries growing overhead. The last scene of all was a triumph, for by the bait of some tempting crumbs laid upon the leaves, Natalie had been able to take a snapshot of a pair of robins that ventured within a few feet of the two little figures lying clasped in each other's arms under a bramble bush. She felt that in this photograph she had almost rivalled the achievements of any famous naturalist, and that she might some day turn her attention to producing a volume of "Wild Nature in the Camera", or some equally ambitious project.

Ivy Linthwaite and her protégée Cissie Milne

were concentrating their energies on wood-carving. Ivy had had a course of lessons the previous winter, and had grown sufficiently accustomed to her tools to be able to undertake quite an elaborate piece of work with deep undercutting; but Cissie, who was a beginner under Ivy's tuition, contented herself with doing a lightly-chipped picture-frame.

Nina Campion was busy with a beautiful set of flower paintings in water-colours. Some were done at school under Miss Whitlock's superintendence and some at home, but to both she gave equal care and her very best endeavours.

Rhoda Somerville, when questioned by Nina as to her capacity for making a model as an exhibit, was at first rather dismayed by the project, but on thinking it over she began to see her way more clearly, and consented to undertake the task. She decided that she would try to construct a miniature edition of Castleford Church. She had the whole outline of it in her mind's eye, as well as possessing photographs which would help if her memory failed. She set about it very systematically. First, she begged an old drawing-board from the studio to act as stand. Then out of stiff cardboard she fashioned the model church, cutting out spaces for the windows and covering them with coloured gelatine paper to represent stained glass. When roof, tower, and walls were all neatly fixed together, she put a thin coating of glue over all, and dusted it well with sand, which made a really excellent imitation of the yellowish stone of which Castleford was built. With the aid of a paint-brush she made the traceries round the windows and some attempt at gargoyles on the tower, and reproduced the dark oak of the heavy door, studded with iron nails. The churchyard next claimed her attention. She mixed a quantity of plaster of Paris, and put it down all round the church, which cemented the model firmly to the board that she had used for a stand, and also gave the effect of uneven ground. She smoothed down the path, and while the plaster was still wet, stuck in little pieces of sanded cardboard for grave-stones, and small twigs of yew to represent the ancient gnarled trees that surrounded the chancel. A coat of green paint, applied to the cement when dry, was supplemented by some beautiful moss, which her mother sent her from the woods at home, and which gave a finishing touch to the whole. The little model was really extremely pretty when all was completed, and such an exact copy in miniature of Castleford Church that Mildred declared she could almost imagine that she heard the organ inside it.

The progress of Rhoda's work had been a subject of intense interest to many of the girls, who had watched it stage by stage from its first rough commencement, and they were agreed that it would be one of the most uncommon exhibits on their special table, if not in the whole of the show.

Mildred, who felt responsible for Rhoda at St. Cyprian's, was glad to find that her friend could make so important a contribution to the Alliance. She realized that any success in the exhibition would be a great point in Rhoda's favour, and likely largely to increase her popularity in the school. Rhoda herself had taken keen pleasure in her construction, independently of its value as an exhibit. Her deft hands enjoyed making things, and her thoughts had all the time been centred at Castleford. She was too happy at St. Cyprian's to be home-sick; nevertheless she missed the Vicarage, and anything which reminded her of it was a doubly-welcome pastime.

Meanwhile the other members of the committee and their protégées were also busily occupied. Pauline Middleton, whose bent was towards figures, had finished a very clever pair of heads executed in pastels, quite the best work she had so far accomplished at school, and a subject of much satisfaction to Miss Whitlock. Meg Croisdale, whose hobby was illumination, had copied a page from an old missal upon a sheet of vellum, and had thoroughly enjoyed herself amongst the quaint Celtic spirals and twists of the capitals, and the strange little animals and figures which composed the interlaced border. She had laid on the bright colours and the gold-paint with a steady hand, marvelling only at the patience of the monks of old who could complete a whole book, one single leaf of which it had cost her so much time and attention to reproduce.

Aveline Wilson and Gertrude Spencer had gone in for pyrography, and shared a poker-work apparatus between them, which they took it in turns to use, the one who was not manipulating it standing near and blowing gentle puffs with a pair of bellows to prevent the smoke from the burnt wood from rising into the face of the worker, a division of labour greatly appreciated after an experience of smarting eyes produced by the fumes. Aveline finished a large photograph frame with a tasteful design of irises, and Gertrude decorated a little corner cupboard with a conventional pattern copied from a piece of antique furniture. Eleanor Duncan concentrated all her energies on an oil-painting of still-life which she did in the school studio, partly during lesson hour and partly during her recreation time. It represented several Venetian jars, with a piece of silk drapery as a background, and a few flowers flung carelessly across the foreground in company with a nautilus shell and a string of beads. The whole made a beautiful harmony of colour, and Miss Whitlock was more than satisfied with the result.

Nancy Rostron had made a complete departure in her exhibit. She had chosen to dress a dozen small dolls as representatives of various European nations, and had made each tiny costume with the greatest elaboration, carrying out every detail with a considerable amount of skill. When finished, the dolls were wired, and placed in a circle round a stand, so that each might equally show its points and claim the judge's attention. With Rhoda's model church, this was perhaps one of the prime favourites among the exhibits, for though it could not claim the artistic merit of some, it certainly possessed the charm of novelty.

The girls had given a great deal of trouble, and had devoted many hours of their spare time to these preparations, and all looked forward eagerly to the day of the "Show". By the kindness of the Mayor, a room in the Exchange Assembly Hall had been lent to the Alliance for the occasion. A small admission fee was to be charged, and the proceeds were to be sent to the Kirkton Guild of

Play, an institution for brightening the lives of the children of the slums. Everybody was pleased with this loan of a room. It put the various schools upon a more equal footing than if the exhibition had been held in one of their own buildings; and the Exchange Assembly Hall was situated in a very central position in the city, easy of access by tram for all the suburbs.

The premises were only available for one day, so the exhibits had to be taken down and arranged during the morning, to be in time for the opening at half-past two. The six members of St. Cyprian's Art Committee were granted a special holiday for the purpose, and a private omnibus was engaged in which to convey them and the various treasures in their charge to the hall. Through Nina Campion's care, Rhoda's model church reached its destination without the displacement of even a tomb-stone, and Eleanor Duncan took equal precautions to preserve Nancy Rostron's set of dolls from injury. Miss Webster, the art mistress from the High School, was in charge of the room, and showed the St. Cyprian's delegates which wall space and table had been allotted to them. They had brought hammer and tacks and other requisites, so they at once set to work. They placed Eleanor's large oil-painting (which she had had framed) as a centre piece of their portion of wall, with Pauline's pastel heads (also framed) on either side. Nina's flower paintings and Natalie's photographic views were accorded the next post of honour, and then all spare space was filled with selections of the best studio work that had been done during the term. The table was certainly not any too large for the twelve exhibits that were to appear upon it. The church and the dolls, being the largest, were placed in the middle, and the other specimens ranged round. Various members of the art class had sent in picked contributions, so there was a good display of carving, poker-work, wood-staining, illuminating, and designs for illustration.

There was no time to compile a catalogue of the "Show", but each exhibit bore a small label with the name of the contributor and her school, and in addition each table and separate wall space was surmounted by a large card bearing the name of its school. The committees did their work thoroughly, and by twelve o'clock the whole room was in order, and ready for the inspection of Mr. Baincroft, the artist who had promised to act as judge.

During the course of the afternoon a very large number of girls from the various schools, together with parents and friends, visited the exhibition. Mrs. Graham accompanied Mildred, for she was anxious to see the St. Cyprian's department, and particularly Rhoda's model church, of which she had heard much.

There were to be no prizes, for the headmistresses of the six schools had agreed that it would be better for the Alliance to work without any definite rewards, but "Honourable Mention" was to be given to the best exhibits, and any of outstanding merit were to be "Specially Commended".

At the door of the hall, Rhoda, who was arriving with the rest of the boarders, in charge of a mistress, happened to meet Mildred and her aunt.

Miss Rowe readily allowed her to join her friends, so she entered the room under Mrs. Graham's escort.

"I can't look at a single thing till I've seen St. Cyprian's table, so let's go there first, please!" declared Mildred, avoiding the attractions of Newington Green on the one hand and Marston Grove on the other, and urging her companions forward. "Oh, here we are! There's the church, Tantie! Isn't it lovely? Oh, Rhoda! It has actually got 'Specially Commended'! I'm so glad; it thoroughly deserved that! What a point for St. Cyprian's! Has anybody else had such luck?"

Freda's illustrations to "The Goose Girl", one of Pauline's pastel heads, and Aveline's poker-work had won "Honourable Mention", so that St. Cyprian's had four honours to its credit, which was as much as any of the other schools had gained. The judge had only given tickets of commendation to exhibits which he considered of quite unusual merit or originality, but he had written a short report, highly praising the general excellence of the work submitted. When Mildred and Rhoda had finished rejoicing over the St. Cyprian's successes, and had shown Mrs. Graham each several contribution to their own portion, they turned their attention to the departments of other schools. It was interesting to see the various hobbies which had been pursued. Templeton girls had evidently been going in for fretwork, while the High School had made a speciality of stencilling and bent-iron work. Some of the Manor House girls had sent exquisite specimens of embroidery and drawn-thread work, and also bore off the palm for cake-baking and sweet-making, a branch which St. Cyprian's had not attempted. Marston Grove excelled in clay-modelling and repoussé brasswork, while Newington Green had produced very excellent results in carpentry, basket-weaving, and bookbinding.

The virtue of the little exhibition was that it gave the girls an opportunity of seeing what was being done by other schools, and supplied them with many hints for future work. Several St. Cyprianites went home resolved to learn bookbinding, while Freda's illustrations were pointed out by the Templeton art mistress to her pupils as something which they might try to emulate. All the various members of the Alliance met on a very friendly footing, and heartily admired each other's exhibits, so perhaps no other department of their mutual league could be regarded as a greater success.

"Well done the Arts and Handicrafts!" said Freda, as she helped to clear St. Cyprian's table after closing time. "It's been an absolutely perfect afternoon, and do you know we've taken twenty pounds in admissions? The Guild of Play ought to bless us!"

"Everyone's enjoyed it," agreed Ivy. "And we've all worked together so amicably, that's the best of it. This 'Show' ought to become an annual affair. It's quite an institution, and if next year we might have it in a larger room, we'd—well, we'd——"

"Astonish the world of Kirkton!" laughed Freda.

CHAPTER XVIII

Twelfth Night Revels

THE autumn term was drawing rapidly to a close and Christmas was near at hand. The Literary branch of the Alliance had been particularly active in preparing a number of the united Magazine, which was now at the printer's, and was to be issued shortly before breaking-up day. The six editresses who were responsible for its production had not found their task a light one. The expense of printing had limited them to one hundred pages, so many of their original plans had had to be curtailed. After much consultation it was decided to allow each school fifteen pages and two illustrations, either in line or half-tone, the spaces for which must be included in their portion. The remaining ten pages of the magazine were to contain a leading article on the Alliance, and special news, such as reports of the Eisteddfod and Exhibition, results of cricket and hockey matches since last Easter, the work of the various leagues and guilds, and announcements for the forthcoming season.

Rachel Hutton, the head girl of the High School, was voted general editress, and appointed to write the leader and the various reports, while each subeditress was responsible for the portion allotted to her school. The work did not sound very formidable, but when Laura Kirby, as editress for St. Cyprian's, began to get her material together she realized some of the thorns which beset the journalistic path. Fifteen pages of print seemed a small allowance, and very limiting to the powers of her contributors. She could almost have filled it on her own account. She wished all the best talent of the school to be represented, and tried to map out her space accordingly. It was most difficult, however, to keep her literary stars within due bounds. Nora Farrar, the generally acknowledged poet laureate of the College, had been put down for a short poem of twelve lines, calculated exactly to fill half a page; but when she handed in her manuscript the dismayed editress found that it contained no less than seven verses.

"You'll have to cut some of it out," she suggested.

"Cut it short! Impossible! Why, it would spoil it entirely," protested the poetess indignantly. "Can't some of the others shorten their things instead?"

"No, indeed! They'd prefer to lengthen them."

"Well, look here, it will ruin my piece utterly if I have to chop out the middle half of it."

"I'm very sorry, but it's got to be done, unless you'd rather write another poem."

Laura found that every contributor committed the same mistake, and each manuscript was apt to overflow its due number of words. The distracted editress had to be very stern in marking out passages which she considered were not strictly necessary, and insisting upon their omission. It was so hard to persuade the budding authoresses that this matter of space was one of real importance, and that they must not exceed their allowance even by a single paragraph. Many were the grumbles and protests, and as Laura was unfortunately not blessed with too large a share of tact, the making of the magazine proved a rather stormy business. The illustrations were another source of difficulty. Freda Kingston brought a quite pretty and clever sketch over which she had spent much time and trouble. She had painted it in brilliant colours to appear in the magazine, and was highly annoyed when she was informed that all drawings meant for reproduction therein must be in black and white, as the Alliance could not run to the expense of colour printing.

"I shall actually have to do it over again! Why didn't you tell me before, and save me all this trouble?" she asked plaintively.

"I didn't know you were going to do it in colour," groaned Laura. "I thought I'd explained to everybody that all the illustrations must be done in black and white. Copy it again in pen and ink, can't you?"

"Bother! Will they spoil my sketch at the printing works? I want to keep it afterwards."

"You'll probably get it back adorned with the impress of the engraver's thumb in black ink! It'll be a chance for you if you want to acquire skill in reading finger-marks, but it won't be an improvement to your design, so you'd best prepare yourself for the worst."

In spite of all these minor troubles Laura managed in the end to arrange her fifteen pages satisfactorily, and sent them off in triumph to the general editress by the appointed day. The printer faithfully fulfilled his part of the bargain, and delivered the copies in good time, so that the magazines were ready for subscribers at the beginning of the last week of the term. It had been impossible to afford anything very grand in the way of a cover, so they had contented themselves with the title *The Alliance Journal*, and the motto "Unitas superabit", which had been chosen as the watchword of the League. Rachel Hutton had written a really capital leading article as an introduction, and had contrived to express a large number of ideas and suggestions in an extremely small space. Each of the separate schools had contributed highly readable matter, and of a very varied character, so that sonnets, lyrics, and parodies, essays, detective stories, adventures, Nature notes, historic dialogues, reminiscences of country rambles, recitations, serious and comic, humorous episodes, and school titbits all found due place.

General opinion voted the magazine "perfect", and the editresses had the proud consciousness of having for once given entire satisfaction to their reading public, a distinction which editors in the real world of journalism might well envy them.

The supreme attraction of the last week of the term was the united dramatic performance that was to be given in aid of the Children's Hospital. It had been no easy matter to find any piece in which six schools could be represented without giving undue prominence to one or other; but the Twelfth Night revels which had been chosen nappily allowed such a wide scope that each was able to undertake a separate department of equal importance. The play was a general combination of a number of old mediaeval festivities, and though it might be somewhat irregular to mingle them, the whole made an excellent entertainment. They were supposed to be acted on Twelfth Night, but as that date would fall during the holidays, it was considered no anomaly to anticipate it, and the event had been fixed for 20th December.

All the schools had been busy practising their parts, and none had worked harder than St. Cyprian's. The special portion of the performance which they had undertaken was the entrance of the King and Queen with their Court, and their enthronement amid due rejoicings. The speeches to be learnt were only short, but there was a very elaborate ceremonial to be observed, a dance to be executed by courtiers, and two part-songs to be sung, therefore many rehearsals were needed before it was perfected. Lottie was indefatigable. She drilled the chorus, trained the dancers, coached the speakers, arranged the costumes, and during rehearsals, at any rate, was sometimes stage-manager, pianist, prompter, dancing mistress, Lord Chamberlain, and principal boy, all combined. She herself was to act King, and Rose Percival, a very pretty girl from IVA Form, had been chosen as the Queen.

Mildred's orchestra was to play during the whole entertainment, so they learnt the music for the songs, dances, and processions of all the schools, also the opening and closing marches. Erica Newstead, Catherine Richardson, and Althea Ledbury, the girls respectively from Templeton, the Manor

House and Newington Green, proved valuable additions, and with their help the little band really sounded quite effective. Elizabeth Chalmers's zealous conductorship had trained them to play in good time, exactly together, and in excellent tune; and if they could not attain to rivalling Professor Hoffmann's Students' Orchestra, they were at least a very welcome augmentation to the musical portion of the performance.

Mildred keenly enjoyed the rehearsals. It is always gratifying when one's pet scheme turns out well, and as she had taken much trouble in arranging the scores, she felt a pardonable pride in the success of her work. She loved the music for its own sake, but she was also very public-spirited, both on behalf of St. Cyprian's and the Alliance, and glad to contribute her share for the common weal. The charity to which the proceeds were to be sent was one that appealed to the schools. The Kirkton Children's Hospital was a new institution that had only lately been opened. Many of the girls had been taken to see it, had walked through the bright sunny wards, and had noticed the little patients wearing the woollen jackets that had been provided by their United Needlecraft Guild. To help to raise funds to keep the cots occupied was an object worth working for, and justified the original intention of the Alliance to be not only an institution for mutual improvement, but to render real aid to their poorer sisters in Kirkton.

The revels were to be held in the Kirkton Assembly Hall, though in a much larger room than that devoted to the Art Exhibition. Tickets had been sent to the various schools, and had sold so well that a good audience was assured beforehand. The Mayoress of Kirkton was to be present, and to bring her children, and several other prominent citizens had also promised their support. As it was essentially a children's entertainment it was decided to hold it in the afternoon, which would greatly simplify the difficulty of arranging for the safe home-going of the performers when it was over.

Twenty girls from St. Cyprian's were to take part, not counting the orchestra, and these were the heroines of the hour at the College. Their dress rehearsal was viewed and approved by a school audience, and the deepest interest taken in their costumes. Many of the details of these were lent for the occasion. There had been dramatic entertainments before at St. Cyprian's, so some of the ex-performers had various properties laid by at home, which proved of valuable assistance to the general effect. Clare Verrall, who had once been the ambassador in "Cinderella", was able to lend her gorgeous trumpet with its silken hangings to Agnes White, who was to act herald. Bess Harrison, who years ago had been one of the "Princes in the Tower", was delighted to find that her velvet doublet and silken hose would exactly fit Lucy Stearne, who made a pretty page. Freda Kingston's artistic skill was requisitioned to provide crowns for the King and Queen, and with cardboard, gilt paper, and cracker jewels she manufactured quite a magnificent regalia. Ivy Linthwaite prepared the Elizabethan ruffs of the courtiers, and stencilled heraldic devices on various banners which were to be used; and as many other girls were ready to contribute beads, knots of ribbon, paste shoe buckles, ornaments for the hair, lace ruffles, and other accessories useful in stage toilets, St. Cyprian's congratulated itself that it would be able to make a brave show.

The six companies of performers went early to the Exchange Assembly Hall, each school in charge of a mistress. The arrangements had been well made, so that there was no confusion over the dressing, though much fun went on behind the scenes. The members of the Alliance had met so often for various functions that they began to know one another, and to exchange greetings almost like old friends. Though each was a stanch supporter of her own school, they were always ready to combine for a general object, and drop any rivalries for the moment. So St. Cyprian's and Templeton girls might be seen chatting about hockey, and Newington Green discussing the magazine with the Manor House, and a general *entente cordiale* reigned supreme.

The members of the orchestra had come in white dresses, and gave quite a festive appearance to the room as they took their places and commenced the overture. Templeton was first on the programme, and opened the proceedings with a procession. Their players were dressed as boys and girls in Old English costume, the former in smock-frocks, large felt hats adorned with bunches of cowslips, and knees tied with knots of gay ribbons; the latter in low-cut dresses, muslin cross-overs, mob-caps and mittens, so that the whole looked exactly as if they had stepped out of a Kate Greenaway picture-book. To celebrate the season they sang a Christmas carol, and then proceeded to give a charming and elaborate exhibition of morris-dancing. They had been carefully drilled, and went through the most intricate steps without a hitch, waving their sprigs of holly, coloured handkerchiefs, or ribbon-tipped wands, according to the requirements of the measure. They sang well, and rendered all their choruses crisply and in exact accordance with the actions of the dances. With the orchestra to augment the music the effect was most gay, and gave a vivid impression of the Merrie England of former days.

Templeton was succeeded by Newington Green, which had taken up a totally different line. It had concentrated its energies on its younger members, and its first item was a dance of fairies and elves by small girls of nine or ten years of age. They had been selected with a view to their appearance. The fairies were all blue-eyed and fair-haired, and in their thin gauzy robes looked true gossamer sprites, as light as air. Their little feet tripped about as if scarcely touching the stage, and they left a general impression among the audience that they were of such sylph-like and ethereal composition that it was almost possible to see through them. Their partners, the elves, were all brunettes, and wore pale-green tights and helmets made to represent big bluebells. Both they and their sister fairies carried long garlands of flowers, which they used in the performance of their dance, now holding them aloft, now waving them to and fro, and now joining them in a floral chain to link the sprites together. The songs chosen were: "The Fairy Pipers", and "The Horns of Elfland", and Mildred had contrived so admirably to arrange the melodies with pizzicato passages on the violins that the ring of the little magic pipes and horns was unmistakable, and the audience listened almost spellbound to the fairy music.

When the pretty scene was over, it was rivalled by another of equal interest. As the fairies and elves danced off the stage, a troupe of butterflies flitted on instead. Their costumes had been prepared by the Newington Green art mistress and her best pupils. They were of thin butter muslin, made extremely full from the neck, and with a thin piece of bamboo stitched down the length of the skirt under each arm. When these bamboos were seized at the bottom, and raised above the level of the head, the skirt extended so as to give an exact impression of wings. All the dresses had been painted with the characteristic markings of certain butterflies, and as their owners gently waved them about, it seemed as if Fritillaries, Tortoiseshells, Purple Emperors, Swallow-tails, Camberwell Beauties, Painted Ladies, Red Admirals, and Peacocks were holding carnival together upon the stage. They danced a charming measure, twisting and turning so as to display the splendour of their wings, and winding in and out as if flitting about among the flowers. Each girl had a helmet contrived to represent a butterfly's head, with long antennæ and large round eyes, which further enhanced the insect effect, and wore long brown stockings drawn over sandals, giving a far more characteristic effect than shoes. The music was dainty and appropriate, and after responding to a vigorous encore, the butterflies flitted away, having covered Newington Green with glory.

It was now the turn of St. Cyprian's. Their chief feature was the grandeur of their procession, so an opening march announced their advent. They filed on to the stage with slow and stately steps, in all the pomp and majesty which they had been able to get together. First came the heralds, magnificent creatures in silk and velvet, holding long trumpets from which hung emblazoned banners; then my Lord Chamberlain, in flowered robe and long cloak, bearing his wand of office, and ushering in with much ceremony the King and Queen. Lottie really looked very fine in her gold-embroidered doublet, crimson cloak, long silk stockings, and magnificent crown; and Rose Percival, in pearl-trimmed white satin, with a mock-diamond necklace, her long flaxen hair arranged to fall over her shoulders below her waist, and her pretty face surmounted by her tiara, was regal enough to rival the monarchs of story-book fame. Their Court was not behind in gorgeousness. The gentlemen-in-waiting looked true cavaliers with their curled lovelocks, lace ruffles, and plumed hats, and the ladies outvied them in the gayness of their colours and the elaboration of their ruffs.

In this part of the revels there were a few speeches; the King and Queen were enthroned, songs were sung, and an old-fashioned dance was performed by the courtiers, such as might have taken place at some pageant of the fifteenth century. At its conclusion, instead of retiring from the platform, the royalties kept their thrones, and their maids of honour and gentlemen-in-waiting grouped themselves picturesquely on either side. They were to act stage audience for the mummers who came to play before the Court. This important department of the entertainment had been undertaken by the High School, which had risen nobly to the occasion. First came St. George of England, St. Andrew of Scotland, St. Patrick of Ireland, and St. David of Wales, all arrayed as knights in armour and all mounted on hobby-horses. They wore surcoats emblazoned with their countries' coats of arms, and carried pikes and shields; and with the permission of the King and Queen they engaged in a spirited tournament, making their hobbies prance about with fiery zeal, and dealing resounding blows on their pasteboard armour. But their internal rivalries were soon put an end to by the entrance of a common enemy—a huge and terrific green dragon, a scaly monster with horrible jaws and businesslike talons with which it suggestively clawed the air. It immediately made for its opponents, and there followed a grand scene of dodging, scuffling, and pursuing before the fabulous beast was finally subdued and bound in chains.

A jester in motley costume, with hood and bauble, was a special feature of the mummers, and provided immense fun as he made his jokes and plied his comic antics upon the other characters, belabouring John Bull with his bladder, rallying the doctor on the virtues of his pills, and tripping up the constable with the easy mirth of the clown in an old-fashioned pantomime. Quite out of breath with their violent exertions, the various champions ranged themselves on the steps of the throne, to give the audience the pleasure of beholding them during the performance of the next item on the programme.

Marston Grove School was in no way behind the others. To make a variety, it had provided a series of "Songs in Character", mostly chosen from nursery rhymes. "Where are you going to, my pretty maid?" was acted with lifelike coyness by a charming country wench swinging her milk can; Jack and Jill came together, bearing their pail between them; little Miss Muffet fled in a panic from the onslaught of a gigantic spider; six pretty innocents danced round a mulberry bush; Bo-Peep lamented the loss of her sheep; and Wee Willie Winkie stole about in his night-gown, blowing sand into the eyes of his companions. The costumes were charming, and each little scene was perfect in itself.

The Manor House, the last on the programme, had arranged a totally different display as a final effect. A large grandfather's clock stood at the back of the platform, and had before appeared only a part of the stage scenery. The space in front of this was now cleared, and after an appropriate speech from the King, and a song from the mummers, all waited with close attention while the chimes rang out and the hour was tolled. As the last stroke died away, the door of the clock-case opened, and out trooped, one after another, a procession of wonderful personages. First came old Father Time, with scythe and hour-glass, and behind him the months of the year, from snowy January to rosy June, corn-crowned October and holly-decked December. Then followed many a well-known nursery character—Little Red Riding Hood, Puss in Boots, Bluebeard, Aladdin, Hop o' my Thumb, the Three Bears, Cinderella, Jack the

Giant Killer, Beauty and the Beast, Catskin, the Snow Queen, Rumpelstiltskin, Robinson Crusoe, Dick Whittington, and Goody Two-Shoes.

Ranging themselves at the front of the stage, they performed a pretty series of short action-songs, very appropriate to the season, and ending in compliments to the audience. As a climax to the whole, Father Christmas made his appearance, bearing in his arms the New Year (a darling three-year-old baby, borrowed for the occasion), and in a little speech thanked everybody for coming to the performance, and gave hearty good wishes to all for the coming holidays. With one final parade round the stage the pageant retired. For the last time the butterflies flitted, the fairies tripped, the dragon roared, and the jester swung his bladder; then amid a storm of clapping and cheering, headed by Father Time and with Father Christmas at the rear, the long procession wound itself off the platform and behind the scenes, to the accompaniment of sprightly music from the band.

"Your orchestra really was a great addition, Mildred," said Mrs. Graham that evening. "It kept everybody together, and made the whole affair sound most gay."

"I'm glad you say so! I think it was worth the trouble. We had a glorious afternoon, and every one of the six schools enjoyed it equally," said Mildred. "Do you know what we did in the dressing-room afterwards? We all joined hands in one big circle and sang 'Auld lang syne', and shouted 'Hip, hip, hip, hooray!' for the Alliance.'

CHAPTER XIX

Winter Sports

AFTER a strenuous term, everybody welcomed the leisure of the holidays. It was a relief not to have to think even of art exhibitions and dramatic performances. For a whole month the monitresses would not need to pounce on Third Form sinners, or write black entries of the misdeeds of certain rebels in IVB. Essay writing gave place to the addressing of Christmas cards, mathematics retired in favour of shopping, and text-books were set aside to make way for magazines. Mildred luxuriated in a thoroughly well-earned rest. Beyond a short daily practice on her violin, nothing was required from her, and she congratulated herself that she was so much more fortunate than Laura Kirby and some other girls who were destined for the matriculation, and who were having special vacation coaching. Mildred, never very robust, felt a reaction follow the strain of so many weeks' hard work, and it was chiefly on account of her white cheeks that her aunt allowed her to accept an invivation which arrived on Christmas morning.

This was from Rhoda Somerville, asking her to spend a week at the Vicarage, and promising the very utmost in the way of outdoor exercise during the visit. To see Castleford again, and especially in its January dress, was an attraction. Though Mildred had not wished to make her home at The Towers, she held the warmest recollections of her stay there, and looked forward to meeting Sir Darcy and Lady Lorraine and Violet equally with the Vicarage family. Rhoda had also invited Kitty Fletcher, with whom she had struck up a strong friendship, and Kitty's brother Neville, who, as it chanced, was a schoolfellow of Diccon's; so it was arranged that the three young people should travel together from Kirkton into Westmorland.

The weather was cold, and the prospect that the frost might continue brought quite an anticipatory glow to Mildred's pale face. She was equipped with a new pair of skates, and had made such provision in the way of strong boots, sports coat, Alpine cap, and warm gloves as to be ready for any variety in the way of exercise. Kitty, equally-well prepared, was expecting ample scope for her energies, and hoping to find adventures that would put even hockey in the shade.

"If we could be snowed up in a cutting, now, and have to dig our way out and tramp to the nearest cottage, it would be fun!" she proclaimed, viewing the landscape from the carriage window as the train sped northwards. "That always used to be the fate, or rather good fortune, of people in the old coaching days. They invariably spent a night at a 'Holly Tree Inn', and either saw a ghost, or found a long-lost will, or restored a runaway heiress to her guardians!"

"There's no romance nowadays," remarked Neville. "If you're looking out for any sensational happenings, you'll be disappointed, Miss Kit. Rich uncles don't meet their disinherited nephews at obscure country inns and melt into bank-notes and blessings; and as for the ghosts, modern hygiene has swept them clean away. I don't suppose you'd find so much as a solitary cavalier with his head under his arm, or a white lady wringing her hands. No, I prophesy that the train will get to Whiterigg station exactly to railway time; and as for being snowed up, there isn't a single flake coming down, and the sky is obstinately blue. Sorry to check your romantic aspirations, Madam, but mine are the words of sober common sense."

"Yes, you always love to tie a string to my imagination and jerk me back. Never mind, if we've no sensation on the journey, perhaps we'll find one at Castleford. A whole week gives one a chance, anyhow!"

If Mother Nature had not been accommodating enough to provide snow for Kitty's delectation, she had done her best in the way of hoar-frost, and the woods were gleaming with sparkling crystals till they resembled the jewelled forests of Grimm's fairy tale. The landscape gained ever in grandeur as the train rushed north, and Mildred, who had seen it in summer, was inclined to accord it the palm of beauty in its winter aspect.

"There's romance enough for you, Kit-cat!" she exclaimed, pointing to a gorge where a swollen rivulet was dashing over a rocky bed. "You ought to find Undines and water-nixies if you watch for them, not to speak of the chance of slipping in, and being rescued from imminent peril of your life. If you're thirsting for dangerous adventures we'd better give the Somervilles warning, and they can go out prepared with a drag, and a stretcher, and an ambulance outfit."

"Oh! but don't you know I'm going to do the miraculous escape?" laughed Kitty.

A very warm welcome awaited the travellers at the Vicarage, where the three boys, as well as Rhoda, were back for the holidays. The Somervilles had the happy knack of making their guests feel at home, and were well able to provide both indoor and outdoor amusements. For the first few days the weather, though fairly keen, did not admit of true Alpine sports. The young people, however, found plenty of enjoyment in long walks over the moors and scrambles up the hills. They would take lunch with them, and pass the whole day in the open air, returning for tea at four o'clock with ravenous appetites for muffins and Yule cakes. Music and games were the order of the evening. Mildred had brought her violin, and was able to convince her friends of her improvement; the Vicar produced his violoncello, Rhoda sang her latest songs, and the rest of the party were always ready with a chorus to the seafaring and hunting ditties which Eric was fond of trolling forth. Diccon was endeavouring to learn the banjo, and though his performances on that instrument still left much to be desired, and were an offence to ears educated to more classical strains, they at any rate provided much merriment. Neville had, as he expressed it, "no parlour tricks", but Kitty was clever at recitation, and declaimed many humorous pieces for the edification of her audience, who waxed enthusiastic over certain American comic gems which were the stars of her repertoire.

But all the time the young folks, while enjoying themselves hugely, were yearning with an almost unreasonable insistence for snow. The British climate, more lavish with rain as a rule, had given a spell of aggravatingly clear skies, but at length, as if relapsing into its usual habit, drew storm clouds across the blue.

"Thermometer below freezing-point, mountains smothered in mist, wind in the south-west!" chuckled Diccon. "If we don't have a good fall of snow before to-morrow morning, you may take me out and roll me down the hill in a sack! I'm not a weather prophet without observation."

Even before bedtime Diccon's hopes were fulfilled. The air was a maze of soft floating flakes, and already the path to the churchyard was covered. He retired in high glee, rubbing his hands in anticipation of the pleasures of the morrow. Next morning everybody awoke to a white world. While her children slept, Nature had slowly and silently accomplished her work; all night there had been a steady fall, and now a foot of snow lay over the landscape. It was for this that the boys had been waiting. Their bobsleighs, if not quite up to the level of those provided at Alpine winter resorts in Switzerland, were at any rate serviceable, and they knew of a good place for a toboggan track. Immediately after breakfast they went off to prepare the slide, choosing a splendid hill slope with a field at the bottom. They hurried back to fetch the girls.

"It's just right. You'd best come along at once

and make the most of it," affirmed Rodney. "One never knows how long this sort of thing is going to last. It might be a melting slough of despond by to-morrow."

"Don't break your precious necks!" said Mrs. Somerville.

"There's no danger at all," laughed Diccon.

Rhoda had enjoyed the pleasures of tobogganing before, but to Mildred and Kitty it was a new and delightful experience. The rapid motion through the frosty air was an intense exhilaration, and the rough-and-tumble part of the performance only made them laugh. With cheeks crimson from excitement, they were ready for any number of repetitions of the experiment.

"Come along with me, Mildred, and I'll take you down like a sheet of greased lightning!" said Rodney. "No, don't go with 'sweet Richard'! He'll spill you overboard, and break your nose, if not your neck!"

"A libel! I'm as steady as a railway truck running through a goods yard!" protested Diccon. "Never mind! I'll take Kitty, and we'll see who's greased lightning!"

"Right you are! We'll have our go first, then you can follow. Eric and Neville can act as judges."

"Suppose they disagree?" laughed Mildred.

"Then Rhoda is final umpire."

"It's the most blissful sport in creation!" declared Mildred, as she tucked herself on to Rodney's sleigh. "It beats swimming and dancing and rowing and hockey, and everything I know except flying, which I've never tried."

"You're going to try it now," said Rodney. "Here goes! Right away!"

Off they went at a most terrific pace. The slide was in good form by now, and Rodney had got into practice.

"How many miles an hour?" gasped Mildred as they glided on.

"Wish I'd a speedometer! About a hundred, I should think. She's going A1. Oh, I say! Look out for yourself! Jemima! That was a narrow shave!"

As he spoke, Rodney had ground his heel heavily into the snow, and the sled slued sharply to the right. They were almost at the bottom of the run, and in another instant were able to stop. Rodney sprang up, and rushing back to the lump of snow which they had just avoided, hastily uncovered a jagged piece of rock.

"Hi! Danger!" he yelled to Diccon, who was about to start down the track. "Look out here for all you're worth!"

"What's the matter?" cried Mildred, who had joined him.

"Matter? Don't you see this boulder? It was completely hidden by the snow. If we'd hit it, I'd have broken your nose for you in good earnest, or something worse. Keep wide, Diccon! It's as nasty a trap as one could find anywhere—it's so innocently covered. There they go, like an express! They'd have smashed straight into it if I hadn't warned them."

"Who's won?" asked Mildred.

"A draw!" shouted Rhoda.

"Then come on, Mildred, and we'll try again.

We know our danger spot now, and I promise I won't run you at it. Are you game for another go?"

"As many as you like!" declared Mildred with sparkling eyes.

That evening the weather behaved with extraordinary caprice. A short thaw, melting the surface of the snow, was succeeded by the sharpest frost of the winter, and for twenty-four hours the thermometer surprised even those case-hardened meteorologists, the oldest inhabitants. The result made all lovers of winter sports chuckle with satisfaction. Every pond and flooded meadow had a surface like glass, and skating, which before had been an illusion, was now a possibility.

"We'll go down to Wilkins's pond," declared Rodney, "it's not bad for a beginning. But to-morrow'll be the day of days! I've just seen Sir Darcy. He says another twelve hours of this frost and the lake will bear. He won't let anybody on to-day, but by to-morrow morning it ought to be in absolutely ripping condition. Then we'll show you what Westmorland skating is like!"

"It's our last day!" sighed Mildred. "I'm glad the grand treat has been saved up for the end."

The Somervilles could all skate well, for Castleford was a cold place in winter, and often registered frost when more southern counties had open weather. Some meadows near the Vicarage were generally flooded in December and January by the overflow of a brook, and the four inches of water that covered them froze rapidly, affording an opportunity for ice lovers ot which they generally availed themselves immediately. Mildred and the two Fletchers had also learned to skate. Kirkton possessed the advantage of a real ice rink, and they had sometimes spent Saturday afternoons there, so though they could not rival the Somervilles, they were not absolute novices, and could look after themselves. The whole party passed the day on a neighbouring pond, and by dusk both Mildred and Kitty had improved so immensely with the practice that they considered themselves thoroughly qualified to appreciate the joys that were promised them on the morrow.

By ten o'clock next morning a very jovial company met at the lake. Sir Darcy had invited a number of other families from the neighbourhood, and young and old were all anxious to try their prowess. The ice had been duly tested with the orthodox gimlet, and passed as absolutely safe; it was in splendid condition, and the smooth expanse presented a most attractive appearance.

"Who need go to Switzerland when they've got this at their very doors?" exulted Rodney. "I don't believe St. Moritz could go one better, and we're not crowded up with a lot of people either. It's wonderful!"

"Yes, if she behaves herself in the matter of frost!" laughed Mildred. "The worst of it is that she keeps up her reputation for a day or two, then gets tired of it, and sends a thaw. By next week this will probably be all water again."

"Prophesy smooth things unto me!" protested Rodney, with mock tragedy. "The fact that you've gone home will be bad enough. Won't you leave the ice to console me?"

"That's out of my dispensation. You must write to the weather office."

"I'm going to try fancy figures!" declared Rhoda. "If you don't see me cut an eight before the day's over, I'll—well—bite an inch off my skates!"

"A discreet promise, Madam Rhoda," said Rodney. "You're generally very ingenious at wriggling out of your bargains."

"Take that back, or I'll put an obstacle in your way when you're cutting your best flourish!" laughed Rhoda.

All the visitors had come determined to enjoy themselves. Sir Darcy and several of his friends had commenced curling, urged on by the enthusiasm of two Scottish gentlemen who were staying with the Tracy family. The Vicar joined them, and soon the elder members of the company were engaged in the sport, as interested and excited as any juveniles. The young people were busy at first helping some of the guests who were not very steady on their skates; but when these had gained sufficient confidence to support one another, their teachers were free to cut figures, get up a hockey match, or practise any other diversion they pleased. Several sledges had been brought to the lake, and children were placed on them and taken for rides, races being organized between the rival sleighs, to the huge delight of their small occupants, who would never have tired of the pastime if their long-suffering entertainers had not at last struck work and left them to amuse themselves.

It was a very gay and pretty scene—the merry groups of skaters, the bright cold January sunshine gleaming on the crystals that decked the boughs of the trees surrounding the lake, The Towers looking like a Christmas card with its ivy-clad turrets, and in the distance the snow-covered hills rising with an Alpine whiteness above the dark patch of the pine woods. On the supposition that frosty air gives keen appetites, Lady Lorraine had made generous provision for her guests. At eleven o'clock hot beef-tea and toast were brought out, and at half-past one everybody went to the house for lunch, while chocolates and toffee were dealt out liberally during the morning. Among all the young people who were assembled together none made a more charming figure than Violet. In a blue-velvet costume, with grey squirrel furs, her eyes shining like stars and her cheeks as pink as carnations, she was the acknowledged belle of the occasion, and "The Lady of the Lake", "The Snow Queen", "The Frost Fairy", and "Venus of the Ice" were but a few of the epithets bestowed upon her. She had no lack of partners to skate with, and was kept so busy among all her many friends that it was not until late afternoon that she was able to get a word with Mildred alone. The cousins had not yet seen much of each other, for during the earlier part of the visit Violet had been away staying with the Tracys, and had just returned home when the frost grew keen. Sir Darcy considered her too precious a treasure to risk her life at bobsleighing, so she had not been allowed to join the Somervilles' tobogganing expeditions; and though all the party at the Vicarage had had tea on Sunday at The Towers, Violet had been too much in request helping her mother to act hostess to allow time for any private talk with Mildred.

"Come along now!" she said brightly, "I've set all those boys to sweep for the curling, so we shall have a few minutes' peace. Let's take a turn together round the lake. I've heaps and heaps of things I want to tell you. I tried to scoot away with you on Sunday, but I never got an opportunity."

Hand in hand the two girls started, and were soon deep in a most interesting conversation Violet had really grown rather fond of Mildred while the latter was staying at The Towers, and had missed her since she went away. She had made a confidante of her cousin during the summer, and she was now anxious to pour into her sympathetic ears the accumulated news of many months. Anxious that their *tête-à-tête* should not be disturbed, they skated as far away from their friends as possible, going towards the lower part of the lake, a portion which had been so far avoided, owing to the roughness of the ice. If it was an unpleasant surface, at least they had it to themselves, so they went on and on, not looking particularly in what direction they were going, Violet talking hard and Mildred listening and putting in comments.

"So you see how it is, and I shouldn't be surprised if Miss Ward doesn't come back at all after the holidays, or at least leaves at Easter," Violet was saying, when Mildred suddenly gave a sharp exclamation and, loosing her hand, cried to her to stop.

It was indeed high time. So engrossed had the

girls been in their conversation that they had not noticed they were approaching the overflow of the lake. The rough ice had grown thinner, and ahead of them, where the brook took its source, it was barely half an inch in thickness, and stretched a smoother but most treacherous surface, narrowing to the half-frozen outlet.

The shock of loosing hands threw Mildred on her back, but Violet, unable to stop herself, skimmed rapidly forward on to the cat-ice. There was a cracking, rending sound, the ice split in all directions like a flawed mirror, and with one piercing terrified shriek Violet disappeared into a pool of water. Mildred was on her feet again in a moment, and grasped the situation in a flash. Crawling on her knees to the edge of the ice, she was able to seize Violet by the hand just as her cousin rose to the surface. But the weight of the two girls was too great for the thin plate of ice; again it cracked, and together they were plunged into the lake. Most mercifully Mildred did not lose her presence of mind. She could swim, and, supporting Violet, she was able to reach a rather thicker portion of the ice. This was not sufficiently firm to allow the girls to scramble upon its surface, but it afforded just enough hold for their fingers to enable them to keep their heads above water. By this time their screams had brought everybody hastening to the spot, and great was the alarm of the skaters at the sight of their peril. Mr. Douglas, a Scottish friend, who arrived first on the scene, at once took command.

"Keep back! Keep back!" he shouted to the distracted oncomers. "You'll only crack the ice and increase their danger. Fetch the ladder and the rope. Hold on, girls, for your lives! We'll have you out in a minute!"

Before his guests arrived that morning Sir Darcy had taken the precaution of causing a ladder and a long coil of rope to be laid on the bank in case of accident, and the wisdom of his proceeding was well justified. In less time than it takes to tell it, a dozen eager hands had seized the ladder, and, skating back with it at lightning speed, pushed it gently across the broken portion of the ice, so that at least its nearer end rested on a secure foundation. By its aid the girls managed to scramble from the water, and were drawn along over the more solid ice till eager hands could snatch them.

Dripping from their freezing plunge, and shivering with cold and fright, they were taken at once to The Towers, and put to bed with warmed blankets and hot-water bottles. The party, in much consternation at the accident, broke up immediately, the various guests returning home. Sir Darcy and Lady Lorraine were greatly upset, and Mr. and Mrs. Somerville hardly less so. The doctor, who had been summoned at once by telephone, gave a good report of the invalids, however, and assured their anxious friends that they seemed likely to do well and take no harm from their wetting, quiet rest and warmth being all they required.

Mildred did not return home with the Fletchers, as had been arranged. Lady Lorraine would not permit her to leave The Towers until the doctor had seen her again and pronounced her fit to travel. Fortunately, owing to the remedies applied so speedily after their ducking, neither of the girls had caught cold or suffered any other ill effects.

"You might have told me you were going to make holes in the ice, and given me a chance to be there to rescue you!" said Rodney reproachfully to Mildred before she left. "That Scotch fellow stole a march on me!"

"I'll give you fair warning next time—if I'm ever so foolish again!" she laughed in reply. "I don't see how I'm to do it on the rink at Kirkton!"

"I'll go and look after you, just as a safeguard, if you'll tell me when you intend skating there. I'm due back at my diggings in a week. I always get Saturday afternoons free, you know."

Mildred left Castleford with regret, even though she was returning to her own dear Meredith Terrace.

"It's not that I don't love home best, Tantie," she was careful to assure Mrs. Graham. "But I've got fond of Westmorland too. There's one thing that's a supreme satisfaction to me — they say I saved Violet's life; and if I really did, it's surely some little return to Uncle Darcy and Aunt Geraldine for their kindness last summer. I always felt they were hurt at mv leaving them, and I wanted to do something to make up. I'm so glad I got the opportunity—it mightn't come again in fifty years!"

CHAPTER XX

A Musical Scholarship

The Spring Term at St. Cyprian's was a stormy one in several respects. The weather during the end of January and beginning of February was atrocious, and resulted for Miss Cartwright in a touch of pneumonia, which laid her aside for a while from her work. The College without its Principal was like a sheepfold without a shepherd; and though the teachers did their best, everybody felt the lack of the strong guiding hand that was accustomed to hold the reins. No sooner was Miss Cartwright back at her post than several girls developed mumps, and a strict period of quarantine followed for any companions who had been in their vicinity—an unexpected holiday which their parents deplored, and they themselves scarcely appreciated, as they were barred from all social intercourse until the due number of days had expired. Owing to this misfortune, and to a scare of measles at Newington Green, all Alliance matches and functions were postponed till the various schools could show clean bills of health, and even the making of charity garments was for the time prohibited.

The girls missed the Alliance meetings dreadfully. They had scarcely realized until now what an intense interest the League supplied, and how extremely flat the term felt without the pleasant competition of the other schools. They were constantly wondering how Templeton's hockey was progressing; if the new photographic club at Marston Grove had held its first exhibition; whether the Manor House had really taken up painting on satin; and how the High School Nature Study Union prospered.

"I believe we were fearfully narrow before, only we didn't know it," said Bess Harrison. "When the Alliance was first suggested, I'm sure we all thought it would be just an easy walk-over for St. Cyprian's in everything."

"We jolly soon found out our mistake!" murmured Kitty Fletcher, who was still smarting over a hockey match in which Newington Green had triumphed. "The Coll. has to look after herself, or take a back seat."

"Somehow it seems uncommonly tame without the others to spur us on," admitted Maudie Stearne.

"Isn't there anything we could do just to liven ourselves up till all these microbes have taken their departure, and we're once more labelled 'safe to meet'? Something, if possible, that the other schools won't have thought of, so that we can surprise them after Easter?"

"Well, of course if you're prepared to go in for prize-fighting or fortune-telling, or the making of artificial wax flowers, you might find an untrodden path, but I think most things have been pretty well exploited already."

"It must be lovely to go out as a missionary to the Cannibal Islands!" sighed Sheila Moore. "Just think of finding people who've never heard, say, of the Foxtrot, and being able to show them how!"

"They'd soon Foxtrot you into their biggest fish kettle, you goose, and dance their original war steps while digesting you! A nice appetizing little morsel you'd be, I expect! Just like tender roast pork!"

"Pig yourself!" retorted Sheila.

"All the same, to go back to my original plaint," urged Bess, "we're pretty well kept within the bounds of our own Coll. this term, so why not do something on our own—something unique?"

"And I return to my original reply, that there isn't a solitary art or handicraft left unappropriated by the other schools," grunted Maudie.

"If we can't do something unique, let's do something commonplace," suggested Eve Mitchell.

"Why shouldn't we sew?" propounded Mildred.

"My sweet innocent, you forget that the garments we fashioned might convey the microbes of mumps to others! All such charitable enterprises are for the moment off."

"I'm afraid I wasn't thinking of charity. I've got an idea—yes, I have really! The school ought to own a banner. I thought at the Arts Show that it looked so ugly just to have a large card with 'St. Cyprian's College' hung up over our exhibits. It ought to be beautifully worked on silk or satin. Suppose we lead the way and make one? I expect the other schools would follow suit."

Mildred's idea appealed strongly to the girls. They considered that a banner would be a great acquisition to their College properties, and with

Miss Cartwright's permission they determined to make one. Such a large and important piece of work naturally required much discussion and planning out. Designs were submitted by members of the Art class, and a select committee appointed to consider them. In the end they decided upon a white satin ground with an appliqué border of some conventional floral pattern. At the centre was to be a coat of arms with four quarterings, the British lion, the crowned unicorn that was the crest of the city of Kirkton, a group of iris, which they chose as the school flower, on the ground that signifying the rainbow it was emblematic of many virtues merged together, and in the last corner a lyre, showing their special bent towards the study of music. At the top "St. Cyprian's College" would appear in large letters, and at the bottom their motto: "Nulli Secundus". The border and the quarterings were to be worked separately in colours on pale-green satin, and appliquéd on after the lettering had been finished.

The border was so designed that it could be made in portions of about four inches square, each to be committed to different hands, and the quarterings also were to be done apart. By this division of labour more than thirty girls were able to help, and it was felt that the banner would be a united effort. By general vote Freda Kingston was given the lettering, and a small band of workers was chosen to stitch the various pieces together when finished.

"If any health inspectors think it likely to hold germs, we can have it disinfected," laughed Bess. "It's going to be absolutely gorgeous, and it's arousing such an amount of school patriotism in my breast that I'm prepared to brave any dangers and defend it to the last drop of my blood."

"I don't know whether I admire the ramping lion or the charging unicorn more. Ivy has given Mr. Leo such a beautifully savage and furious eye!" said Maudie.

"Apollo's lyre with its golden strings for me!" proclaimed Mildred. "Nina has made them so splendidly straight and taut, I'm sure they're in tune."

Naturally the construction of the banner was an affair of many weeks; but when it was at last completed it was really a very handsome object, and quite a work of art. It was placed on view in the lecture hall, and visited by crowds of admiring girls, after which it was put safely away in folds of tissue-paper, to be kept for some great occasion when it could do honour to St. Cyprian's.

"It will be a nice little surprise for the other schools when we trot it out at the next Alliance function!" exulted Bess.

"They'll be absolutely green with envy!" affirmed Ivy. "I prophesy they'll all try to go one better."

"Let them try, then! We shall have had first start, and they can't get over that, anyway."

"I expect it will end in all the schools joining in an Alliance banner."

"Then there'd be six quarterings, and that's not heraldic!"

"No, no, there'd be eight, because the British lion and the Kirkton unicorn would still have to come in, and each school could have its emblem or its flower."

"Right you are, my youthful Solomon!"

Like all other terms, the spring session came at last to an end. The sufferers from mumps and measles had returned to their respective schools duly armed with doctors' certificates, quarantine was over, and after the interval of the Easter holidays the Alliance was able to meet again, and pursue its various avocations with renewed vigour. It had been a great source of regret to Kitty Fletcher, as head of the Games department, that St. Cyprian's had had no opportunity of wiping the stain off its reputation in regard to hockey. By next season she would have left the College, and could no longer "lead her hosts to battle as of yore". She impressed upon Edna Carson, who would succeed her in office, the mission of supremacy in the hockey field, urging her to spare no efforts to make the team realize its responsibilities. Meantime she turned her attention to cricket, determined to do the best for St. Cyprian's in the one term which remained to her.

As she had prophesied, Rhoda Somerville was a great source of strength, and promised to rival Joan Richards in batting. Under Kitty's careful tuition she improved immensely, and the captain began to regard her new pupil with much complacency. Edna Carson, of "hat-trick" fame, Daisy Holt, nicknamed "the Lobster", and Peggie Potter were well up to their last year's form, so there seemed reasonable hope that the College would win its due share of matches. At tennis, too, it was not behindhand. Lottie and Carrie Lowman had come to the fore, and proved the best champions that St. Cyprian's had yet had. Lottie had a more than usually good opportunity for practice this summer. She had been unwell in the spring, and the doctor had advised that she should not attempt to go in for public exams, as had been intended, recommending as much outdoor exercise as possible. She gleefully took him at his word, and, curtailing her hours of home preparation, played singles with her sister Carrie till both reached a pitch of excellence that caused Kitty to purr with delight. As Games delegate Kitty did not approve of any girl trying to sit on two stools. She had sternly discouraged Daisy Holt and Peggie Potter from, as she said, "wasting valuable time at the courts"; but as the reproach had been thrown at her that she encouraged cricket to the detriment of tennis, she was thankful that two such champions had arisen to give their whole-hearted attention to the latter without drawing from the team of the former.

Mildred formed one of the rank and file at games; she had not the skill to excel, nor could she spare the hours required for practice. Her violin required all her present energies; Professor Hoffmann was inexorable in his demands, and kept her rigidly up to the mark. Her music time-sheet was now a very different affair from the irregular register she had shown when this story began, and was indeed the best in the school, not excepting that of Elizabeth Chalmers, who had always been held up as a model for slack workers to emulate.

Laura Kirby was concentrating all her powers on studying for a Girton scholarship under Miss Cartwright's special coaching, so, beyond a little tennis for exercise, she was too busy to think of maintaining the physical reputation of the College, though there was a feeling among the girls that she would probably establish an intellectual record, and cover the school with glory.

"I never saw anyone swot like you, Laura," said Lottie Lowman at one of the monitresses' meetings. "You're going ahead like a house on fire, and if you're not established in your own diggings at Girton by next October, I shall say the examiners cheated."

"That remains to be seen," replied Laura rather wearily. "I'm not the only one who's swotting, you may depend upon it, and some people's brains may be more curly than mine. Oh, but I should like to go to Girton! I'd a cousin there, and she used to make me just wild with her accounts. She said it was the time of her life. I shan't be content till I've taken my tripos."

"What will you do then?"

"I don't know. I'm ambitious. I'd like to be principal of a college some day, or else go in for scientific research work. Don't laugh!"

"We're not laughing. Why shouldn't you realize your ambition? We'll see you come out top yet!"

"I don't hanker after college," said Lottie, "but I just love tennis above everything, and I'd like to be county champion. I'm afraid I've not much chance—Carrie's really better than I am—but that's my dream. What's yours, Freda?"

"Oh, to be a great artist, of course; either to paint animals, like Rosa Bonheur, or to go in for book illustration, and make a special line for myself, like Kate Greenaway. I'm to study at the School of Art as soon as I leave St. Cyprian's. It will be blissful to do nothing but paint all day."

"If I can only scrape through the Froebel exams. I'm going to be a Kindergarten teacher and Games mistress both together. There are good openings for anyone who can combine the two, and it would just suit me. I'd like to get a post at a big High School where there are hundreds and hundreds of girls, then wouldn't I just train them at cricket and hockey, and pick my teams carefully—rather!" said Kitty.

"How about the Kindergarten part of the business?"

"Oh, that would be all right! I'm fond of kiddies, and should be quite at home amongst them."

"It's a very sad thing, but I've no ambitions,' acknowledged Bess; "and I don't believe Maudie has either, except to go to dances. Confess now, Maudie, that's the summit of your dreams."

"Well, I don't want to go to Girton at any rate," laughed Maudie, "or to study at the School of Art, or teach Kindergarten. I guess we all know Mildred's vocation."

"Rather! If she doesn't study music it will be a criminal offence against the College. We look to her to be the star of St. Cyprian's, and have her name painted in special gold letters on the board in the lecture hall. Do you hear, Mildred? You've got to distinguish yourself, or perish in the attempt!"

"Don't expect too much from me, please. Perhaps I shall go off, and disappoint you horribly. Lots of people have assured me that youthful prodigies generally turn into nonentities when they're older."

"The sour-hearted brutes!"

"Well, it isn't encouraging, certainly, to be told so. But I don't care a button! I shall just go on working for the sake of the music. I love that, quite independently of success or failure."

One day when Mildred went for her violin lesson she found Herr Hoffman in quite a state of excitement. He had a piece of news to communicate, and he was evidently brimming over with it. He began to tell it to her immediately she came into the room. He had learned only the evening before that Mr. Macmillan, the Scottish gentleman who for many years had been president both of the Crawford Concerts and the College of Music, and was now Mayor of Kirkton, wished to celebrate his year of mayoralty by encouraging musical talent in the city. He therefore offered a scholarship, tenable for three years in the Paris Conservatoire, to the best student on any instrument. The conditions were simple. The candidate must be under twenty-one years of age, and must have resided in Kirkton for a period of not less than seven years. Either sex was equally eligible, and no preference would be given to those who had studied at any special school of music. The examination was to be held at the beginning of July, and the decision of the judges was to be final.

"It is as if it had been made for you! Yes, made for you!" urged the Professor. "Hitherto the musical scholarships in the city have only been obtainable through the Crawford College, but this is open to all. You are under the age, you have resided more than seven years in Kirkton—I ask, then, what hinders?"

"My own incompetence," protested Mildred. "All the clever students in the city will be going in for it. Why, it would never be given to a girl of hardly seventeen. The thing's impossible!"

"Age is no matter!" grunted Herr Hoffmann. "I do not often praise you, but you can play what many who are older dare not attempt. You shall try it? Yes? I go myself to see your good aunt, and persuade her. Have I not always said that you should study in Paris? Kalovski is now teaching at the Conservatoire. Himmel! It is the opportunity of a lifetime! He is the one master to whom I would send you."

Herr Hoffmann lost no time in visiting Dr. and Mrs. Graham, and advising them to allow their niece to go in for the scholarship. After thinking the matter over for a few days they agreed. There seemed no objection to her trying, and if she failed no harm would be done. An hour's extra practice daily the Professor required, but that could be arranged with Miss Cartwright, who was willing to let Mildred's music take the first place in her education, and who, they knew, would encourage her to enter as a candidate. Mildred herself was almost appalled at the prospect, but it was settled for her by her elders, so she was obliged to fall in with their plans. After all, the Professor's enthusiasm was infectious, and though she might not share his sanguine hopes, she was at least willing to try her best.

The test piece for the examination was the "Valse Triste" by Sibelius, and she set to work at once to wrestle with it. It was a composition that it would tax the powers of a first-rate concert player to render adequately, so she had no light task before her. Herr Hoffmann, in his anxiety for her to excel, alternately cajoled and raved, so that her lessons were a series of sunshine and storm. By this time, however, she knew her master's idiosyncrasies, and neither his impatience nor his bursts of temper could put her out. She had discovered what a kind heart he held under his rough manner, and was well aware that he spent an amount of time and trouble over her which was altogether above and beyond what could be expected by even the most exacting of pupils. So she worked away, trying to do justice to his tuition, but viewing it almost as a piece of presumption on her part to attempt the examination.

The weeks passed along quickly—too rapidly for the amount Mildred wished to do in them—and the beginning of July drew near. The candidates were to be examined in one of the smaller rooms at the Town Hall, the judges being Monsieur Diegeryck, a well-known Belgian violinist, Monsieur Stenovitch, a Russian pianist, and Mr. Macmillan himself.

"I shall fail, Tantie—I know I shall!" declared Mildred. "It's ridiculous my going in at all! I only do it to please you and the Professor. You wouldn't be satisfied if I didn't try. I only hope the judges won't crush me too utterly, and tell me it's wasting their time to listen to me. No, I'm not even nervous, because I feel the chance is too remote. If I'd greater expectations I should mind far more; as it is, I shall just play my piece in the best fashion I can, and accept any snubbing that's offered me afterwards. I've got to the point where I simply don't care."

"Then by all means let us leave it at that," said Mrs. Graham, who, after previous experiences of Mildred's apprehensions, had no wish to rouse fresh fears.

On the 4th of July, therefore, Mildred, fortified by the Professor's very latest instructions and directions presented herself and her Stradivarius at the Town Hall at the time which had been appointed for her. She had to wait a few minutes while a piano student finished playing, but her turn came next, and she was very soon ushered into the examination room. She looked round eagerly. A Bechstein grand piano stood open, after the last candidate's ordeal, and Signor Marziani, one of the teachers at the Crawford College, who was to play the accompaniments to the stringed instruments, was in the act of closing the top. Mildred had been very anxious to know who was to accompany her, and was rejoiced to find that it would be Signor Marziani, for she knew from Herr Hoffmann's accounts that he had a sympathetic touch, and was far more skilful at his task than Mr. Joynson, who shared the duty with him at most musical examinations in Kirkton. She glanced hurriedly at her three judges. Mr. Macmillan she had seen before—a pleasant, cheery-faced elderly man with kindly blue eyes; but the two others were strangers. Monsieur Diegeryck was a typical Belgian—big and fair and stout, with a bland smile that seemed to seek to reassure her; Monsieur Stenovitch, on the contrary, was thin and dark, with long hair and bushy eyebrows, under which a pair of keen eyes surveyed her with an almost cynical expression of criticism. All three had pencils and paper, and appeared to have been comparing notes on their reports of the performance of the last candidate. They composed themselves to listen, and Signor Marziani struck a few preliminary chords on the piano.

"Now for it!" thought Mildred. "Well! They can't do more than pluck me, and I'm quite prepared for it."

For perhaps the first time in her life she did not feel nervous before an audience of strangers. She played exactly as if she were having a lesson from the Professor, or practising in her bedroom at Meredith Terrace. She was surprised at her own confidence, and went through the Valse Triste so easily that it was over almost before she realized what she was doing. The judges looked at one another, but made no remarks. Each scribbled rapidly for a moment, then they told her that she might go, and bowed her politely from the room.

"How did you get on?" asked a student who was waiting outside.

"I haven't the least idea. They said nothing, but I expect I've failed. I can't flatter myself they looked encouraging. I'm only thankful they didn't squash me quite flat."

It would be a day or two before the result of the examination was made known, and Mildred waited, not exactly in suspense, for she was so sure of failure, but with the feeling that she would be glad to get the bad news over and done with. She minded the Professor's disappointment more than her own, for he had been the keener on the event.

On the Tuesday following, as she was sitting at drawing in the studio, she received a summons to the Principal's study, and, entering, found Miss Cartwright and Herr Hoffmann in animated conversation.

"Mildred, my dear child, we have to congratulate you!" began the headmistress smilingly.

"Did I not tell you, Freundchen, it was the chance of a lifetime?" beamed the Professor. "Hein! You shall see the letter for yourself."

"I—I—surely—is it true?" gasped Mildred, as she read the short but businesslike communication. "I can't believe it. Oh, have I really and truly and actually won the scholarship?"

CHAPTER XXI

Harvest

St. Cyprian's decided that Mildred's success was so far the greatest triumph the College had had, and a worthy finish to a term in which they had beaten Newington Green at cricket and vanquished Marston Grove at tennis; and when later on came the news that Laura Kirby had won the Girton Scholarship, and that even Kitty Fletcher had managed to get a second class in her examination, Miss Cartwright felt the year's work had been eminently satisfactory. All her Sixth Form girls were leaving, some to continue their studies elsewhere, and others to find their vocations at home; but all carried away the warmest recollections of the school which had laid the foundations of their education, and many left a tradition of strenuousness which would be handed on to future monitresses, and so maintain the high tone which they had established.

Mildred was overwhelmed with amazement that she had been actually selected from among forty candidates to win Mr. Macmillan's open exhibition. She had hoped after leaving St. Cyprian's to study at the Crawford College, or possibly at the Academy of Music in London, but to go to Paris was a far higher opportunity. Herr Kalovski, one of the most celebrated violinists in Europe, was at present teaching at the Conservatoire, and through the powerful influence of Mr. Macmillan could be persuaded to receive her as a pupil, a privilege only conferred on a favoured few. As Herr Hoffmann had always founded his style on Kalovski's, it would be a particular advantage for Mildred to study under the latter, for she would not be required to change her present system of bowing, and though she would have much to learn she would not be put back to the very beginning, as might be the case if she selected a teacher with different methods. As the Professor had said, it was the chance of a lifetime. She was indeed young, but with Kalovski that was a point in her favour, not a drawback, for he was well known to confer his rather capricious interest upon those of his pupils who were still in their teens.

Naturally the event was of supreme importance at Meredith Terrace. Mildred would be away for three years, or probably more, only returning to Kirkton for holidays, so it seemed a great break in her home life. But Dr. and Mrs. Graham had always intended her to take up a musical career, and resigned themselves to the parting as the inevitable consequence of their choice on her behalf. It was arranged that she was to board with a widowed sister of Herr Hoffmann, who lived in Paris, and who promised to look after her as if she were her own daughter. Dr. and Mrs. Graham gave themselves a short holiday to escort their niece to France, and after a tour up the Seine, which pleasure she shared with them, they returned to England, leaving her safely in charge of Madame Dulac.

September, therefore, saw Mildred settled at Avenue Marceau, 24, and beginning an entirely new phase in her existence. She had been taken to the Conservatoire and introduced to Herr Kalovski, who, after hearing her play, admitted that Herr Hoffmann had laid a good foundation, and formally consented to place her under his tuition. It was considered a great honour to become his pupil, so Mildred at once aroused interest at the Conservatoire, and found herself in the midst of a delightful musical coterie. It was a keen stimulus and inspiration to hear the playing of other students and masters, and to be able to attend some of the beautiful concerts and operas which were given almost every evening in the city. The quartet class, in which she was placed, helped her enormously, and also the class for reading at sight. The whole musical atmosphere of the place was a revelation to her; she was wild with enthusiasm, and wrote home such ecstatic accounts that her aunt was more than satisfied.

Kalovski proved a stern, even a severe teacher; but here Mildred's drilling under Professor Hoffmann stood her in good stead, and instead of trembling at his snubs and frequent tirades, she took them all as part of the lesson with perfect equanimity—a method of treating him which, she afterwards heard, raised her immensely in his estimation. She learnt much from Kalovski, for he was able to show her many technicalities only known to a virtuoso, and he would often play for her himself, which she found the best lesson of all. He was a strange man, like all great artists full of whims and caprices and moods, but he took a genuine interest in his English pupil, and in spite of his habitually peppery manner gave her great encouragement. After a time Mildred ventured to show him some of her own compositions, and here his deep knowledge of music was of great service to her, and the hints he gave her were of the utmost value. Gradually she came to be regarded as one of his favourite pupils, and though it was against his method to bestow praise, he began to regard her playing with complacency.

Mildred had had a fair knowledge of French before she came to Paris, and with constant practice she soon spoke it fluently and easily. She was very happy with Madame Dulac, and readily adapted herself to French life, accepting all national differences as part of her education, learning to like strange dishes and to submit to many rules which Mrs. Graham would have laughed at, but which her chaperon considered absolutely necessary.

In this new and busy world time slipped rapidly away. The three years of her scholarship came to an end, but as Kalovski would not hear of parting with his pupil, her course was extended for two years more. Under her brilliant teacher Mildred not only gained a marvellous mastery over her instrument, but his personal magnetism was so inspiring that she won a new insight into music, and besides acquiring technique, grasped the spirit of true exposition. She worked indefatigably, and when at length her long period of training was finished, there were few students at the Conservatoire who could show such a record of all-round improvement.

She left Paris with regret. Her stay there had been a memorable experience, and one which would last for the rest of her life. She had made many musical friendships, and for her teacher had formed the intense appreciation and reverence only yielded to a great artist whose ideals exceeded her own. Her time of sowing had indeed been of great promise, and she was now to return to reap the harvest.

During her absence from Kirkton Mildred had not dropped any of her old friends. She had corresponded regularly with the Somervilles and with several of her school friends, and had kept in touch with Miss Cartwright and the world of St. Cyprian's, enjoying the brief meetings that were possible during her holidays in England. The five years had brought changes to many of her former fellow monitresses and class-mates. Laura Kirby had taken a First in her tripos, and was now engaged in entomological research under a celebrated Cambridge professor—a form of work that exactly suited her, and for which she showed the greatest aptitude. Kitty Fletcher had passed through her training for Kindergarten teaching with credit, and had just found the post which she had always coveted, that of Kindergarten and Games mistress combined, in a large High School of eight hundred girls. Eve Mitchell had studied at the Women's Department of the Kirkton University, and had taken her B.A. degree. She was now a teacher at Newington Green, and doing well.

Bess Harrison and Maudie Stearne were both married, and Bess had a pretty little curly-headed boy to show proudly to her friends. Lottie Lowman was engaged to a gentleman in India, and her wedding was to take place very soon. Neither she nor Carrie had realized her dream of being county champion, but they were the best players in their tennis club, and greatly in request for local tournaments. Freda Kingston was in London, studying book illustration at a very well-known studio, and Ivy Linthwaite was still working at the Kirkton School of Art. Elizabeth Chalmers was engaged to one of the piano masters at the Crawford School of Music, and Edna Carson was married to a clergyman.

Rhoda Somerville had sustained a great loss in the death of her mother, and was now indispensable at home, looking after her father, and helping in the parish. Her three brothers had done well; Eric was just ordained, Diccon was at Oxford, and Rodney had a good berth with the Phœnix Motor Engineering Company in Kirkton. He was still a great favourite with Dr. and Mrs. Graham, and was always welcome at Meredith Terrace. His ingenuity and many original ideas, and his capacity for hard work were well appreciated by his firm, and there was every likelihood of his pushing on to a most successful business career.

Violet Lorraine had grown into a very beautiful and charming girl. She was much admired in society, and was very soon to be married to her old friend Maurice Tracy, whose father's estate adjoined Sir Darcy's. This engagement was highly satisfactory to her parents, for as Maurice was the eldest son the two properties would some day be united.

Mildred had returned from Paris with the laurels of the Conservatoire. Her teachers recognized in her a genius such as they had found in few of even the most gifted pupils who had passed through their hands. Both in the brilliance of her execution and the beauty and originality of her compositions they considered she had few equals, and they had the highest hopes for her future success. It had been arranged that she was to make her debut at a recital at the Kirkton Town Hall. The opinion of her masters as to her talent being well known, her appearance was expected to cause quite a sensation, and was awaited with interest by the music-loving world. Professor Hoffmann rubbed his hands with delight at the sight of his pupil's name placarded on the hoardings, and could not conceal his satisfaction at the fulfilment of his desires.

"It was I who first taught you to bow!" he declared. "Ach! you were a little Mädchen then, and now you are so grown I scarce know you! Do you forget how you played at my Students' Concert? Himmel! You were afraid that night! But you made success, all the same. You told me your Stradivarius was your very good friend. Believe me, it will be so again!"

All Mildred's friends were to be present at the recital. Dr. and Mrs. Graham of course headed the list, the Lorraines and the Somervilles were coming to Kirkton on purpose for the occasion, Miss Cartwright was nearly as much excited as Herr Hoffmann, and St. Cyprianites both past and present were anxious to witness the success of their former schoolfellow.

The big Town Hall was filled to the last seat on the evening of the concert, and in the galleries there was barely even standing room for the many listeners who had thronged to hear the new and unknown performer. Every face was turned towards the platform, and a burst of applause greeted the appearance of the conductor, leading the young violinist who was that night to make her first bow to the public—a slight, girlish figure, whose wonderful dark eyes, soft gold hair, and very simple and unaffected, yet perfectly self-possessed, manner at once made a favourable impression. The vast audience listened with keen attention as, drawing her bow across the strings, she brought out the first liquid notes of Lalo's "Symphonie Espagnole". Her clear, full-blooded, luscious tone, southern in its depth and richness, bewitching, sad, sparkling, and bizarre by turns, served to show not only her exquisite mastery of the instrument, but her wonderful interpretation of the music she was playing. Such strength and yet such melting sweetness of tone, such lucid phrasing, and such delicate feeling for every nicety of accentuation and rhythm her listeners had never heard before, and they realized that they were in the presence of a performer of the very first rank. The short encore scarcely satisfied the zeal of the delighted audience, and Mildred was recalled again and again, till, growing desperate, the conductor was at last obliged to lead on the pianist whose solo was the next item on the programme.

In her second piece, the "Kreutzer Sonata" of Beethoven, Mildred was able to give even a better idea of the scope of her playing than had been possible in the "Symphonie". Her rendering of it was masterly in the fullest sense of the word—so independent and original a performance, with such faultless phrasing of the variations, such a high level of pure loveliness throughout, and such a glorious finale that the very spirit of Beethoven seemed to linger in the notes, and breathe through her beautiful and eloquent reading of the sonata. Warm as it had been before, the audience was now twice as enthusiastic, and deafening cheers began to ring through the hall when, for the third and last time in the evening, Mildred appeared with her violin upon the platform.

The fact that the "Legende" which she was about to play was her own composition raised the interest to its highest pitch, and all waited with anxiety to learn if this marvellous young performer were equally endowed with the gift that can create as well as interpret music. It was an ambitious theme—the story of Undine and the Knight—and it was unfolded with a strength and yet a delicacy of fancy, and a wealth of poetic feeling and imagination which almost took the breath away by the fire of its passion and the daring of its originality. It began very softly, conveying to the listeners the weird and uncanny impression of the haunted German forest; there was moonlight in the music, and the minor key gave that suggestion of sadness which was the motive of the "Legende". The wild fear of the supernatural, which caused the knight to urge his horse with frantic speed through these unknown shades, throbbed in the restrained power of the opening passages, and burst out into a panic of emotion as the vengeful phantom of the foaming waterfall dissolved itself into showers of spray between the rustling branches. The very essence of elvish roguery and frolic rang in the notes when "Undine", the lovely, wayward sylph, charmed the knight with her coquetry and unearthly beauty; the courtship of the changeling water-sprite, her wild whims, her light-hearted gaiety, the strange beings which ever accompanied her from the spirit world, and the sudden change in her bearing when at length she gains a human soul, were portrayed with such fidelity in the airy, elusive character of the music, that the whole of the tender love story seemed to live to the hearers. It was instinct with graceful and piquant fancy, carried out with an exquisite refinement of feeling which never degenerated into sentimentality. In the latter part, where "Undine", the unhappy wife, tries to appease her husband's anger, and to curb the revenge of the supernatural friends who resent her ill treatment, the dramatic fire of the composition rose to a pitch of surpassing grandeur, changing to a dirge-like wail of infinite sadness as, neglected and despised, the once bright sylph melts into the element from which she was first formed, the "Legende" breaking into a finale of such inspired pathos that it seemed as if the spirits of the air above and the water below were joining in a requiem for the soul that had been won at the cost of all earthly joy.

There was dead silence for a moment at the conclusion of the piece, then the audience broke into a roar of applause such as was not often heard in the Town Hall. People cheered and cheered yet again, clapping, stamping, shouting, waving their handkerchiefs, and standing on the seats in the wild enthusiasm of their approval. Bowing again and again at each fresh outburst, Mildred stood on the platform with quivering lips. She felt it was indeed a wonderful power that had been given her, to be able to sway so vast a gathering, to hold her listeners spellbound while she played, and to rouse them to such a height of intense feeling. It was beyond her wildest dreams of success. She had hoped for appreciation and perhaps applause, and she had met with an ovation only accorded to a great master of music.

She ran away at last from the excited crowd, for it appeared as if the cheering would never stop, and in the anteroom behind found a gathering of those friends who had come to wish her joy. To Dr. and Mrs. Graham, her nearest and dearest, to whom she owed the cultivation of her musical talent, she turned first in the hour of her triumph.

"I don't deserve it, Tantie!" she murmured. "They ought to cheer you instead. I should never have played at all if you hadn't made me. The praise is all due to you, and what you have done for me."

Mr. Macmillan was warm in his congratulations, and Herr Hoffmann, whose eyes were wet with emotion, held out his hand to Mildred, saying: "To tell you I am proud would be but a poor way to tell you what I feel. Ach! The 'Legende' was a masterpiece! You are a great exponent of your art, you have the soul of a poet, and the technique of a finished musician. I rejoice that it has been my privilege to take a share in your training. I now with reverence stand aside. The pupil is greater than the master. Go on to still more fame; you rise to heights where I cannot follow you."

Sir Darcy, Lady Lorraine, and Violet were all hearty and enthusiastic in their greetings. They realized at last the extent of Mildred's genius, and acknowledged the wisdom of having cultivated it. The Somervilles seemed as delighted at her reception as if she were one of their own family. Rodney said little, but his few words meant much; and Rhoda kissed Mildred like a sister. Miss Cartwright was overflowing with smiles.

"Your name is to be painted on our board of successes to-morrow," she declared. "You are indeed a credit to St. Cyprian's, and we are proud to count you as a former pupil."

As Mildred stood thus, the centre of so much congratulation and so many good wishes, she felt that she had indeed reaped a rich harvest for the perseverance and hard work of the last few years. It had been worth the doing, and her toil was repaid now a thousandfold. Her father's dying words came rushing into her memory: her strenuous effort should atone for the life which he had wasted so sadly. Surely she had discovered the Count's secret. The Stradivarius had in her hands been the key to fame and success, and at length she had entered into her inheritance.